Steal a Few Cents

T0127486

Steal a Few Cents

Rupert Smith

Winchester, UK
Washington, USA

First published by Roundfire Books, 2017
Roundfire Books is an imprint of John Hunt Publishing Ltd., Laurel House, Station Approach,
Alresford, Hants, SO24 9JH, UK
office1@jhpbooks.net
www.johnhuntpublishing.com
www.roundfire-books.com

For distributor details and how to order please visit the 'Ordering' section on our website.

Text copyright: Rupert Smith 2016

ISBN: 978 1 78535 607 0
978 1 78535 608 7 (ebook)
Library of Congress Control Number: 2016954755

A CIP catalogue record for this book is available from the British Library.

Design: Stuart Davies

Printed and bound by CPI Group (UK) Ltd, Croydon, CR0 4YY, UK

We operate a distinctive and ethical publishing philosophy in all
areas of our business, from our global network of authors to
production and worldwide distribution.

Chapter 1

"I never met my father," he said, keeping his eyes on the road.

They were heading west, toward a thin seam of fading crimson where the towering dome of darkening sky touched the horizon. Serried ranks of grass along the edges of the highway flickered stiffly as they sped past. Behind them the fields relaxed, sighing in the coolness after another November afternoon under the busy African sun.

Stephen stole a glance at the middle-age man behind the wheel, softly outlined in the green glow of the dash. "How so?"

"We lived in the township," he began. Then, almost as if he were talking to himself, he muttered, "My mother died when I was seven, and my grandmother brought me up."

The big car sped on, swallowing a pulse of white dashes on the road surface.

"That old lady," he went on, "early every morning she'd take me by the shoulder like this"—he made a grabbing action with his right hand—"and shake me awake." He shook his head almost imperceptibly. "She taught me everything I know."

Stephen waited, but that was it. In silence once more, he gazed straight ahead. His expectation of how people behave kept him from asking to hear more. If someone wants to tell you his secrets, he will, without your saying a word. If he wants to keep them to himself, he won't tell you even if you ask all day.

The younger man, settled into the plush upholstery of the driver's seat, gripped the wheel with an intensity that made Stephen wonder. Thuli Mpongose was in his early forties. He stood five foot ten in his Givenchy slip-ons and was slight of build, though the beginnings of a middle-age spread had pushed back his matching belt a notch or two. Dark complexioned and hair shaved to a stubble, he stared down the world with steely determination and an impenetrable reserve. In the photograph on the cover of a recent *Finance Week*, he stands at a lectern, gazing confidently over the heads of his investors, the poster boy for a new generation of successful businessmen. A man with the world at his feet, confidence in his eye, and change to spare in his pocket.

Stephen lost himself to the road ahead, hypnotised by the bright white cone of halogen headlights that scurried through the dusk ahead of the speeding car. Something in the pattern of the taillights of a truck lumbering ahead of them in the left lane, and the loneliness of the open road, took him back to an earlier time when his world was small and dependable, and his father came home after dark with his newspaper tucked under one arm and the smell of the paper factory on his clothes. Their little town had run on the clockwork of that factory, setting its watches to the deep bass of its foghorn that called the beginning and end of each shift, and tailoring its hopes and plans to the rhythm of its massive presence. At night a sprinkle of red lights blinked on the tall stacks and high roofs, telling an age-old tale of the slow grinding of the years. Lying in bed he'd hear the sirens wailing in the night, passing on unimaginable messages; and then the hammering breath of a steam locomotive drifting further and further away until he'd slip into sleep in the silence.

"So what do you make of this?" Stephen asked, as they slid past the turnoff for Bapsfontein.

"Hah! I'm not like other CEOs. I don't hide behind the HR manager." Thuli shifted his grip on the wheel and glanced in the rear-view mirror. "I was there last night. I went to visit his mother. She's an old lady. They were all there and they were crying."

Stephen heard the smugness in the man's voice; ignored it. "Was he married?"

"No. He has a brother who is at university and doesn't live with his mother." He shook his head and said again, "She is an old lady."

"He was only twenty-eight," Stephen murmured, remembering the entry in the file. "It's a real sadness."

"He was a bright young man," Thuli replied, nodding his head. "He worked himself out of poverty, just like me."

Pensively, Stephen stared off into the distance, tracking the sliding progress of a dark cove of trees that stood far out into the night against the lights of a farmhouse.

"I just can't make out how it happened," he said at last. "What was he doing out there in the middle of the night? He had no business wandering around the mining area, hours after he should've been home. And I don't understand how he got himself killed."

"These young men," Thuli said, "they think they're bulletproof, they think the rules don't apply to them. Then this sort of thing happens."

"I don't know if he thought he was tough or not, but he was an accountant. An accountant! What was an accountant doing removing an obstruction from a moving conveyer belt in the middle of the night?" Stephen semaphored his exasperation with one raised open palm. "That's what the security report says: *Removing an obstruction from a moving conveyer belt.* Who in his right senses would do something like that?" He shook his head. "Jonny's report just doesn't make sense."

It was Thuli's turn to glance at his travelling companion.

"Well, I don't know what else it could be," he said. "These young guys moonlight. They work overtime on someone else's ID, and then split the income. That's what he was doing there. He didn't stop the conveyer because if you cut production, you cut everyone's month-end bonus, and his mates wouldn't have forgiven him for that."

Stephen sighed. "So now the whole mine's shut for twenty-four hours while the dicks from the Department swagger around the place. How's that for false economy?"

The inspectors employed by the Department were notoriously

officious. Stephen felt glum about the prospect of having to deal with them about an incident he really could not make head or tail of. He shook his head and went on: "If Jonny's story comes out in the inquiry, or if Mamela was working under someone else's name, they'll be all over us like a rash. Just think of the implications: no proper training, no controls over who is on shift, no security, no safety equipment, no nothing. They'll have a field day."

Thuli pursed his lips. He couldn't abide criticism and this sounded very much like it. Stephen was about the only person in the company who could speak to him, the CEO, like this and get away with it. At sixty-three and nominally retired, Stephen was the senior statesman of the company, the cool head to go to when things got tough. But Thuli didn't like this kind of talk.

"That's why we have to prepare properly," he answered, allowing a touch of authority to creep into his voice.

Stephen said nothing. Being told, after a lifetime in legal practice, that he should prepare for a hearing didn't warrant a reply. Instead he said: "We have to tread carefully with the unions as well."

"The unions will be all right. I've already phoned Fana, and he's okay. He didn't much like Mamela, thought he was a troublemaker. He always had his own ideas about what the unions should do. And the smaller unions will also be okay. They know this happens and they know what their members do."

Thuli shifted lanes to overtake an old Kombi lumbering ahead in the slow lane. As Stephen mulled over what Thuli had said, his mobile beeped; it was Lisa asking when he'd be home. *Home in an hour*, he texted, then returned to the conversation.

"I've asked for full reports from everyone, not just from Jonny. And I want the clock cards and records for the last six months. I'll be back at the mine in the morning to talk to anyone who can tell me what happened here. We've got to come up with a proper explanation, one that doesn't make us look like a bunch of

Charlies. But I think we'll have our hands full."

Thuli grunted his agreement and turned his full attention to the road which was now getting busier as they neared civilisation. Soon they slid past the airport turnoff and then under the overpass at Gilooley's where the rush-hour stragglers still lingered. Between the Kensington ridge and the buttress of Linksfield nestled the city lights of old Johannesburg. Thuli pointed the sleek Mercedes north to Sandton where all the action is nowadays. At Linksfield he slipped off the N3.

"I'm in a board meeting for Richard's Bay tomorrow," Thuli said, "and I'll try to see the Minister after that. He likes being kept informed. And if we run into trouble it's good to have him on our side. Keep in touch. How long do you think you'll be?"

"Depends on what I find. I'd be surprised if it takes more than two days. Especially if I start first thing in the morning. Tell Xoli to give this priority, won't you? Sometimes he behaves as if anyone from head office is just in his way."

"Sure. I'll tell him. I want this dealt with properly. I built this company and I don't want anything to damage it." Thuli set his jaw like a tank commander: there's no can't in African.

He really believes this stuff he says, Stephen marvelled, but said nothing further until, many traffic lights later, they swung into the basement garage in Rosebank. "Okay, cheers then. See you in a few days. Say hi to the pretty coal terminal for me."

"Thanks, old man. I'm sure Richards Bay will miss you too. Regards to Lisa. We'll talk tomorrow."

Stephen watched the big Merc fishtail out of the garage as Thuli set off in a squeal of tyres. He hopped into his own car for the short drive home. It had been a long day and tomorrow he'd leave well before dawn.

Chapter 2

Electricity sneaks into your house and into your dreams, whisper-quiet, leaving no sticky fingerprints, not tracking in mud. She is well-mannered and polite: she asks no questions, makes no mess; and then she is gone again, without fuss and without complaint. She twitters on your phone; she mixes your muesli; she blends your single malt; she designs your jeans; she froths your cappuccino. Without her your creepy doesn't crawl, your shower makes no steam, your fridge turns nasty. She is your silent and permanent companion, and when load-shedding spoils your party, you miss her more than you can imagine. As her extra gift to you, as a kind of additional spiritual bonus, she keeps your hands clean and your conscience clear. And to keep her in step and faithful to your every need, you need coal. Lots of it.

Coal is her dark twin, the dirty scoundrel, the pirate who plunders, the dark lord who leaves behind a bitter wake of destruction. He rips up the land and belches forth his filthy offering from deep gashes in her sides; he spreads his choking blackness over the swathe of his passing; and the scars of his parade never heal. From the temples of his massive furnaces, kilns and boilers, his fiery breath yells abuse at the blue sky; and the powdered bones of his reign spread far and wide, carried on an unwilling wind. And where he stomped over the country, the rivers and streams weep sad and distorted tears forever after.

In Mpumalanga, where the sun comes strolling through the front door every morning, nameplates tell the story of a beautiful green place, a place of fertile valleys and verdant plains: Syferfontein, Anysspruit, Kleinkopje, and Bettiesdam. The grasslands of a high plateau roll eastward from Johannesburg for hundreds of kilometres to the edge of an immense escarpment, undulating over fertile sweeps of green where farms and fields lie side-by-side, thrumming with the pulse of a quiet life. Brooks and streams tumble and fall to join bigger rivers on their way to the sea; and the sky is broad and blue and clear. Under these beautiful fields lie the fossilised remains of ancient forests and wetlands, of the wide and shallow seas of three hundred million years ago. And in so many places brimming with such beauty, bespoke by such happy names, the ground has been torn open to get at the offering of the land's ancient carboniferous past. Where leviathan generations once plodded through their slow lives, massive drag lines and heavy machines now lumber, hacking black and grudging coal from open pits, and disgorging it into lines of dirty wagons on their way to power stations with tall towers that pour billowing clouds of smoke into the blue yonder.

When Stephen pulled up at one of the few traffic lights in Crosby, the sun had only recently stuck its head over the horizon. It was a pretty how town with clouds floating above it and the bells of the old stone church chiming the pace of the hours. In the new morning, an out-of-date road sign pointed left, in the direction of Biesiesfontein. Next to it, a bigger and brighter sign bore a company logo—the head of a cheetah in bold profile, with one blue and one black shadow, each slightly below the image above it. SETHEMBA LIMITED 7KM, it directed. The light changed and Stephen rolled forward, to the Biesiesfontein Colliery, to meet the day.

The guard at the gate greeted him by name, "Mr. Wakefield," nodded and lifted the boom for Stephen. He nodded back as he drove in, and reversed into his bay, as safety officers on all mines insist, pulling into the shade of an old pin oak. A *swamp Spanish oak*, he remembered Lisa telling him they were sometimes called. A big one of those stood over the drive in front of his house in Saxonwold.

He found Jonny van Straten in his office, chewing on a toasted egg-and-bacon sandwich. At his elbow on the table perched a black rubber flashlight, at least a foot long, like the ones tough cops in the movies have.

"Hey, old timer!" the man behind the desk beamed, lumbering to his feet and wiping his mouth with the back of his hand. He grabbed Stephen's hand in a meaty fist. In his younger days, Jonny played lock for the Falcons for several seasons and since then his massive frame had thickened around him to justify his nickname, Thaba, given to him by the workers. "That means 'mountain'," he'd told Stephen proudly when they first met years back. Stephen's six foot one of his youth had slimmed down to spry slenderness; next to Jonny-the-mountain he looked fragile.

A framed Springbok rugby jersey on the wall behind the desk had, so said the signature, once belonged to Mark Andrews. In an emergency Jonny could break the glass and put it on—it looked about the right size. Square wooden shelves against the walls kept dozens of files in well-ordered ranks, holding the secrets of many years. The two men stood across from each other, the top of Stephen's head level with Jonny's chin.

"How long have you been in this office now?" Stephen asked.

"I don't know," Jonny said, frowning. "I joined the company in '94, but first I had other offices. I've been in this one for about ten or twelve years I suppose. Why do you ask?"

"Twelve years in the same office and you still haven't managed to get a chair for your visitors to sit in?"

Jonny laughed. "My visitors are usually in trouble and it's better that they stand. It reminds them of their sins." Grinning, he spun open the door to his secretary's office, yanked a chair one-handed through it and plonked it front of Stephen. "There you go."

"Thanks." Stephen sat, and then smiled at the young man. "How's the crew?"

Jonny's sons, who were now even bigger than he was, played in schoolboy provincial sides, a source of much pride to the old player. Brimming with pleasure he gave an update of the latest news, what the boys were up to; and then turned the conversation back to Stephen. "How's the missus?"

"She's well," Stephen said. "She wants me to quit and go to Cape Town. I'm thinking of it seriously."

"Ja, good idea," Jonny said with a chuckle. "You're over the hill and then you can fall asleep with the rest of them!" He evidently enjoyed his own joke, laughing heartily. "Daarso in Slaapstad," he guffawed. *There in the Sleepy City.*

"Thanks a lot. I'll tell her you agree," Stephen drawled.

When Jonny had his giggles under control, Stephen asked, "Now, this Mamela thing. What do we know?"

One of those well-ordered files yielded the bald facts. Joseph Mpho Mamela, company number 0217/07, born in Tsakane, Brakpan, on 17 July 1987. Matriculated from Tsakane Secondary School in December 2006 with one D, three Cs, one B, and a distinction for Accountancy. Started working at the company in June 2007 as a labourer, at the number 1 Stacker Reclaimer. Good reports from his superiors, no incidents of misconduct. Received a study grant, first payment in March 2008 from the Sethemba Workers Trust for a correspondence course through UNISA in Financial Accounting. Joined the administration department as a junior salaries clerk in July 2008. Promoted to accountant in March 2009. Member of the National Union of Mineworkers, elected as workers' representative in June 2011. Received a diploma in Advanced Accounting Services in November 2013. Promoted to senior accountant at the end of the same month. Regular increases and glowing reports since then.

"I see he became an accountant around the time Sethemba bought the mine. Is there a connection?" Stephen asked. "Did the new management promote him?"

"Don't know, boss. He was part of the accounting hand-over team."

"And now he's Panico's 2IC?"

Jonny nodded. "They liked him a lot."

"What do we know, Jonny? What kind of a guy was he? Did

you know him?"

"I know everybody. That's being the safety officer. But I never had anything directly to do with him, which is, you know, good. I only get to see the troublemakers in here. But he was always polite and the assessments from his bosses, as you see, were always good."

"Are we seeing Panico later?"

"He's already waiting for us," Jonny confirmed.

"And Mamela was a shop steward?"

"He was." Jonny stroked his chin thoughtfully. "He was always quiet at meetings, followed the protocol. You know, lots of these guys go out of their way to be rude. Some even refuse to have personal dealings with management. They'll only speak in formal meetings, and then do their best to be difficult. Mamela wasn't like that."

"He was a good guy?"

"Yes, I thought so. Not that he was on management's side. He was always ready to try to get more for the workers. Always wanted more."

"So, sort of what he was supposed to do?" Smiley wrinkles in the older man's face showed he was teasing.

"Ja! I suppose you're right. He wanted more for everyone, not just for himself. He was a bit of an idealist, not like so many of the others who'll sell out their comrades for extra beer money."

"If there's a horse called Self-Interest, back it?"

Jonny chuckled again as Stephen reached for the document on the desk in front of him: the *Preliminary Report on Fatality*. It was dated 3 November 2015.

"So, Big Jon, tell me what happened."

"Gee, the boss he comes here and he asks hard questions."

He was quiet for a moment, thinking.

"I don't really know. Two guys in a bakkie going on shift at six o'clock on Friday morning saw his vehicle next to the conveyor belt. The door was open, engine still running, but he was nowhere to be seen. They didn't think much of that to start with, and stopped to see if they could help. They thought there was a problem with the belt."

Everyone on the mine drove a pick-up truck, a *bakkie*.

"Where was this?"

"Middle of nowhere, which is really confusing."

The belt, he explained, ran for thirteen kilometres in all, from the high wall on North Section all the way to the power station fence. There was a service road next to it, though only a small section of the belt ran through the operational area.

"They found the vehicle about halfway along, in the middle of the veld. That's really odd because nothing happens there. It's just the belt on its own in the middle of nothing."

"And the belt's covered?"

The big man nodded. "It runs under its own roof most of the way. I asked Jozi if they often have problems there, and he said never. It's in the middle of a long stretch where nothing ever goes wrong. According to him, if the belt breaks, it doesn't break there."

"So was there a problem with the belt?" Stephen frowned.

"No one could find anything wrong. Not the guys who found him, and not the inspection team that went there afterwards."

"So there's no engineering incident report?"

"No, boss. There isn't anything to report."

"Then, please tell me matey, what made you say in your report" — Stephen lifted the document a few inches off the table — "that Mamela had stopped *to remove an obstruction from the moving conveyor belt* quote unquote?"

Jonny eased back in his chair, aware that his ears were being pulled.

"It's a guess, boss. I don't know what else it could have been."

"An experienced copper like you," Stephen drawled.

Silence settled in the little office as Jonny fidgeted sheepishly and Stephen watched him, a tiny smile hovering in the corners of his mouth.

"You know what the real boss says?" Stephen asked.

The young man sat forward again, keen to know.

"He says our man moonlights. He says because his first job was in coal feed, he clocks in as one of his mates, and they share the overtime."

"Well, you could say the boss is always right. Except this time, he's not."

"Why's that?"

"Maybe a few years ago you could do that, but not anymore. Not unless you want to take your mate's thumb with you on shift. Because that's how you clock in nowadays—with your thumbprint on a scanner." He sat back and beamed. "Biometrics," he explained, as if he'd invented it.

"Hmm. Well, we've got to check it out anyway. I asked for all the clock cards, and will you and your people please go through them to check if His Lordship is right. Jonny, quite apart from this incident, we need to find out whether a scam like that is possible. Because if it is, we have to stop it."

"I'll check," Jonny said, "but this is a hard system to break— when you swipe your thumb, you're also on video. You can't have one guy swipe his thumb and another one go on duty. And I've looked at Thursday night's recordings already. The people who were supposed to be on duty were on duty." Johnny sat back again, this time looking pleased with himself.

"Thanks, Sherlock," Stephen said. "That knocks the scam idea over, but it doesn't help us to figure out what was he doing there. Do we know what time it happened?"

"We don't. Sometime during the night, definitely before six o'clock on Friday morning."

"And what exactly happened to him?"

Jonny became sombre.

"Ah. You don't want to know. I took photographs, and I'll show you if you want, but I don't recommend it. It's not a pretty sight. Basically, as I see it, he got his hand caught between the belt and the rollers, and it just pulled him in." Jonny illustrated the fatal mechanics by grabbing his left wrist with his right hand, and lurching across the table, as if pulled by an irresistible force. "He was crushed." He shook his head. "I've seen many gruesome sights over the years, and this one's right up there."

"The belt meters didn't register anything?"

"Nope. There's thousands of tonnes of coal on that belt. The monitors only register a complete tear or a total stoppage. Or spontaneous combustion."

Sometimes coal on the belt bursts into flames all on its own, Stephen remembered. A dangerous business, this mining.

"So what's your guess, Big Man?" he asked.

"I've already told you, and then you cast aspersions on my being a policeman and all," Jonny replied with a grin. "Look, I think what happened is that our man was going home on Thursday night, and for some reason decided to take a drive along the belt—maybe he was nostalgic, maybe there was some other reason, I don't know. But there he is, and he sees something on the belt, and because he's a good employee, he stops to remove the obstacle. He would've known how to do it, from when he worked at the stacker reclaimer. And then his arm got caught. That's all there is to it. It was an accident, but it really was his own fault."

"How is it his own fault?"

"He should've contacted the control room. At the very least, he should've stopped the belt before trying to clear an obstacle."

"And what's an obstacle? What would he have been trying to clear?"

"Oh. It's usually just a chunk of coal caught between the belt and the rollers. It falls off the belt and bounces up funny. And if it stays there long enough and doesn't work itself free, the belt can tear. It happens."

Stephen mulled over Jonny's speculative account of what had

happened. It wasn't altogether unlikely, except for one thing. Looking askance at the huge man across the desk, he drawled laconically, "Nostalgic?"

"Well, all right. I admit that's a bit thin." Jonny looked down at his fingernails. "To be honest, I've no idea why he was there. It's miles out of his way, and in the wrong direction. But I can't think of any other reason."

Chapter 3

The passage was tiled in light brown ceramic; the walls were beige; and curtains, short falls of hessian in single ply, covered small windows, set at shoulder level every ten paces. The ceiling hadn't been repainted in many years and had faded to dull off-white. The place was the colour of latte. Stephen followed Jonny past the office with the sign that said: Stationary. He'd been itching to change it for years.

Around the corner was another sign: ACCOUNTS–Authorised Personnel Only.

"We're authorised." Jonny winked, reaching for the door handle.

The room was a large rectangle divided into eight open-plan workstations, all of them facing inward to a single chest-high partition that ran down the centre of the room. Rows of dull grey metal filing cabinets lined the walls, and on the desk in front of every chair blinked a computer screen. The room, in contrast to the passage, was the sober grey of dedicated administration—the walls were zircon, the carpet tiles slate, the partitions flint. Each desk was occupied, and each groaned under a load of invoices, journals, lists, and registers. Keyboards clicked under flying fingers, forms were being completed in triplicate, calculators were doing overtime. A chubby young girl in a red and blue T-shirt with shiny silver sequins sparkling across it was pulling open, and banging shut, the drawers of a filing cabinet.

"Morning pen pushers!" Jonny boomed. He seldom moved quietly.

"Hey, Mr. van Straten!" Smiled a pretty girl with short dark bangs seated closest to the door. Several others, young people manning the busy office, waved and said hi and then got on with their work. Panico's office was the only one with a door and it was at the back, furthest from the passage. Jonny knocked twice, shouldered the door open, and went in.

Panico Georgiou rose from behind his desk wearing his habitual smile. To look at Panico was to get a smile from him. Stocky, with a serious pair of biceps on him, he wore trendy round horn-rimmed readers that he now took off to look at his visitors. He was in his early forties and was the only member of the senior management team on the mine to dress even remotely stylishly—and he had style in buckets. His trousers were tailored, his pure cotton shirt crisp, his shoes Italian. Whenever Stephen saw him, he had a three-day stubble that made him look like someone accustomed to dodging the paparazzi at Cannes. He'd taken over the accounts office in a crisis of mismanagement eighteen months earlier and now it ran like a high-precision machine, with a happy contingent of employees and a high reputation for efficiency. Dov Weinberg, the financial director, never got tired of singing his praises and it was no secret that Panico would move into Dov's role when he retired any day now. The only real question was who on earth could fill those fine Italian shoes here at the coal face, particularly now that his 2IC was gone.

"The Silver Fox himself!" Panico said, squeezing Stephen's hand affectionately, nodding at the crop of snow-white hair.

"This colour isn't natural," said Stephen, pointing at his head. "I spend hours every morning disguising the black underneath." He'd started going grey in his early thirties and had all but forgotten what his original hair colour had been. In the wedding portrait on the wall in his and Lisa's bedroom, among the gallery of family pictures, he has a head of dark brown, almost black hair. He looked so young and optimistic, it had to have been a long time ago.

"Ja, Sissie." Jonny grabbed Panico's hand, almost pulling him off his feet.

Panico laughed, and replied, "Ja, Skaap," trying to rescue his hand. *Yes, Sheep.*

They took their seats around the tiny table in the office. "How's the family?" Stephen asked, eyeing the framed picture of Panico and his sons, and another of his wife, both in pride of place behind the desk.

"I tell you no secrets that Crosby isn't Helen's favourite place." He grinned. "She spends most of our disposable income driving to Jozi and back. But the boys are so well. They love it here. They're out on their bikes all afternoon and they grunt away in that odd guttural noise that passes as a language for our friend here." He nodded in Jonny's direction.

"Mooiste taal in die wêreld," Jonny confirmed. *Most beautiful language in the world.* Then, looking around the spic-and-span office, asked with incredulity, "You ever do any work in here?"

"In February I did the crossword puzzle." Panico smiled. "And then the whole office took off a month from our usual duties to answer your safety questionnaire."

Jonny pulled a face. It was his form but not his doing. The Board had decided that every department on the mine needed a quarterly risk assessment, and Jonny, the Chief Safety Officer, was in charge of it. Dutifully enough, he'd circulated a list of detailed questions about risk profiles to each and every department, though of course the questions were aimed primarily at the operations, where dangerous machines lurked and injury hid around every corner. Not much of it applied in any realistic way to the Accounts Department, but Panico and his team had had to complete it anyway.

"I hope we passed?" Panico asked, poker-faced.

"Ja, jong," was all Jonny said. *Yes, well.*

Stephen chuckled, then turned serious: "Panico, we are preparing for the inquiry into what happened to Joseph Mamela."

"Mpho," corrected Panico. "His name was Mpho." He shook his head. "It's a shame. He was my star performer. I hoped he'd take over from me when the time came for me to move on. He's going to be difficult to replace."

"Tell me about him," Stephen said evenly.

"He was an amazing young man," Panico began. "His mother was a domestic servant and his father a taxi driver. They scrimped and saved to put their children through school. When Mpho was in high school, his father was killed. After Matric, he came to work here and put himself through a correspondence degree. That takes a lot. His brother is studying to be a doctor and Mpho was paying his bills. His mother is still a domestic worker, but she's almost too old to work."

Panico said that when he took over, Mpho was the only person he could trust to know what he was doing. "He was really quiet, made no noise. So quiet I think Cocky hadn't noticed really that he was there."

Panico's predecessor, Koketso Khuzwayo, was called "Cocky" by all and sundry. He was a nice man, but not a careful accountant. "When I got here, Mpho was doing much of what I now do. He was handling stuff way above his paygrade, and doing it well. He's the reason why there wasn't more of a crisis before Cocky left."

"What happened last week? Do you know?"

"I wish I did. Mpho worked a lot of overtime. He never got paid to do it, but we are short-staffed and he carried one or two of the new appointees who aren't quite up to getting through what they're supposed to do. We're really going to miss him."

Panico looked genuinely distressed. But there was something more. Stephen had watched and listened to people his whole life and saw the young man was nervous. He decided to wait for it to come out on its own.

"On Thursday I left here at about four-thirty." The day-shift began at six in the morning and ended at four. To fit in, the admin staff kept the same hours. "I was last to leave except for Mpho who was still busy at his desk. I said goodbye as I left, and I never saw him again. If I'd known, I would've spoken to him a bit longer. But truth is, I was in a rush and just barged out of here."

Stephen waited in silence, waiting for Panico to work through the issue on his own.

"Look, Stephen, is there a problem about the bakkie?" Panico blurted out.

There it is, Stephen thought to himself. "What do you mean? What about the bakkie?"

Panico looked down at the blotter in front of him. He hadn't written anything on it and certainly hadn't blotted it. The blotter on Stephen's desk crawled with telephone numbers and reminders to himself, along with his speciality doodle, a three-dimensional cube with windows on all six sides. That's how he kept himself occupied while waiting for the person on the other end of the line to come to the point.

"I know it wasn't exactly right, but Mpho didn't have a car and he often worked overtime. He lived in Crosby and if he missed the shuttle he'd have to wait for the shift bus at nine. Every department is allowed to requisition a vehicle and that's what I did. It was only ever used for Mpho to get home after working late if he missed the shuttle."

The poor man looked as if he'd just pleaded guilty to a terrible crime. Stephen waved his anxiety away with a sideways gesture of his hand.

"No, no," he said. "Nothing to do with the bakkie. You did the right thing. No complaints, and I'll speak to the safety officer myself about this. Tell him this is none of his business." He stared, mock-serious at Jonny who held up his hands and said: "Bullied into submission again."

Across the table the relief was palpable. Where superiors were officious, careers had been bent out of shape for less.

"But what was he doing at the conveyor belt? Do you know?" Stephen pressed.

"I haven't a clue. He was the type of guy who would've tried to help if he saw there was a problem, but I just don't know. I can't even think why he would've been there."

Stephen thought about that for a bit. "How had he been around the office? Anything that caught your attention?"

"No. As I say, he was very quiet. In fact, he'd become even quieter once the thing with Frankie Mabena happened."

"What exactly happened there? Lisa and I were in Italy when that went down."

The holiday had been the longest of Stephen's life. He and Lisa had spent six weeks in southern Tuscany, living in a rented villa, and walking through the deep-green country with its terraced fields, gnarled vines and massive fig trees. In the ancient stone villages with nary a green blade of grass from northeast to southwest, they drank coffee next to little fountains in the piazza, and in the evenings they ate under the stars on their stony veranda. It was only when he got back to the office that he heard the bones of the story: that Frankie had been sent to prison for three years. He was sorry that he hadn't been around to intervene.

"It was a sad thing," said Panico. "Frankie worked here as a junior accountant while finishing his studies through correspondence. He came from a very poor family, just like Mpho, and he was equally conscientious. He was everyone's darling. The whole office liked him. Mpho was his closest friend. The two of them got on like a house on fire, always chatting and laughing together. At lunch they sat together in the courtyard with the smokers, eating their sandwiches. The *rokers* teased them because they didn't smoke, but they always took their ribbing with smiles.

"Then, one day, while I was checking through the payments file, I saw a double payment. I went to the source documents and found that one of the payments had been made to a private bank account. It didn't take me long to find whose account that was—Frankie's. As an attempted fraud, it was really amateurish. And it was the first time he tried it. I called him into my office, and he burst out crying almost as he walked through the door—he knew

I had found out.

"He sat here sobbing. His whole family, his entire clan wanted money from him—he was the golden boy who had managed to get a university education. And now he worked in an office, an actual office. None of the rest of them had jobs, but if they did, they did menial things—they were cleaners and security guards. That type of thing. And Frankie was supposed to pay for everybody, whenever they needed money. A relative died, and he'd had to cough up for the funeral. His sister was ill, and he had to pay for her treatment. His mother was old and he had to care for her. And the only way he could cope, really, was to steal."

"He was a little crook," said Jonny.

"Yes, he was. He did try to steal. But I felt sorry for him. I put in a recommendation, directly to Thuli, asking that we not press charges. I knew we had to fire him from the Accounts Department, but I didn't want to ruin his life by sending him to jail as well. But the company decided that it would be a slippery slide to nowhere. It was Thuli himself who made that decision—he rang me and told me stuff about how he'd grown up poor and that if you allow people from the townships a finger, they'll grab the whole hand. That kind of thing. *Open the floodgates*, is what he said, if we didn't charge that poor boy."

Panico looked down at his desk, silent for a while. He didn't want to criticise the CEO, but it was clear that he didn't agree with how things had been done. Then he shook his head and added: "And now he's in jail and his life is in tatters." Even Jonny said nothing.

Stephen nodded.

"Were Mpho and Frankie more than friends?" he asked. Next to him, Jonny snorted. Stephen looked at him coolly and with half a smile said: "Jonny, can you organise me a cup of coffee please? I'm parched." Jonny, nothing if not aware what was happening, lumbered to his feet, left the office and closed the door behind him.

"So?" Stephen pressed.

"Hell, Stephen. I don't know. I mean, how can I say?"

"Well, you *are* Greek," Stephen said, holding the young man's gaze. Panico laughed, the tension draining out of him.

"Yes, I think they were more than friends. Certainly Frankie behaved like a girl and it was an open secret that he was gay; and Mpho was probably gay as well, although from just meeting him once or twice you wouldn't have known. There was a gentleness about him that made you think he was different—no testosterone-fuelled machismo. You know, he wasn't your average rugby player. I didn't ever ask, because it's none of my business; and if I knew it wouldn't have made an ounce of difference to me. And, Stephen, just to be clear—I liked them both, they were good employees and they did their work well. Until, of course, life legged that poor boy over."

"Do you think any of this could be relevant to Mpho's death?"

"I can't see how."

Stephen couldn't either.

Chapter 4

"The university I went to," Jozi Moloi told Stephen, "the University of the North, was established in 1959. The village around the university used to be called Sovenga, which stood for Sotho, Venda and Tsonga. But nowadays people call it Mankweng."

He went there to study engineering in the early 1980s, when the country was being pulled apart by civil war, and the Nats still thought their independent republic of arrogance and apartheid would last forever. To get there from home he lugged his suitcase on a bus to Germiston, and then took the train. The carriage danced over switch-points outside the station, following the locomotive briefly to Johannesburg, then veered north. Stop after stop they crept through Pretoria, and later sped through the shimmering evening over the Springbok flats, past Warmbad and the foothills of the Waterberg.

"Our campus was forty kilometres east of Pietersburg," he said, "in the first swell of the Hwiti mountain range." After the 1994 elections the town changed its name to Polokwane.

He was not a big man, but his chin was made for the movies. His face shone with good health and prosperity as if he polished himself in the mirror every morning. He kept his hair as neat as a military parade, and considered the world from behind aristocratically high cheekbones. He drew his own conclusions, was convinced of their correctness, and then kept them to himself. While he was making up his mind about Stephen, he rolled a red-and-white pencil around in his bony fingers.

"There was political trouble and while I was there they closed the university several times because of the protests and the violence. I was worried that I wouldn't ever qualify because I was running out of money. But in the end I got an honours degree in Mining Engineering." He motioned in the direction of the framed degree certificate on the wall. "It was at university that people first called me 'Jozi.' My first name is Cebile, but one day in class I said that I wanted to work in the city, in Johannesburg. So people started calling me Jozi, and the name stuck."

"You're the section engineer for Biesies North?" Stephen asked. Every part of the mine has somebody appointed as the so-called *Responsible Person*.

"That's me. I'm appointed for Biesies Main and Biesies North," Jozi sighed.

The formal legal appointment went with the position. It carried no status—only obligations. Stephen took over the explanation.

"You know that in the eyes of the law whatever happens in your section is your responsibility. If it's serious enough, as in the case of a fatality, Theuns and Xoli could be held responsible as well."

The three people in the direct firing line for the death of Joseph Mpho Mamela were Jozi; Theuns Myburgh, who was the Chief Engineer for the mine; and Xoli Sibeko, the General Manager and big boss of the whole operation. All three could be charged personally in a criminal court if the mine was suspected of having been negligent in Mamela's death, or if a mining or safety regulation hadn't been followed to the letter. For this reason alone, the book of mining regulations was sacred, as if bound in blood and skin; and by its stern code the mine and the people on it lived their lives. The mantra chanted at every management meeting was *Safety, Tonnes and Cost*. Keep your people safe, mine as much coal as possible, and keep your eye on overheads that sneak in like a thief in the night. But always in that order: Safety first; then the rest.

"What happened?" Stephen asked.

"I don't know." Jozi shook his head. "I can't begin to tell you what this guy thought he was doing or how he managed to get himself killed." He steepled his fingers, still holding the pencil between the index and middle finger of his right hand, like an extra spar in the roof of the building his fingers described.

"It's not the type of place you get to accidentally. You don't just wander around and suddenly there you are. You specifically have to go there—it's far from anywhere else. Even if you did go there, it's just not that dangerous, except if you really go out of your way to be stupid about it. You actually have to stick your hand into the moving parts to be injured; and you have to be suicidally foolish to do that." He was quiet for a second or two before he continued: "He was an *accountant*." Jozi spat out the second syllable for emphasis: ac-COUNT-ant. He shook his head once in disbelief. "He had no business being there. He wasn't allowed to be near the belt, let alone to interfere with it. He got himself killed through dedicated stupidity."

"How did he get to where he was killed?"

"He drove. The stupid man drove."

"But how was he not stopped for being in an unauthorised place?"

"Let me show you." Jozi got up and moved over to a large scale map of the mine pinned on a brown soft board covering most of the wall furthest from the window. It was a working document, not meant for show. Several coloured pins were stuck into it, here, there, and everywhere. Someone had pointed things out on it, emphatically stabbing a grubby finger at the chart. Perhaps the same person had drawn a series of black arrows, showing the movement of something in a prevailing north-easterly direction. In the bottom left-hand corner, someone had written *10/8 ROM trgt 18.5.*

"This"—Jozi traced his finger along the outline of black that circled almost the entire map—"is the perimeter fence." The whole mine was contained within it. "Here"—he stabbed an index finger in the bottom left corner of the map—"is the main gate to the administrative block." Stephen noticed that Jozi's fingers left no marks; those dirty fingerprints were someone else's.

"Over here" — Jozi circled four separate enclosed areas: two in the bottom right-hand corner, one at the top, and the biggest by far slap bang in the middle of the map — "are the operational areas. The big one is Biesies Main, these ones are Modder 1 and Modder 2, and this one" — again he stabbed his smudge-free finger — "is Biesies North. Each one of the operational areas is enclosed by its own separate safety fence, and you can get inside only by going through a checkpoint. You don't get through unless you can say exactly who you are and what you want, and you have the necessary permission. With very few exceptions only working vehicles are let through. We keep a tight control on that. There are other areas" — Jozi outlined three much smaller areas with circular motions of his hand — "that are also access controlled: the plant, engineering works, and the back-fill area."

The engineer stood back from the map, frowning at it suspiciously. Then he continued. "This is the conveyor that runs from the high wall on Biesies North to the power station fence. Here," he stabbed again at the map, "is where we deliver to Eskom. From there on it's their problem. You'll see the conveyor," he traced a dark red line from the operational area in the north all the way to the delivery point on the western edge of the mining area, "all-in-all is just over thirteen kilometres long. It obviously isn't just one belt, but where it's relatively flat, sections are up to just over a kilometre long. Where this guy got himself killed is right in the middle of the longest section.

"The belt there runs at something like four hundred feet per minute. That's seven feet per second. When you stand next to it, it doesn't look that fast. But it's faster than you can react to if you get pinched between the rollers. Just think about it: It would pull you through from top to toe in less than a second. And, obviously, the thing weighs hundreds of tonnes. Not only the belt itself, but over a kilometre of coal piled on top. It would pull an ox through the rollers without registering a blip."

"The entire length of the conveyor is inside the mining area, but outside the operational areas?" Stephen asked.

"Exactly. If we want to fence it off, we would need to run a thirteen kilometre fence for no particular purpose. Worse than that: the fence would interfere with access to the conveyor." He traced his finger along the service road that ran the length of the belt.

"One more thing: the belt is covered for most of the way. Here, where the incident happened, it has its own roof; and its structure makes it difficult to get to. It runs a metre-and-a-half above the ground, but it's supported by a criss-crossed metal structure that leaves no room for strolling through. You have to duck in under the support struts if you want to get at either the rollers or the belt. It's only the maintenance crews that get in there from time to time. Everyone else keeps away. And the maintenance crew, I can assure you"—Jozi turned exasperated eyes to Stephen—"switch the thing off first. No one in his right senses fiddles with a conveyor while it's running."

"I can imagine." Stephen nodded. "So how did this guy get there?"

"Well, he comes to work in the morning and parks next to the Admin block, over here," Jozi pointed at the map again. "He comes in the main gate the same way as you do—he shows his identity card at the boom. And, of course, he drives a company vehicle. So, no problem for him to get inside the main fence. When he goes home again, he is supposed to go back out of the main gate. There's no other way out. Everything on the mine comes through that gate—maybe not the one you use, but the big one next to it for moving the really big stuff through."

The main gate, Stephen knew, was like the entrance to a busy port: a regular-sized gate for ordinary traffic, and another, which looked as if it had been built in Brobdingnag, for everything else. Between the gates was a security office manned by several men and women in uniform who tried the patience of everyone who wanted to come in, by insisting that you comply precisely with their every requirement. If you got fed-up, well, that was your choice: you could come inside after you did what they wanted you to do, or you could stay outside forever.

Jozi went on, "Someone like Mamela could drive around the mine all day without being asked where he was going, but when he got to one of the restricted areas, he wouldn't be allowed to go any further."

Stephen considered the layout. "The conveyor isn't in a restricted area. So, Mamela could get to it quite easily. All he had to do was get inside the main gate?"

"Yes, I suppose that's right. If he wanted to be an idiot, he could access the belt."

"Well, we know he did, even if we don't know why," Stephen said. "Isn't that a problem for us? It's a potentially dangerous thing, and it isn't properly access-controlled? Didn't you tell me once that if it was possible to do something stupid, somebody would do it sooner or later?"

"Yes, I did. And it looks as if I was right." He frowned and massaged his temples. "But look at it this way: If he wanted to be stupid, he could've injured himself anywhere – he could've crashed his car, he could've tripped over his own feet, he could've set himself on fire. Anywhere. But the mine is only responsible if we added to the danger. If he did himself in all on his own, that's not our concern."

"I wish it was that simple."

"But Stephen," Jozi said, visibly irked, "if this idiot behaved anywhere near responsibly, he'd still be okay. He's constantly reminded of his absolute duty to be safe. We drill it into the lot of them morning, noon and night. Like everyone else, he signed a piece of paper saying he knows this. I've seen it on his file. Jonny will show it to you. Every employee on the mine has to do that."

Jozi flung his pencil onto the desk. It bounced and rolled off the other side, landing on the floor at Stephen's feet. He bent down, picked it up, put it down in front of him.

In the somewhat awkward silence, Stephen said, "And then this guy comes along and fucks up your safety record?" A ghost of a smile hovered near the corners of his mouth.

"Well, yes," Jozi said, and had the good grace to look sheepish. His frustration gave way to resignation. "You know, we work at it, very hard. And it's a big thing for us. All day, every day, we say: *Safety, safety, safety.* We were getting close to three thousand incident-free hours. You've seen the board where we write it up. It's a competition between the sections. When we get there, we have a little party—a *braai*, and everybody gets a few Rand as a bonus. So we do our best. But now we have to start again from the beginning because an accountant, an *accountant*, managed to get himself killed in one of my belts." Stephen wondered how Panico would've felt about the disdain Jozi had for his profession.

"Will you show me where it happened?"

"Sure. Let's go."

On the way they picked up Jonny, and all three of them went in his bakkie. It would've been easy to miss the forest by staring at the trees. Not that there was a tree in sight as they drove out slowly toward the western boundary of the mining area.

They passed a work gang fixing a section of road, another bunch doing something to a complicated structure a few paces away from the road; they drove past enormous machines parked next to a workshop, and several machines passed them: bakkies like Jonny's, heavy service vehicles, and a backactor. They drove past the spiral plant and the dense medium wash plant; from some way off the bright eye of a welder's torch stabbed at them like an awl; somewhere else someone was beating a metal plate with what sounded like Thor's hammer. In the distance they saw a gargantuan dragline ripping up the land, and massive haul vehicles lumbering down a much bigger road. On a pitch black field, a bulldozer was levelling mounds of coal chips; on another field, mobile drills bored down into the ground. A crusher was swallowing mounds of coal, chewing them with a great gnashing of its teeth and spitting them onto an incline belt that was building a neat conical pile ready to be gathered in as today's harvest. And everywhere pulleys whirred, sirens wailed, motors whined, conveyors muttered, engines chuntered, heavy machines groaned, and hooters blasted out their sundry warnings. Everyone was doing his own little thing and only the guys in charge, guys like Jozi, knew how it all fitted together and what had to be done next.

They drove to an area where Stephen had never been, close to the boundary fence. Jonny turned onto a service road next to a covered conveyor that looked as Jozi had described it, except that it was longer than Stephen had expected. They drove slowly along it for several kilometres, truly out into the sticks. There was only the veld and the covered conveyor. Eventually Jonny slowed and pulled off to the side, leaving his bakkie half-in and half-out the road. He turned to Stephen. "This is where they found his vehicle, exactly like we are now, parked like this. The driver's door was open, the motor was still running, but he wasn't anywhere to be seen."

"Like the *Marie Celeste*," Stephen said.

"I don't know her. Who's she?" Jonny asked.

"The youth of today." Stephen sighed. "Don't know a thing. The *Marie Celeste* was a nineteenth century sailing ship that was found making her way along under full sail, but without its crew. Apparently there was still food on the table, but the crew was gone."

"No, man. He didn't come in a ship. He drove here in his bakkie," Jonny laughed, and turned off the engine. All three of them got out, still grinning. "Now be careful, old boy. We don't want you tripping over your feet and falling into the conveyor. I wouldn't know what to say to your missus."

"I'll be on my best behaviour," said Stephen. He saw that

Jozi's description had been accurate—the carrying surface of the conveyor was supported by a lattice of metal struts, which made the belt really difficult to get to. Also, it ran under a simple pitched roof, triangular in cross-section. The lip of the roof extended below the level of the belt, so that if you wanted to see the belt at all, you actually had to duck your head under the roof.

"Where was he? Where did they find him?"

"He was here," Jonny said. He squatted, close to the conveyor, and pointed up at a section of the supporting structure—two sturdy vertical poles on either side of the conveyor, the double load-bearing support that carried the massive weight of the belt and its cargo. Attached to the frame were several horizontal rollers over which the belt moved. The same design was repeated every few metres, and in between the belt was supported by a metal bed, cross buttressed for maximum rigidity.

"His injuries were severe?"

"Let me put it this way, he was almost unrecognisable. They only identified him by his name tag that was still on a lanyard around his neck. Somehow that was still in one piece."

Stephen stared at the contraption in silence.

"What can we tell from all of this?"

It was Jozi who answered: "Absolutely nothing. We don't know why he was here or what he was doing. You won't discover any hidden clues here."

Jonny nodded.

"Our detective friend here thinks Mamela was removing an obstruction from the belt. What do you think?" Stephen asked Jozi.

"It's possible. But that doesn't tell us what he was doing here or how he knew there was an obstruction at this exact spot, or how or why he thought he should try to remove it." The glance that passed between Jozi and Jonny confirmed that they agreed on this.

"Come gents. We have to have a theory at least. Did he kill

himself deliberately?" Stephen was trying to plan ahead for what he'd tell the Inspectorate.

"You mean like suicide?" Jonny looked pensive.

"I don't mean 'like suicide.' I mean suicide, plain and simple."

"Hell of a way to do it, boss," the big man said, shaking his head.

Chapter 5

The two men were waiting in the passage outside Jonny's office when he and Stephen got back from their drive with Jozi.

"Afternoon, gents," Jonny boomed.

"Afternoon, Mr. van Straten," they said.

"Let's go sit in the committee room."

Jonny led the way. Four doors down from his office he turned the handle on an unmarked door. They walked into that smell you get when a lot of paper and office furniture have been left in a small sealed room for days on end. Jonny went straight to the windows and opened them. The room was drab. There were dark-blue carpet tiles on the floor, nothing at all on the off-white walls, piles of old files along one wall, and a round table in the middle of the room with five regulation office chairs around it. The blinds, vertical slats of fabric, astoundingly were violet.

Jonny was all business: "This is Mr. Wakefield from head office. He's here to speak to you about the fatality."

Stephen had seen this before. If these two had been office workers, they would've been offered tea first and perhaps even cookies. But they were not from the Admin complex, so no attempt was made to make them feel at home. He supposed it had something to do with the dichotomy of labour and management, the perennial divide between bosses and workers. Never the twain shall meet, and if they do, don't expect tea. Both men looked at Stephen in trepidation, their apprehension showing in their faces and in the way they sat on the edge of their seats.

"Thank you for your time in coming to speak to me." Stephen nodded. Neither responded. "I'm Stephen Wakefield and I'm helping the company prepare for the inquiry into Mpho Mamela's death. You were the ones who found his body?" They both nodded. "Can we begin with your names, please?"

"Lebohang Duma," the man on the left said with a nod. He was in blue overalls unbuttoned down the front, and under it, an old khaki T-shirt full of holes and stretched in the collar. On his head was a knitted beanie, despite the heat of the afternoon. He looked to be in his fifties and had the sort of face that showed neither emotion nor interest. He'd speak when spoken to; and the sooner he could be away from here, the better.

"Jumpy Mashishi," said the younger of the two, in a more confident voice. He wore a standard issue open-necked work shirt with the company's double-shadowed cheetah logo on the left pocket, under the name Sethemba Collieries. He was much younger than his companion, probably still in his twenties, part of the new generation that had not had its confidence systematically ground out over decades. He had no hat, and looked like the one who would be prepared to talk to this white man from the city.

"What's your first name, please?"

"Bandile."

"Thanks. Last Friday the two of you found Mpho Mamela's body. Please tell me what happened." As Stephen had expected, Jumpy was the one who took up the invitation to speak.

"It was early in the morning, seven o'clock, something like that. We were checking the conveyor. We do this every morning. We were at the long section and we saw the company bakkie. It was parked on the grass half in the road. The engine was on. The door was open but we saw nobody." He stopped speaking and looked at Stephen.

"Who was driving your car?"

"I was," Jumpy answered. "Lebo doesn't have a licence."

"So what did you do then?"

"I stopped the car and we got out. We didn't see anybody. I hooted to see if somebody would hear. But nobody came. So we looked inside the bakkie but there was nothing. We didn't know what to do. We walked to the conveyor and looked under it. Lebo saw him first." The man fell silent again.

"What did you see?"

"*Hayi*," the older man said, shaking his head. "He was fucked up." Stephen waited, but Lebo said nothing further. He looked at Jumpy, who took over again.

"We saw a body lying under the conveyor. He was pulled through the rollers. There was a lot of blood, and the man, he was dead." His head dropped as he recalled the horror. "I want to rip the memory from my eyes." The silence that followed made it clear to Stephen that neither man was about to add any further detail.

"So what happened to him?"

Neither man responded, so he tried again: "Was he on duty, or was he working there? What was he doing? How did he get killed like that?" Again a curtain of silence.

"Hey, man!" Jonny barked. "Answer Mr. Wakefield. Did you kill him?"

The men grunted in surprise and denial, shaking their heads and looking at each other in alarm.

"No!" Jumpy said, shaking his head. "We just found him. We don't know what happened. We weren't there."

This is hopeless, Stephen thought. But the inquiry will insist on establishing a chain of continuity, as they called it. From the scene of death to the mortuary and a name on the death certificate.

"What did you do then?"

The two men looked at each other in confusion.

"Well, did you radio your control room, or did you phone? Or did you drive there? Did you tell someone? What did you do?"

"We don't have a radio," the young man said.

"So what did you do?"

"We both got in the bakkie and drove to the control room. We fetched Amos."

"Why did you both go?" Stephen asked.

Neither man answered. *Well, why not*, Stephen thought to

himself. There wasn't really anything they could do at that stage. And by the sounds of it, Mamela wasn't going anywhere.

"Who is Amos?"

"He's the superintendent. Amos Hlongwane."

"What did he do?"

"He phoned security and first aid. We didn't go back there."

Stephen came to a decision to put both himself and the reluctant duo out of their respective miseries. "Okay, that will be all, thank you very much. You've been very helpful. Thank you for your time."

In the passage they turned left, and Jonny and Stephen turned right. As they walked along, Jonny stared quizzically at Stephen from under a raised eyebrow. "*You've been very helpful?*" he repeated the older man's words. "Are you getting too old for this job? Shall we get you an assistant?"

Stephen smiled sheepishly as Jonny continued: "You think it could have been possible for them to be less helpful?"

"Perhaps not, Mr. Thin Blue Line. I actually don't think they have anything useful to say, really. They'll be witnesses at the inquiry, but just to repeat that they found the body. They know nothing further. And I'd rather do without their fantastical theories of what actually happened."

Back in his office Jonny sat down heavily and said: "I suppose you want to talk to the titivating *doos* as well?" He meant Trevor Hodges, the prissy and officious HR manager.

"It's been a long day, Tonto. Can we keep that exquisite pleasure for tomorrow?"

"Kemosabe, I like a man with a good plan."

Chapter 6

Stephen's B&B in Crosby was in the middle of town, opposite the small post office and next to an old-fashioned second-hand book dealer who kept a display of old coins and medals in glass-topped cabinets against the furthest wall. Next to that was *Hengel en Haarkapper*, the multipurpose shop where you could get your hair cut and everything you needed for your next fly-fishing trip. The corner belonged to a general dealer that smelled of newspapers and tobacco.

Stephen left his overnight bag on the bed and made his way downstairs. Crosby was a town that went to bed early and he didn't want to miss dinner. Cecelia, the plump and pretty owner, cooked breakfast only. She ran a bed-and-breakfast, not a bed-and-supper.

"I won't be late," he told her at the door, turning an old-fashioned brass doorknob and stepping out into the early evening. The hot afternoon had let go of its sweaty hold on the day. Five minutes and three-and-a-half blocks brought him to the front door of a whitewashed building beckoning from behind a handmade wooden sign that told him he'd reached the *Commando & Arms*. An old short-barrelled field canon on two metal wheels pointed jauntily over the roofs of the buildings across the road. The gun hadn't been fired in a hundred years and probably hadn't moved from that spot in twenty-five.

The town of Crosby had seen much action in the war between Great Britain and the Boer Republics at the turn of the nineteenth century. On 26 June 1901 General Ben Viljoen attacked a British column not a stone's throw from the playing fields of the primary school Panico's children attended. The Boers killed forty of their enemy and wounded three times as many. They also captured 275 men, took their weapons, and set them free. They knew they would soon face their short-term prisoners in the field again unless they shot them on the spot. But that's just not how they rolled.

The British said thank you by building, only a few miles from the town centre, the largest concentration camp of the war for Boer women and children. At one time it had 7750 inmates, 1381 of whom didn't make it through the war. Emily Hobhouse visited and took pictures of emaciated children who look to us now as if they were at Treblinka or Dachau. The great British war machine also caught and executed Commandant Johannes Lotter, who, in the picture on the wall of the Commando & Arms, is a young man in a worn shirt, clutching his waistcoat with an enormous farmer's hand. Determination and sadness are etched in his narrowed eyes.

A gallery of pictures around him shows *burghers* in various poses and groups, young and old men in rough handmade clothes, holding rifles with which they hoped to fight off the foreign invader. Most of them have beards; all of them have wide-brimmed hats; and the fashion ran to cross-bandoliers bristling with bullets.

The photo that always drew Stephen's eye was of seven tough men, daring the world to come get them. In the front row a young man who couldn't be more than seventeen stares fearfully at the camera. Eternity knows what we did to him. The photo right next to the young man is of Lord Kitchener, well-fed and self-satisfied, congratulating himself on his handlebar moustache and collection of medals, braid, and rosettes. Idi Amin made many of his more inspired wardrobe choices after seeing that picture.

"Hey, Stephen," Hannes greeted him from behind the bar. Hannes had big shoulders, big arms, a big face, and a big grin. "Good to see you. Are you well?"

"Yes, thank you. And you?"

"Yup. Always well. Kannie moan met 'n bek vol tande nie." *Can't complain with my mouth still full of teeth.* "What can I get you?" He listened to Stephen's order, grinned for good measure, and opened the fridge with a big hand that he wrapped around a bottle of beer. With his other hand, no smaller, he plucked a glass off the shelf and put it in front of Stephen.

"Daar's hy," he said, in a big voice. *There you go.*

Stephen settled at a table at the open window with his beer and the menu. His choices were steak, lamb chops, wors, beef curry or, incongruously, macaroni-and-cheese. The Commando special was steak, chops, and wors. The food was always excellent, but you had to be careful of the coffee. Stephen studied the menu, trying to choose the smallest portion. Hannes didn't do small of anything and regarded it as a personal insult if the plate you sent back to the kitchen wasn't licked clean.

Stephen looked up at the scrape of a chair being pulled back. A tall, thick-set man looked at him from under a lowered brow. He was six foot two and as wide as a barn door.

"Good evening, Mr. Wakefield. Would you mind if I join you for a minute?"

"Not at all." Stephen got to his feet and extended his right hand. "Stephen Wakefield," he said.

"Ronald Ncube," the big man replied, as they shook hands. Everything he wore was formal and black, except the white of his priest's collar. A silver crucifix on a long chain dangled on his chest. His face was blunt and his head completely bald, down to the rings of fat above his neck. His fingers were thick and his eyes walnut-brown. He beamed kindness like a lighthouse on the darkest of nights. He looked like the father everyone should have—big and solid and dependable; a man to stand between you and the world when you're alone and frightened.

"Sorry to disturb, but I was told I may be able to find you here. I'd like to talk to you. I'm the priest at the church where Mpho Mamela worshipped. We were friends and I hoped I could spend a few minutes talking to you about him?"

"Certainly, please go right ahead. Can I get you anything?" Stephen asked.

"No thank you. I won't be long. I don't want to take much of your time." The man stared pensively at Stephen. "Actually, can I change my mind? Can I have a cup of coffee, please?"

"I'd be wary of the coffee here if I were you." Stephen chuckled. "We can get you one, but are you sure you won't have something else instead?"

"Oh, very well," the man replied with a chuckle. "Please can I have a large Coke? In a beer mug with lots of ice. I have been sweating all day. Old Man Sun hit me all day with that long stick of his." He showed how, tracing the hitting motion and snapping his right index finger against the others. "*Shaya!*" he said with a laugh, squeezing one eye shut. Stephen laughed with him.

Ronald fell on his drink, slurping half of it in the first long draft without drawing breath. He set the tankard down on the table, wiped his mouth with the back of his hand and sighed, "Aaahhh!" like they do in the adverts.

Stephen watched in fascination. Hannes, who was also watching, winked and smiled in acknowledgement when Stephen raised a surreptitious finger, ordering a refill. It didn't come too soon. Hannes arrived with the full tankard at the very moment Ronald put the empty one down. They looked at each other and both of them burst out laughing, two huge men enjoying a joke. Ronald looked abashed, and Hannes was in his element: here was a fellow traveller who knew how to knock back a drink. He waited for people like this from behind his mahogany fortress with all its colourful bottles and rows of polished glasses. When he found one, it confirmed his faith in humanity.

Ronald wiped a tear of laughter from the corner of his eye and said: "Thanks, man. Thanks." Hannes clapped him on the shoulder with a meaty palm and went happily back to his post behind the bar.

Ronald was still chuckling and shaking his head when Stephen said: "I didn't know Mpho personally, but everyone I come across speaks highly of him."

"Yes, I'm not surprised. He's a remarkable young man. Was."
Ronald sighed the weight of the world off his shoulders. "I met
him a few years ago. Just when he started working at the mine.
He was a labourer, did you know that?"

"I did."

"His job was to roll drums that had been painted that day
from outside in the yard into a furnace for them to cure. He'd just
moved to town and he didn't know anyone. He came to church
on the first Sunday he was here."

"That would've been in June 2007?"

Ronald nodded. "He told me he was the older of two brothers.
His mother worked as a domestic in Brakpan. His father had
passed away many years ago. He was determined to get an
education so that he wouldn't have to be a labourer for the rest of
his life." During the long winter nights when he froze in the yard,
and baked like a gingerbread man at the furnace into which he
had to roll the drums, he made his wish on a sliver of moonlight.
He made a pact with himself under the bowl of stars: *See this
through, Buddy, and then we'll leave the bones of this heartbreak behind
forever.*

"But here's the thing. What he really wanted to do was to help
other people. He loved his mother and felt desperately sorry for
her. He wanted to save her from what he saw as indentured
labour; and he wanted to help his brother, who was much
younger than him, to get a university degree. But not just that. He
wanted to help all poor people. He was a socialist at heart with a
true concern for his fellow man. He was born to be a priest, you
know."

Ronald took a smaller sip from his now half-empty drink.

"He was such a kind man. His agenda was always about
others, never about himself. I've seen many trade union leaders
and shop stewards, and most of them have some commitment to
the cause of their fellow workers. Nothing a thousand Rand
won't fix, though. But Mpho wasn't like that. He wanted the

world to be fair and everyone to get an honest shake out of the system."

Ronald had helped Mpho to register for a correspondence course in accountancy, and because he'd been around the mine for a while, he knew how to apply for a study grant for the young man, from the Workers Trust. "He was so excited. He came to show me his books when they came in the post. He worked hard at that course. He had a physically demanding job at the company, always night shift. But when he was done, he came to sit in the office at the church hall and he worked and worked. He said he couldn't work in the hostel because they wouldn't leave him in peace."

Because he was studying and had passed his first exams, the HR department arranged a position for him in accounts. It made things easier because the work was less physically demanding. "You know, some people are made for hard physical work and others not. I'm too lazy to work hard," he guffawed, then went on, "but Mpho was skinny and not suited to manual labour. After every shift he was hammered. So the job at a desk was much better for him. And the pay was better."

Hannes had come shuffling back to the table. "Sorry to interrupt, gents, but can I take your orders, please? The kitchen will go on strike if I don't tell them soon what to make you."

"Join me for supper?" Stephen asked.

"No, no. You eat while I talk."

"Ag rubbish, man." Hannes said *man* in Afrikaans.

"Yes, absolutely," Stephen agreed. "Order something. The food is outstanding."

Next to him Hannes preened. When Ronald ordered the Commando special, he almost shook him by the hand. That was the only right choice as far as he was concerned.

The story emerged as Ronald tucked in without restraint, and with a third tankard of Coke and ice. Mpho became involved in Ronald's church as an organiser. His energy and compassion made him perfect for the job.

"He arranged a feeding scheme at the local primary school. He always said that you can't make sense of what the teacher says if all you can think of is how hungry you are; when your stomach feels as if there's a wild animal inside you trying to rip it to pieces. Hungry kids learn nothing. He arranged a grant through the mine's CSI program. You know what that is? The Corporate Social Investment program. And he got sponsors. A grocery store donated peanut butter, a bakery gave bread, a dairy sent milk. That sort of thing. Mpho put the logistics in place: ladies who volunteered to make sandwiches; and a vehicle and a driver to deliver the stuff to school. Now every kid gets a peanut butter sandwich and a glass of milk at break. The academic results have shot up. The headmaster tells me just about all the kids have improved. I'm so proud of that boy. The scheme has been running for about four years now."

Feeling as if he really could make a difference, Mpho became involved in the trade union. "It was important, he said, that the workers be treated fairly. He was elected as a representative and helped by doing admin and logistics. The union is hierarchical and only the senior members do the shouting. I know Mpho waited for his turn one day. He told me often that he'd be less confrontational and would achieve more. If you behave reasonably and don't shout, he used to tell me, then people listen better and you manage to do a lot more. Shouting your mouth off sometimes feels satisfying, but it's always the wrong thing to do." Ronald shook his head. "Such wisdom in one so young."

In his job it went better and better. He graduated, was promoted, and soon became a trusted employee, to the extent that his boss arranged a vehicle for his personal use. "You might think it would've gone to his head, but it didn't. He refused to use the bakkie other than for company affairs, and he used his much bigger salary to support his mother and put his younger brother through medical school."

"Sounds like a wonderful young man. All the more pity for this dreadful loss." Stephen frowned. Ronald looked pensive, clearly trying to decide how to phrase what he was about to say next. He sighed, massaged his temples with an enormous hand, and continued with his tale.

"About a year ago some things changed. Not with how he was and what he believed in. All that stayed the same. But there were two big changes. Maybe more, but two main things. The first is that he suddenly had more money. He tried not to show it, but he had enough to start buying himself some treats. He'd never spent anything on himself, but now he bought himself stuff. Not big things, but last winter, for example, he bought himself a stylish coat. He was so proud of it."

Like Akaky Akakievich, Stephen thought. At university he'd read Gogol's short story in which a poor loser, Akaky Akakievich, dreams of having a better coat because his is old and the winters in St. Petersburg are harsh. He saves for years, goes hungry to set aside money, and finally buys the coat of his dreams. The first day he wears it he feels special, like a new man. And on his way home that night, two thugs jump him and take his coat off him. That's Russian literature for you.

Stephen kept quiet, carried on listening.

"He also sent more home to his mother and brother. I know this because I saw a bank slip in the church office once. He was sending the majority of his salary, and still he had money left." Ronald paused in his story. Then, as if coming to a decision, he continued: "The second thing that happened was that he fell in love."

Ronald turned the full force of his empathy on Stephen. "Mr. Wakefield, I'm a priest and you may expect me to be judgemental and disapproving about this, but please be kind in your heart. We are all different and in God's eyes we are all the same."

"Stephen. Please call me Stephen. And if you wait for moral judgements from me, you'll wait a long time."

"The person Mpho fell in love with was just as nice as him. They were very much the same. They both came from poor backgrounds, they both spent almost all their money supporting their families, they both put themselves through correspondence university, and they were both the kindest, most soft-hearted people you'll ever come across. The love of Mpho's life was Frankie Mabena."

"They worked together?"

"Precisely." The priest sat quietly for a moment, gathering his thoughts.

"Stephen." Ronald looked across the table with the sadness of ages gathered in his dark eyes. "You know what happened to Frankie. It's not fair, brother. It's just not fair. Mpho took it really hard. Deep unhappiness overcame him, it undid him. And a steely resolve about something I'm not sure of settled over him. He changed."

One night the two of them had sat up for hours talking about life and sadness and how the loaded dice always tumbled against good people. "He was so bitter that night, not at all the way he usually was. I remember him saying to me: '*Steal a few cents and they put you in jail; steal a few million and they put you in charge.*' He recited it, almost like a mantra. He was such a private person and was never indiscreet, and wouldn't tell me what he meant, wouldn't tell me who he was talking about. But he had something on his mind; something that sapped his good humour and made him bitter and angry." Ronald sighed deeply, shaking his head. "And I don't know what."

"Then he died, all of a sudden?" Stephen said the words the priest didn't want to say.

Ronald nodded, almost imperceptibly.

"What are you telling me?" Stephen frowned, filling out his question with concern in his eyes.

The huge man on the other side of the table heaved another sigh, as big as the barrel of his chest. "I don't know. But something wasn't right."

"Do you think he committed suicide?"

"Absolutely not. He was consumed with responsibility. He'd never in a million years give up on his mother or his brother or on Frankie. And on all the people he cared for. He could no more do that than walk a tightrope from here to Cairo. No, he certainly didn't kill himself."

Stephen let the silence settle. After a moment he said: "My friend, it looks as if Mpho died by accident. There really is nothing to let me think otherwise. But I'll follow up on what you have told me. Thank you for coming, I really appreciate your time. I'll keep in contact and I'll take what you have told me seriously."

"Thanks." Ronald nodded. He stood up and took Stephen's hand in his thick-fingered mitt. "I know you will. That's what people who've told me about you also said."

Chapter 7

Stephen woke to the silence of the small town. A turtledove outside his open window swapping stories with a wagtail, the far-off gear change of a car, the sun pouring down like silver.

When they were first married, Stephen and Lisa got a phone call before six every morning, Lisa's folks back on the farm near Underberg checking that all was well. The cows had been awake for ever so long, the milking was done, and with breakfast on the table, it was time to share the news. If the telephone in the farmstead rang after half past seven at night, it was death or serious illness. Even insolvency was discussed while the sun was still up.

But folks on a farm phone for any reason from dawn's early light. It took a while for Farmer Charles to realise how urban his new son-in-law was, hearing to his astonishment that Stephen went to bed after midnight. From then on he was too polite to make any noise early in the morning; and his daughter was too fond of her parents not to have their early morning chat. She'd slip out of bed when the first shadows slid silver-grey along the wall, and ring from the kitchen after putting on the kettle to boil.

Now that those before-breakfast calls were only a bittersweet memory, at first light she still left the night owl beside her dreaming his deepest dreams, and padded down the passage to meet her circle of admirers. In the kitchen the cats arched their backs and purred; and at the back door in a circle of expectant faces and wagging tails, the dogs waited in ill-contained excitement for the key to turn in the lock. They'd swarm in, chirruping their joy at this reunion as if Lisa had been gone for a month. They bashed their thick tails against the door and kitchen cabinets, all three trying to be patted first. The cats would watch in disdain from their high perch on the counter, but made no comment. Such silliness warranted none.

Stephen knew that when the sun was up, so was his wife. He reached for his phone and dialled.

"Hey, you're up early," said the woman he loved so well.

"Yup. Thought I'd catch you before your tea got cold."

"Almost too late." There was nothing to tell but much to say. Yesterday had been full, not hectic; she thought today would be the same. His day? Well, things were going slowly, and some of it was a bit puzzling. Since forever Lisa had known not to ask after details—discretion was the better part of his valour, and also his way of life.

"When am I expecting you?" she asked.

"I'll ring before I leave. But I'll try to get away by four. So expect me at seven or so?" Then they would have dinner together.

Stephen rolled out of bed and woke up properly under the shower. He kept breakfast to a minimum, after the mountain of his dinner the night before. Then he jumped into his car and set off for the mine. His appointment was for eight o'clock.

On the short drive he remembered that Johnny Hodges played the alto sax in Duke Ellington's band. He was an interesting man, an artist. His namesake, Trevor Hodges, was the HR manager at Sethemba Collieries. He was neither interesting nor an artist; and it was generally acknowledged that he could make a monkey bite its mother. He got to the office early so that he could tell everyone that he got to the office early. He wore a different cravat every day, often with a paisley design. That alone was enough to disqualify him as fully human in Jonny van Straten's eyes. But that alone wasn't what made people avoid him like typhus.

Stephen pushed open the door of Hodges's office a few minutes early. The desk was neater than any desk should ever be. In the middle of it stood a miniature shiny golden golf bag in which an assortment of pens was neatly arranged; and a miniature white plastic golf ball was the calendar. Next to it a slogan encased in acrylic glass said: "Either you run the day, or the day runs you." On the walls were several framed photographs of Hodges in smiling poses at various company functions. Directly behind his chair was another slogan in curly copperplate: "Time is the wisest counsellor of all."

Trevor Hodges was a short man who had over the previous three or so years lost about forty kilograms. When he'd still been short and fat, thought Stephen, there was a type of pathos about him, an indefinable something that made you feel sorry enough to listen to his interminable stories. But now that he was svelte, at least in his own eyes, he dressed like a dandy and handed out style and diet advice to anyone he could corner for long enough. In his job he was meticulous to an improbable degree, and in his reports he never used one word when twelve would do. His officiousness was only exceeded by his sycophancy. He fawned obsequiously over anyone he thought senior to him, Stephen definitely included. He was correspondingly searingly rude to those he regarded as his inferiors.

But his biggest failing, the one Stephen couldn't forgive him for, was that he couldn't keep quiet. If he so much as saw you, he started on an endless story with no point other than that Trevor was the hero of some or other HR coup. He answered every question by saying, "Let me give you some background." Stephen was really scared of those words. They presaged a torrent of irrelevant twaddle as surely as dark clouds and a sudden drop in temperature on a Highveld summer afternoon foretold a thunderstorm. Because nobody would stand still for long enough for him to end a story, if indeed they ever ended, he loved nothing better than to be asked for information. Then he blossomed into the diamond class bore he longed to be.

"Trevor, is there anything on Mamela's file that could be relevant to his accident last week?" Stephen hoped against hope that the prissy little man sitting in front of him heard and took note of his emphasis of the word *relevant*.

"Let me put it to you this way. Before the company transferred its systems onto the new HR Standard Acceptance Practice and Procedures, I attended a conference that was given by the Institute in Sandton. We spent three days designing the standard-isation of protocols and processes. Marius van Druten was in the chair, and we went through every single step of the processes in an attempt to set an industry standard for all of us to follow. The document that came out of that was a draft that was circulated to all participating delegates. We all submitted comments, and my comments were the ones on which we started emphasising the second draft."

Stephen felt a general itch develop somewhere between his seat and his trousers. He interrupted: "When was that, Trevor?"

"It was, now let me see, 1986. It was in July. No, wait, it was in August, because we had a second drafting meeting in September."

I can't get pissed off with him so early in the conversation, Stephen forced himself to subvocalise. "Yes, thank you. Can we move it up a little, though? Mamela was born in 1987 and started working here in June 2007. He moved into the Accounts Department about a year later. Can we take it from there, please? What were his annual assessments and are there any out-of-the-ordinary issues or events on file?"

"Well, as I was saying." Hodges sat back in his chair, legs crossed daintily at the knees, with a pinched expression on his face, clearly offended that he'd been cut short. "One of the most fundamental things in the HR Standard Acceptance Practice and Procedures relates to the protection of personal information and the maintenance of strict confidentiality. It's the mainstay of our departmental processes and procedures, and without it we simply cannot operate on any sound or sustainable basis. The platform so created is sacrosanct, and cannot be undone for any reason at all."

"Are you telling me that the contents of his file are confi-dential?"

"Our function is dependent on the maintenance of the trust of our employees and they must be comfortable that there's no disclosure of their personal information. The HR SAP and P specify clearly as an industry standard that personal information is proprietary to each individual and his entitlement to confidentiality is entrenched in the principle of freedom of information."

"Even when they're dead?"

"Yes." Hodges nodded staccato-crisp and straightened the pen and pencil lying next to the file so they were exactly aligned.

"So you won't tell me what's in the file?"

Stephen felt as if he'd been wrong-footed despite himself and despite his having dealt with this man and his department before.

"It's not that I *won't* tell you. It's that I *cannot*. The integrity of the system, and my own personal integrity will absolutely forbid it, and will prevent me from making any disclosure. The HR system constitutes a closed homogeneity and if you were to remove one of its most fundamental elements, then it collapses and we are without any system whatsoever."

"I see. We keep a system but no one is allowed to know what's in it?"

"It's not that *no one* is allowed to know what's inside it. *I* know what's inside it. And the unions and employee representatives have confirmed their confidence in my integrity on many occasions. We have a very good understanding and the company benefits on an ongoing basis from my being the most trusted representative in the eyes of the workers." The HR man folded his arms and set his mouth in a thin line.

Stephen was temporarily at a loss. *Jonny would know how to deal with this*, he thought. But he had absolutely, point-blank, refused to join Stephen in the meeting. "My life is too short for that," he had said. "If he accidentally says anything useful or interesting, please let me know? In summary form." Then he'd laughed, clapped Stephen heartily on the shoulder, and pushed him in the direction of the HR Department.

"Trevor, I can't have this conversation with you. You keep the files not for yourself, but for the company. I need to know the answer to my question. What's in the file that you won't tell me about?"

"The standardisation of the protocols maintains the integrity . . ." he began.

"No." Stephen interrupted, feeling himself losing his cool, despite his earlier resolve. "You have to tell me. In fact, not just tell me. I need to see what you're hiding in that file. You must give it to me right now. This isn't a game."

Hodges stiffened even further, if that seemed possible. "I'm not *hiding* anything. It's standard industry protocol that I can't make disclosures of the contents of a personal file to just every Tom, Dick and Harry! The contents of that file will remain confidential and the integrity of the system and my own integrity will not be compromised without the proper process and procedure."

"I'm neither Tom, Dick, nor Harry." Stephen gazed levelly at the man across the table, who realised belatedly that he may have been pushing his luck. "I'm a director of this company and I'm investigating a matter of grave concern and consequence. To the company. What's in the file you're not telling me?"

"That is something I can't tell you. I need a proper instruction before I can disclose the contents of the personal file to you."

"What constitutes a proper instruction?" Stephen sat firmly on his impulse to shout at this pompous little man.

"I need an instruction from the very top."

Stephen gazed at Hodges across the desk, inwardly counting first to three, and then to ten. Without saying a further word, he pulled out his mobile and dialled. His call was answered on the third ring.

"Xoli? It's Stephen. I'm sitting with Trevor Hodges, about the Mamela fatality. There's information on his confidential file that may be crucial to the investigation, but Trevor needs an instruction from you before he can disclose it to me. Can I give him the telephone?"

Stephen leaned across the desk and handed over the phone. Hodges took it nervously, his whole being now transformed to that of a cowering puppy, eager to please but fearful of a possible beating.

"Good morning, Mr. Sibeko. Yes, Mr. Sibeko. Right, Mr. Sibeko. Very well. Immediately, Mr. Sibeko. Thank you, sir. Goodbye, Mr. Sibeko." Then he handed the phone back to Stephen. "Thank you. That was very important. Now we have the procedural aspects squared away, and I can disclose the contents of the file. Which, of course, will remain confidential, even if you know them." He made an attempt to smile at Stephen, who wasn't ready for smiling yet.

"Thank you, Trevor. So, let me have it. What's in the file that is so important?"

"I didn't say there was anything important in the file. I said I couldn't tell you whether there was anything important. In fact, there isn't anything unusual in the file at all."

Stephen stared at him in dumbfounded silence. "You made me go through that whole performance only to tell me there's nothing on the file?" Stephen frowned and looked sideways at Hodges, nodding once for emphasis.

"It's a procedural requirement, Mr. Wakefield. But now that we've squared it away, I can disclose to you that this file is perfectly straightforward. There have never been any complaints about him, and he has never made any complaints about anybody. This file is clean as a whistle." Hodges nodded obsequiously, pulling the corners of his mouth into the tiniest of experimental grins.

"Jesus Christ," Stephen said under his breath, as he exhaled slowly. *No wonder van Straten wouldn't come with me,* he thought. "Very well, then. Please tell me when last Mr. Mamela had a salary increase."

Now Hodges was keen to show how efficient he was, and astoundingly gave a straight answer: "In November 2013 he was promoted to a senior position in the Accounts Department. He got an increase because he went onto a different pay scale. He got a big increase then. In February this year, 2015, he got an inflationary increase, same as the rest of the company. His was on the higher end of the scale. He got 8 percent."

"Thanks. Nothing else on the file? No notes, no letters, no nothing?"

"Nothing. Here, have a look." Hodges handed over the file. And, truly, there wasn't anything else on it.

"Well, thank you for your help. The information has been most useful. I'll get back to you if I need anything else." Stephen got up to leave.

"It was a pleasure. Always happy to help. That's what we're here for." Hodges bounced out of his chair, rubbing his hands like a Dickensian shopkeeper. "I thought to myself that this young man won't get up to any good by arguing with Mr. Mpongose. I have never seen Mr. Mpongose cross, because he is such a fair man. But he was very angry with Mamela when he chased him out of his office."

Thuli Mpongose, the CEO, kept an office down one end of the passage, near the HR department, when he was at the mine.

"What's that?" Stephen asked.

"Oh, I'm sure it's nothing, now that he isn't around anymore. But last week on Wednesday evening it was at about ten past six. No, it was about twenty past six, I had packed up and was going home. You know I come in at six in the morning, so I had been in my office for just over twelve hours. I walked down the passage and outside Mr. Mpongose's office I heard him shouting at somebody. And then the door opened and Mamela came walking out. He looked as if he'd just been shouted at. Probably deserved it too."

"Did you hear what they were saying?"

"Oh no. I only heard raised voices, and then this Mamela comes walking out of the office. You could see that he'd just received a tongue lashing. He looked as if he'd been properly reprimanded, and his head was hanging. It serves him right not being respectful to Mr. Mpongose."

"How do you know he wasn't respectful?"

"Well, I don't know. But Mr. Mpongose won't say anything if you treat him properly. I know this. He has never been unfair or unreasonable to me. We get on like a house on fire. He respects my advice and doesn't move without consulting me first. So it must have been Mamela's fault. But I don't know what they were arguing about."

"And neither of them reported this to you?"

"No, definitely not. As I say, I just heard it in the corridor."

"Thanks," Stephen said thoughtfully. And then he made his escape.

Chapter 8

"You're back earlier than I thought. I was expecting you next week," Jonny deadpanned as Stephen collapsed into the chair which, in deference to his visit, had stayed in place.

"That guy," Stephen let out a slow breath. "You had better start planning what you'll write in the murder docket one day when someone strangles him."

"I'll say it was self-defence. He had to kill him or die of boredom."

"The boredom is the easy part. It's his officiousness that really gets me."

Jonny grinned ruefully. "He won't give you anything unless you fill out the form he made up. It asks about a thousand questions that have nothing to do with what you want. And if you don't fill it out exactly the way he wants you to, he refuses to give you the information. He alone decides if you have filled the form out properly. No appeal process."

Stephen lifted an eyebrow. "Yes, I remember you once discussed that with him without formal constraint?"

What Stephen had heard was that one day Jonny, after having had his request for the service record of a man he'd arrested for theft turned down the fourth or fifth time, because he hadn't completed the HR form to Hodges's liking, had crumpled the self-same form in one massive hand and had pushed it into Hodges's shirt pocket. Then he said, according to the complaint lodged against him: "Give me the fucking file right now or I'll rip your ears off."

The complaint had landed on Stephen's desk with a note from Xoli Sibeko, the GM, saying that his sympathy was with Jonny, but would Stephen deal with the incident? Stephen sent Hodges a series of questions about what had happened, putting all the emphasis on the reasons why the docket had taken so long to be handed over, and what could be done to remedy the inefficiencies in the cooperation between the HR department and the rest of the mine. Hodges had seen the writing on the proverbial wall, and being astute about the look of a record of an incident, sent Stephen a magnanimous withdrawal of the complaint, explaining at length why a "synergistic cooperative platform of interdepartmental operating protocols" was more important than an unfortunate misunderstanding among colleagues. He was bigger than that.

Since then Jonny had refused to deal with Hodges. When he wanted something, he told Xoli, and the GM ordered HR to jump. Jonny knew he owed Stephen, but they never talked about it. Now he only said: "Ja jong." *Yes, well.* He shook his head at the memory. "But did you get what you wanted?"

"Not really, but then I didn't know what I wanted."

Jonny's phone rang. He winked an apology at Stephen and picked up the receiver. "Jonny." He listened in silence to the voice at the other end.

Stephen picked up an old *Newsweek* lying on the desk. The cover story was about Greece. The Eurozone had agreed to a bailout of €86 billion for the country. A picture showed Greek PM Alexis Tsipras shaking hands with Angela Merkel, while Francois Hollande looked down his Gallic nose at them. The editorial comment observed drily that if a country elects fools to lead it, those leaders will do foolish things. Perhaps other countries will watch and learn.

Jonny finished his call. "Sorry about that. So, our HR man wasn't that helpful? Unexpectedly disappointing." He shook his head again.

"I did get something I didn't want, though."

"And what's that?"

"I'm not sure. A red herring. Was there an issue between Mamela and Thuli?"

"What kind of an issue?"

"I don't know." Stephen sighed. "Some kind of a disagreement, or maybe a fight? I didn't even know they dealt with each other."

"Is that what Poepies says?" *The Little Fart.*

"Yes. He said he walked past Thuli's office one afternoon and heard him shouting at someone. And then Mamela came out of the office, looking like he'd just been caned. This was last week on Wednesday, the day before he died."

"What was he shouting about?"

"Hodges doesn't know. Didn't hear."

"He didn't ask?"

"No. Not his place to interfere, because he and Thuli have this mutual respect thing going." Jonny snorted. Stephen made a serious face. "Thuli doesn't move without consulting Hodges first."

"Oh yes, I know. Bill Gates also phones here regularly for advice." They both laughed, Stephen finding to his relief that his irritation was disappearing like chocolate cookies after a PTA meeting.

"Did either of them come talk to you about it?" Stephen asked.

"Nope. First I'm hearing about it." Jonny considered the coffee mug in his hand. *California 1, Carmel,* it said. On the back it described the highway: *The Pacific Coast Highway runs north from Leggett, 1 210 kilometres to San Juan Capistrano in the south.* "Thuli was here that day, I remember. We bumped into each other outside Xoli's office when I was coming out."

"So what do you make of the story?"

Jonny looked back up at Stephen. "Hodges is not only a prick, he is a conspiracy theorist as well. He always knows about secret decisions made only by those who really know what's going on, like him; and it's always about a bunch of people who will lose their jobs when a section is closed; or about how there'll never be an increase for some guy ever again. He once made up a story about the Share Incentive Scheme having been secretly changed to favour only the Vendas. They blackmailed the Union and the Board's hands are tied, so he said. It almost caused a riot." He pulled a face.

"But it's always bullshit. Always. I've had to put out the fires of several rumours he started. Why no one has shut him down is beyond me. The stewards can't stand him and refuse to have anything to do with him. So I wouldn't take him too seriously if I were you. I doubt Thuli has ever spoken more than a few words to Mamela. He certainly knew he existed—he makes a point of knowing everyone. But I'd be surprised if they ever had much to do with each other."

Stephen nodded, turning over in his mind what Jonny had said. It certainly sounded right, exactly in keeping with Stephen's own assessment of the little creep. The easy thing to think was that Hodges had in fact made up the whole story. But then, why would he? Even a man as odd as Hodges, why would he make up such a story? And what would it mean? Also, although it didn't seem in any way likely, could it be relevant to the inquiry? Could Mamela have been upset and done something he shouldn't have, because the big boss shouted at him? Stephen filed his thoughts away and turned to the other thing that had been on his mind all of the previous night.

"More seriously though, Jonny. We have a problem. A big one, I think. Do you know Robert Ncube, the priest?"

Jonny frowned, but nodded. "Bakgat kêrel." *Shit-hot fellow.* "For a priest," he qualified.

"He came to see me last night. He told me a long story about Mamela. Says the boy sort of out of the blue had extra money to spend, and there was something on his mind. He wasn't a happy chappie. You know anything about that?"

"Ag, Jisis." Jonny sighed. He shook his head and got up to look out the window. A man with a weed-eater was trimming the edges outside.

"A guy in Accounts Department suddenly has money for one

reason only, and that is that it looks better in his pocket than in the company's bank account. And then if he's worried about it as well, it means that he isn't the only one who is stealing." He sat down and swiveled his chair to face Stephen directly. "You're right, this isn't good news."

Stephen nodded. "Robert seems to have his feet firmly on the ground, and thinks the little guy was as honest as Abraham Lincoln. He didn't abuse his company vehicle, he wouldn't take pencil stubs from the company, worked only for the betterment of his fellow man."

"Good PR," agreed Jonny the cynic.

"We have to tell Panico. Well, we have to tell Xoli and Dov and Thuli as well, but Panico first."

"Yup," the big man said. He picked up the receiver and dialled. "Ja, Seun van Griekeland. Is jy besig?" *Yes, Son of Greece. Are you busy?* Panico could see them right away. No need to fill in a form.

This morning Panico was wearing a slim-fit blush-pink long-sleeved cotton shirt with a button-down collar, his trendy round horn-rimmed specs, and his habitual lopsided grin. He was up to his eyeballs in paper that he abandoned on the spot when his visitors came in.

"I'm starting to feel important. A policeman and a boss. Twice in two days. What extra things might I be able to help you with?"

"Nothing good, I'm sorry," Stephen replied, shaking his head.

"Oh?" Panico frowned. Stephen told him of Robert's visit and what the priest had told him about Mamela and the obvious signs, a year earlier, of suddenly having a lot more money at his disposal. Although the priest hadn't realized the implication of his story, it wasn't necessary to connect the dots for Panico.

"Fuck!" he said, peeling off his glasses and tossing them down on his desk. He sat back with a groan and ran his fingers through his hair.

"It's possible he was stealing?" Stephen asked.

"People who work with money all day have plenty of opportunity to steal it. There are checks and balances, but this office is complicated as hell. Lots of money goes through here. Lots. There are so many possibilities we have to check. Ah, shit man." He shook his head again, picked up his glasses and balanced them back on his nose.

"And, another thing," Stephen continued. "The priest told me Mamela was worried about something. Something was eating him up. He didn't know what."

"No, man. Darn it!" Panico sounded quite old-fashioned to Stephen, using such a quaint expression in this place where language was mostly either forthright or brutal. It was testimony to how bad the news was that he'd sworn like a real miner. Twice.

"That probably means he wasn't alone. He was scared someone was going to rat him out." Then, with an effort of will, Panico composed himself. He turned to the tall security officer and said in a businesslike tone: "Jonny, I need to see his personal bank account. Can you get me access?"

Jonny looked steely-eyed at Panico. "You ask me such a thing in front of this old man from head office. What are you thinking?" Then he winked. "Of course I can. But you can't tell anyone. Including him," and he jerked a thumb in Stephen's direction.

"Stephen, I have to do a full forensic audit. It's like looking for a needle in a haystack. But I have to start as soon as possible. I need authorisation from the audit committee and I need a reason for doing it. I don't want to say I'm looking to see if the guy who has just died was stealing. He was well liked and he was my 2IC. I need a cover story."

"Sure. I'll sort that. I'll get back to you as soon as I speak to Xoli and Dov. And Thuli. In the meanwhile, Jonny, can you jump onto not getting the confidential bank statements? We don't want to do anything that invades anybody's right to privacy. How soon can you not get them? It could tell Panico what he's looking for."

"Who did he bank with?" Jonny asked.

Panico didn't know, but said he'd look it up. "How can you get into his account?"

"Wat die oog nie sien nie huil die hart nie oor nie." *What the eye doesn't see, the heart doesn't cry over.*

"Okay, well. Let's get busy," Stephen said. "I think though, that we have two separate things on the go here now: I'm still looking into the accident and preparing for the inquiry. I'll stay busy with that. And the two of you have a different thing: You're looking for fraud and theft. I can't see how the two could be related, can you?"

Both men shook their heads. "So let's keep them separate, okay? Unless we come to a different conclusion later. But we'll keep in touch." The other two agreed.

In the passage, on their way back to Jonny's office, the big man asked: "Who else do you want to see? I mean for the inquiry."

"I want a word with Theuns, if he's around. I need to tell him something he's not going to like. And later I'm seeing Xoli."

Chapter 9

On both coffee tables in the head office reception area there were several copies of a glossy booklet that provided Sethemba Collieries with its own hallelujah chorus. It was a slick publication, high-resolution printing, and thick, smart covers, with the cheetah logo, complete with both of its shadows, embossed on the front. The cost of producing it had been substantial, its purpose debatable. A good third of the first page was a head-and-shoulders colour photograph of Thuli Mpongose, smiling at the world and his minions. His "message" as Chief Executive Officer went on until the bottom of the third page. The prose was purple, the authenticity doubtful—it had been written by the flowery pen of a corporate communications consultancy. What, in summary, it said was, this company is the real deal.

On the less important pages, there were much smaller photographs of the directors and senior managers, in that order. Each had his own bio, and, for the managers, a description of what they did. They were all there: The chairman, Dikotso "Shakes" Hlongwane, smiling like an amiable pirate; Dov Weinberg, the FD in conservative pinstripe; Xoli Sibeko, the COO, looking as if he were in a tearing hurry; and Zinhle Ncube, the pretty HR director, in neat braids and with a sparkle in her smile. The non-execs looked serious, every one of them, as if the camera had accused them of freeloading. Theuns Myburgh, the chief engineer, looked as if he'd been standing in a stiff breeze when the camera caught him unawares.

The booklet described what the chief engineer did: Theuns's special obligation was to deliver optimised long- and short-term mine plans and schedules, be accountable for layouts, surveying control, ventilation, ground and cost control, coordination of construction and improvement projects, and internal and external technical resources; and ensure that systems and processes met the highest standards. No wonder he looked depressed in the photo.

Sitting in his battered high-backed swivel chair amid the debris that collects around a hands-on engineer, he looked no less windswept, but considerably better at ease. A stout man in his mid-fifties, no novice at the braaivleis fire, he wore a striped short-sleeved shirt and khaki trousers gathered by a belt under the weight of his belly. Greying hair on his chest filled the V of his shirt. Wedged into the joint between the index and middle finger on his puffy right hand he held a lit cigarette. Everyone else could go outside to smoke if they liked, but this was his office and here he'd do as he pleased. And that he clearly did: there were oil stains on the carpet, bits of a gearbox in the corner behind his desk, a box of assorted bearings next to that, an ancient red grease-gun on the windowsill, cigarette burns on the desk. On the floor near the door was a section of a large tyre with unevenly worn tread. Elsewhere, were lengths of electrical cable of varying gauges, plastic containers with nuts, bolts and washers, a mess of loosely rolled engineering drawings and maps, and, just about wherever you looked, disorganised mounds of paper.

"Jozi tells me an accountant managed to get himself killed on my conveyor belt," Theuns grunted at Stephen. "What was he doing there?"

"Hey, don't steal my lines. I'm here to ask you that."

"I see." Theuns laughed, coughing at the same time. Having cleared a little space for it, he filled his lungs again with a long drag from his smoke. "What do you want me to tell you?"

"Well, there's going to be an inquiry. I hear they're sending Kraai."

"*That* prick!" Theuns took another drag to get the taste of the man's name out his mouth.

"He'll climb all over us, and I think we're in trouble with at least one thing."

"What's that?" The engineer sat forward to listen. Despite the gruffness of his manner and practised lack of sophistication, he was by no means stupid. Where working men gathered for a drink or three in the Middelburg coalfields, they talked about him as one of the best engineers ever.

"I've heard you guys didn't know about this man, don't know who he is, why he was there, or what he was doing," Stephen began.

"Being a dumbass," Theuns interjected.

"Apart from that," Stephen replied with a smile. Sympathy wasn't anything Mamela was likely to get in this office. "The thing we have problems with, or potential problems, is that he managed to gain access to the conveyor at all. It's a dangerous installation, and I think the inquiry will likely say that there should've been controlled access."

"Ag, bullshit, man. It's not possible to control access to the conveyor—the thing is thirteen kilometres long. How do I control access to that? I'd need a thirteen kilometre fence. And, in any event, the access is controlled—the conveyor is inside the mining area."

"We couldn't ever argue that it was too difficult or expensive to control access. We're meant to do that anyway, no matter what." The chief engineer nodded stoically as Stephen went on: "Being inside the mining area helps a bit, but not enough. And we don't need a thirteen kilometre fence to control access—all we need is an extra gate."

Theuns raised an eyebrow, took a last puff before grinding the butt into the chunk of an old crank-case that served as his ashtray. There were several other stompies in there already. "Where?" he asked.

Stephen got up and went to the map on the far wall of the office. It was the same as the one in Jozi's office, but this one had many extra miles on it. The top right-hand corner had pulled away from the stem of a thumb tack that had held it in place originally; many people had written many different things on it;

oil stains from the carpet appeared to have spread to it; a portion of Biesies North had been shaded in with vertical lines in a heavy black marker; Modder 1 and Modder 2 were cross-scored with the same heavy pen, and the outline of the operational areas had been heavily edited.

"Here." Stephen pointed at the engineering works. "If you put up at checkpoint on the road right there, you control access to the mining area. Secondary access control that will stop all unauthorised vehicles. You'd need a fence of, what? About twenty metres. And a gate."

"Yes, a gate and people to open and close it and check who goes in and out. And everybody who does go in and out has to stop there, and I have a whole new kerfuffle on my hands."

Theuns's complaint was almost formulaic—Stephen could see from his expression that there was no need to belabour the point. The chunky engineer agreed, even if he couldn't say so immediately.

"You think Kraai will say I must put a gate there?" the engineer mused after considering the idea.

"No, not quite. Kraai will say only that we allowed uncontrolled access to the conveyor and that's a breach of our obligations."

"Okay. I get it. Let's go look. Have you got time?"

"Sure." Together they headed out to Theuns's bakkie in the shaded carport. The engineer fired up the engine, lit a ciggie, and on the drive asked Stephen: "So what happens in the inquiry?"

"There's a long version for the lawyers and administrators, but a short one for engineers. The inquiry decides whether the mine did anything wrong by not following a mine regulation or by being negligent. The finding is in the form of a recommendation to the state prosecutor either to prosecute or not. Kraai will suggest, if he thinks the mine is at fault, that there must be criminal charges."

"Against?"

"Xoli, you, and Jozi."

"You think he'll recommend prosecution?"

"Maybe. The prosecutor doesn't have to bring charges, but he'd normally follow the inquiry's recommendation."

Stephen thought he had Theuns's undivided attention, but he was wrong. The engineer unexpectedly turned off the road and stopped next to an artisan cutting through a steel pipe with an angle grinder. He was wearing safety goggles and thick protective gloves. He was so intent on what he was doing that he only noticed them when Theuns hooted, two short bursts. The man looked up and Theuns beckoned him over. The man put down his power tool, pushed his goggles onto his forehead, and came slouching over.

"Why aren't you wearing hearing protection?" Theuns asked him, none too friendly.

"Uh. It's only one pipe," the man mumbled.

"Se gat," Theuns snapped. *Bullshit.* "Put on protection. And if I catch you without safety equipment again, I'll put you on charge." With that he wound up the window and pulled off slowly. The workman stood back, watching them go.

"So why must I have a gate?" he asked Stephen, as if there hadn't been an interruption. "I mean if the inquiry doesn't tell me to get one?"

"The inquiry will only say what we have is not enough. It's up to us to do the rest." Stephen looked at the man beside him, smiled, and with an upward nod of his head said: "You know why we must get a gate."

"Biesiesfontein has been operating as a colliery for thirty-five years without a gate here. And then this *poepol* comes along, whatever the fuck he was doing, and gets himself killed. And now we need a gate?"

"No," Stephen answered. "We needed a gate thirty-five years ago. We've been lucky so far. But we are all out of luck right now. That's why we need a gate."

They arrived at the place Stephen had pointed out on the map. Behind them were the engineering works and the plant, each with its own fence and security control. The two areas came close together, creating a natural throat down which the road made its steady way. And had done so, apparently, for thirty-five years. On the other side of the bottleneck was only the mining area.

"Here's where you think?" Theuns asked. Seeing him nod, the engineer continued, "If we put it here, all traffic to the works and the plant will be unaffected. Only mining vehicles will move through here, and the majority of them of course stay there. It's only the people carriers that will come through here." He looked up at Stephen and smiled a lazy smile. "For a *ou* from head office you have a smart idea or two. This is the most sensible suggestion I've ever had from you whole bunch." He thought about the practicality for a moment and asked, "But if we put it up now, do we make it worse at the inquiry?"

"Maybe. Maybe they don't see it the way I do, and just let us off. But if there's a brand-new gate where last week there wasn't one, even the dullest of the dull will see the point. I think we must start doing drawings and making the logistics arrangements with security for personnel to man the new gate. And we need a protocol for how the gate will be controlled, and you must tell Jonny and Trevor Hodges." At the mention of the HR manikin Theuns made a groaning noise deep in his chest. "This should be a priority job, but I'm sure we'll only be able to start putting the fence up toward the back end of next week. By then Kraai will have done his worst."

Stephen put on his most serious face. "Theuns, in the meanwhile, we just can't afford another incident. You have to be sure of that."

"Ja. I know." They got into the vehicle and started back to the office buildings. "So you think there'll be a prosecution?"

"I think it's possible. Likely. We have to get lucky for there not to be one. We'll try to head it off, but I think they'll decide it was just too easy to get to the conveyor."

"I see," Theuns muttered, digesting this morsel of bad news. "And do we have any idea what the little fuck thought he was doing?"

"We don't. But that, I think, is actually in our favour. If we can get them to believe Mamela was way out of line, doing his own thing, against every rule in the book, they may just decide our existing access control is okay after all."

"You lawyers." Theuns shook his head. "You do realise that doesn't actually make sense?"

"Yes I do, but maybe Kraai doesn't."

Chapter 10

"Every one of those Komatsus hauls 200 tonnes."

Xoli Sibeko stood near the edge of the pit, surveying his kingdom. In a world where we've democratised every process and every opinion and where one man's views are as valid as the next man's, an operating mine just doesn't work that way. There's a boss, and he is in charge; and what he says, goes. Bra Xoli, as the workers called him, was no exception. Permanently in general-issue khaki clothes, he stood five foot nine in his steel-capped safety boots. The relentlessness of his authority had hollowed out his cheeks and compressed his mouth into a thin line. A half-frown drew wavy lines between the greying temples, visible under his white safety helmet. His slow gaze drifted over the busy scene.

A giant front-end loader, crablike, was piling coal onto the load body of a massive yellow truck; one, two, three shovels and then it was good to go. It set off in a crawl diagonally up the incline, bench after bench toward the level ground, following the one before it that was even now cresting the steep incline onto the flat part of the road. Already the next truck had moved up to the loader that swung its articulated body smoothly through half a turn, holding its brimming bucket high while bits of pitch black coal slopped over the sides. The bucket up-ended over the waiting truck, rocking it on its suspension with a crash of stone on metal. Where Xoli, Stephen, and Jonny stood watching, hundreds of metres away, the sound took a while to get to them: each bucket of black landed in silence, exhaling its own cloud of dust, and only then they'd hear the deep report.

"Who's that, and why doesn't he have a flag up?" Xoli pointed at a bakkie rolling sedately down the steep decline of the haul road, down into the pit.

"Don't know." Jonny shook his head. "Ek gaan nou sy bal

trap." *I'm on my way to stand on his nuts.* In three strides the big man was at his own bakkie. He yanked the door open, folded fluidly into the seat that seemed almost too small for him, started the engine before the door was properly closed and set off after the distant culprit. Xoli and Stephen stood in silence, watching him go.

"What have you found out?" Xoli asked, when Jonny turned left onto the bigger road. He stood squinting into the sun over Stephen's left shoulder.

"It depends what you're interested in. The main charge is that we were negligent in causing Mamela's death. It's difficult to say what the mine did wrong. He was in an unauthorised place, and whatever he was doing was unauthorised as well. Not to mention against every rule in the book. He was bizarrely out of line with safety regulations and, let's face it, basic common sense. So, in short, I don't think the mine was negligent. That would be the main charge, the one to fear most."

Stephen turned to look directly at the GM, now that he had to break the bad news as well. "But I think we have a problem with the regulations. I think the inquiry may find that access to the conveyor wasn't properly controlled."

"How so?" asked Xoli.

"It was just too easy for him to get to the scene of the fatality. All Mamela had had to do was get in the main gate. Lots of people do that every day—me, the secretaries in the typing pool, the guy who delivers Cokes to the canteen, the aunties who come here to give their Bible class on Fridays."

Perhaps it was unfair of Stephen to use that last example, because the idea that on Friday mornings some interfering old biddies from Crosby came to pray for the workers irritated Xoli beyond measure. The only thing that consoled him to a degree was that easily three people turned up every week.

"For Mamela it was laughably easy. He was in a company vehicle, and he worked in Admin. So to get in the gate wasn't a problem. From there nothing stopped him. Not even in theory."

Stephen and Xoli stared off into the distance where Jonny had caught up with his quarry, and now stood towering over him, conducting an animated soliloquy, and repeatedly thrusting an accusatory finger at the poor man who wilted like lettuce on a hot day. Xoli, despite his ingrained gravitas, smiled at the safety officer's antics. Then he turned a quizzical look at Stephen, frowned and shook his head. "Mamela knew he shouldn't have gone there."

"Of course he knew. He had had all the training and refresher courses. The last one was in July. But that's not relevant to whether the layout of the mine complies with the safety regulations. I don't think they do, and I think there's a reasonable chance the inspectors will come to the same conclusion, even if they don't send Kraai."

Kraai Serfontein was the man from the Inspectorate they disliked most. Years ago, when the mine was still called Biesiesfontein and the world worked differently, he was fired by Hugh Kitchener, the then-GM, for incompetence and for generally being impossible to get along with. Kraai had a head like a skull with sallow skin taut over hollow temples, and expressionless obsidian eyes deep-set on either side of his bony hooked nose. He embodied his nickname, Crow. After being fired he knocked about for a while as a consultant, but no one wanted to know what he had to say. Then he joined the department as a health and safety inspector. From that day on, he'd been out to prove a point to the world generally, but specifically to his old employer. In doing so, he confirmed the old saying in the mining world: Those who can't do, consult; and those who can't consult, become inspectors.

"I chatted to Theuns this afternoon about access control," Stephen went on. He recapped his conversation for Xoli, and told him of their plan to put up another control point, but only after the inquiry was finished with its stuff.

"That sounds reasonable." Xoli nodded.

Jonny's victim was now back in his vehicle, which described a slow U-turn and headed back up the slope, out of the pit. Van Straten stood staring after it, hands on his hips as if waiting for the opposing side to dare kick the ball in his direction. Even at this distance he looked menacing in the luminous yellow of his reflective jacket, under the extra few inches of his safety helmet. Sometimes when they were face-to-face and Jonny grinned, as he often did, he reminded Stephen of a housetrained bear.

Stephen rounded the corner to what bothered him most: "The thing that really puzzles me is why Mamela was there at all. I don't know what he was doing; and I don't know what happened."

"Is that really our concern?" Xoli asked, frowning quizzically. Stephen didn't answer immediately, still staring out toward the pit and its never-ending buzz, where Jonny was getting back into his bakkie. Something in Xoli's tone maybe, perhaps in the don't-care attitude with which the young man's gruesome death was being treated as an administrative inconvenience, stuck crosswise in his craw. When Jonny was back in his bakkie and had started on his way back, Stephen replied: "The inspectors next week are sure to ask what Mamela was doing at the conveyor, and we need to have an answer."

He tore his gaze from the horizon and turned to face Xoli. "If we don't answer, they may very well find that we've been negligent. If that happens, there'll be charges against you. You and Theuns and Jozi. The charge will be culpable homicide. The negligent killing of a human being. So to answer your question: Yes, it is very much our concern. Or more succinctly, it's very much *your* concern."

A note of irritation had crept into Stephen's voice despite his usual monumental calm. His reputation was that of the ultimate Mister Nice Guy, the one who never took offence, who always listened and did his best to accommodate. Stephen saw the younger man wince, and immediately regretted speaking harshly. Xoli's job was impossible to do without offending somebody. As the general manager of this mine he had to keep the shareholders, the board, his managers, and his workforce happy. That was easier said than done, and the poor man was the picture of an overstressed GM. Stephen softened his tone. "We are still working on it and I think there won't be a finding of negligence. But that still leaves the matter of not having complied with the regulations. I think on that score there probably will be charges against only Jozi, but perhaps also against Theuns and you, if they're in a vindictive mood. Much less serious. But nevertheless. And we'll try to plea-bargain it."

Xoli nodded. He'd been there before.

"Xoli, unfortunately that's not the end of the bad news." Stephen held the younger man's gaze for a minute. "I think there's fraud in the Accounts Department." He told the GM about his meeting with Robert, the priest, and of the subsequent discussion between him, Jonny, and Panico. "I'll speak to the audit committee and to Thuli when I get back to Johannesburg, but there's no way we can avoid looking into this properly."

Xoli just looked tired. He nodded without comment. He drew the heaviest of all his sighs, mustered a smile from somewhere, and asked: "Are you going to the funeral? It's on Saturday."

"Yes, I'll come along. Thuli and I have made plans to go together. And you and Jonny and Theuns will be there?"

Xoli nodded again, and added, "A few of the other guys will be there as well. The people in the accounts office and his trade union pals. We are sending a bus. I think you should be ready for some politics in the speeches. It won't be a short service." He sighed again, but this time lightly, without the cares of the world on his shoulders.

"There isn't such a thing as a short service at a black man's funeral," Stephen chuckled. "Least, I've never been to one."

"Nope, you're right there." Xoli smiled. "And I should know. I go to them all the time." Together they turned and got into their bakkie. "Have you ever been to a township funeral? I mean, not just the church and the burial. The whole thing?"

"I didn't even know there was a whole thing."

Xoli started the engine. "In black culture death is a serious business."

On the way back to the office buildings he told Stephen of the wake and how the women pray and sing all night in a room with the coffin. All the furniture is taken out, a sheet is hung across the door, and candles are set out, one at the head and one at the foot of the coffin. Beyond this room people stay awake all night, feasting. Usually a beast is slaughtered that day, and the meat is cooked for everyone. Of course some of the men drink a drop or two.

"Then, in the morning, people get dressed for the funeral and get in the buses. In the township you need buses to get everyone to church. And when they get to church they see you guys, who pop in for the last stretch and think it takes a long time."

Stephen laughed and Xoli was pleased to have teased the old guy.

Chapter 11

Sometimes when the night was still and he lay alone in the dark wondering where the time had gone, Stephen heard the lions. When they were restless, stirred by an ancient memory of a honey-coloured savannah spreading in the silence of a moonlit night, endlessly, past the thin line of a far horizon, it was then that he heard their question shivering on the rising air. They called to the land and the vast open sky, asking why they'd been abandoned. Where, they asked, had the time gone?

The lion of Boaz-Jachin, thought Stephen when he heard them. Boaz-Jachin, when his son was born, decided to make him a map on which his precious child could find all the things he needed, a map for finding his way and his dreams. His son set his heart on finding a lion, which in the country of their story had become extinct, all but mythical, like a dragon. When Stephen's children were born he yearned to give them such a map. Over the years he'd done what he could, trying to find the ladders and stay away from the snakes, and hoping not to repeat the mistakes of his own father. Now that they were both out of the house and on their own, he wondered how well he'd done.

His house stood patiently through the years on an acre of deep-green Saxonwold, north of where the first Mining Commissioner of Johannesburg had stayed in von Brandis Square, which now was a bus terminus in the CBD. The first wealthy folk of the new mining town that never slept, so the story goes, wanted to get away from the noise and the dust. One day Florence Phillips, a well-to-do lady, rode her horse north over to the lip of the ridge at the edge of town, from where she saw to her delight the distant blue line of the Magaliesberg. She bossed her husband into building their house in the country, in what is now Parktown. Soon their wealthy friends followed, finding as an extra bonus that it was cooler out north. In the century and a bit since then, the little town had grown into a city, spreading many miles to Sandton and Midrand, halfway to Pretoria, in one continuous urban sprawl.

Where once there was only veld, the commercial powerhouse of Sandton had thrust its roots deep into rocky Highveld ground. Stephen's house, when it was built in the late 1940s, had looked south to the city. Now it looked north from its perch halfway between the two poles of modern-day Jozi, to the concrete and steel of Africa's commercial capital. The streets of Saxonwold wait each year for the purple carpet of flowers to drop from the canopy of jacarandas that line the streets and confirm the local belief that Johannesburg is the world's biggest man-made forest. The trees stand unmoving on both pavements, spreading, in their thousands, deep purple flowers that pop like bubble-wrap when cars drive over them. Every student knows that if you haven't started learning for the exams by the time those flowers first peek out at the world, it's too late.

Directly in front of the house, the thick arms of a stately Liquidambar still gently rocked the treehouse where no young ones had played for many a long year. In the cool evenings, Stephen and Lisa sat on the veranda, listening to the garden. Silence echoed in the courtyard and whispered among the leaves. Then it settled from the edges, and into its stillness they dropped their conversation like pebbles into a quiet pond. The ripples of their words spread and disappeared in the fading light reflected off its smooth surface. A ginger kitten purred on Lisa's lap and the grey cat stared like yon Cassius at the space where he would've liked to be. He settled instead for second best, on Stephen's lap. An ancient long-haired German shepherd lay at Lisa's feet, making conversational noises in the back of her throat that had for years sounded to Stephen like an unspecified complaint. Lisa chatted back: "Hey, Chip Chap. What's up then?" To which the big dog replied with what sounded to Stephen like a further complaint. Two black Labradors, plump and content, lay snoring under the coffee table. When Lisa got up, all five animals followed like a comet's tail.

"You whites are really odd about your animals," Thuli had said to Stephen once, when he'd dropped in to talk about a letter the company had received from a disgruntled farmer next to whose farm they mined. "You introduce your dogs to your visitors as if they're people."

Stephen felt a little silly, having done just that. "Meet Cindy," he'd said, pointing at the long-haired shep, "and Angus and Findlay," nodding at the labs. He felt relieved that he hadn't introduced the cats as well. A least he knew they wouldn't have said a thing.

Lisa had been looking at Google images of Austria all day. "I spoke to Gavin on the phone this afternoon," she told Stephen, "and he's sending through the final itinerary. He has put us into the most beautiful little pension in Salzburg. We're there for three days."

Lisa, Michelle, and Lexy—companions in art, literature, and empty nests—were arranging a winter week in Austria. Arranging with unbridled enthusiasm and uninhibited discussion. They would leave on a Thursday evening, the first in December, Lufthansa bound for Salzburg, for the Arts & Culture Fair. Two days in Ischgl in picture-postcard Tyrol would lead them to Hallstat in Salzkammergut, where they intended to explore the old town on the shores of the most beautiful lake in the world. "I have chatted to Martin and Soula and they'll come through for the day on Saturday," she told Stephen of the arrangement with old friends who had retired to Switzerland. After nine days in winter wonderland, they would retrace their tracks to the airport and wing their way back south in time for cozzies and sundowners on the sunny beaches in Plett. It was tough, but someone had to do it.

"Will you be okay, though? You'll be alone for a week. We leave on Thursday, and are back the next Sunday morning." This was a discussion they'd often had, when Lisa went to explore the far reaches of the globe with her travelling companions.

"I think I'll probably manage." Stephen smiled. "Just don't leave any biryani." On one of her first trips, Lisa had left vegetable biryani in the fridge, concerned that Stephen wouldn't be able to feed himself otherwise. He'd tucked in dutifully every day she was gone, but there was still some left when she got back.

"Yes, but will you be lonely?"

"There are so many animals in this house, how could I possibly be lonely?" The right answer: Lisa would do fine in solitary confinement on Devil's Island if she had her dogs and cats with her. The conversation shifted to what he'd been doing all week.

"Lisa, I know you said you'd come to the funeral tomorrow, but it really isn't necessary. It's a work thing, and I don't expect it will be a whole lot of fun."

"Are you sure?" She frowned at him. He knew her well enough to know she'd go to the funeral without a murmur if he asked her to; but he also knew the are-you-sure game. You play that game when you manoeuvre someone into a corner of your devising, and then you pretend it was his idea. "Are you sure?" gives him a last opportunity to change his mind. Lisa was such a kind person, she played the game even if she hadn't devised the corner in the first place; but she nevertheless didn't want Stephen to step out of it, now she could see the benefits.

"Yes, I'm sure, thanks. Thuli is picking me up and we're going together."

"What will you wear?" Lisa asked the thing Stephen would otherwise have thought of when he stepped out of the shower the next morning. After as much thought as he would've given the matter a day later, he said: "A tie and a jacket." He watched to see if that answer would do. It was in the frame, but not a bull's-eye.

"Obviously, duh," her eyes said. "Which jacket?" To Stephen all his jackets looked the same. There were minor differences in colour, but not so he could tell them apart. Lisa had tried over the years to make him wear different, more stylish things, but they'd hung in the back of his wardrobe until she gave them away. How he would've decided which jacket to wear was simple: the one most recently returned from the cleaners. Whichever one that was. But, being an experienced husband, and being deeply fond of this kindest of all people, his wife, he asked instead: "Which one do you think?"

"How about the one you got in Cape Town?" She liked that one; she'd chosen it herself.

"Good idea, thanks," he said, with the slightest of smiles in the corner of his eyes. Lisa, aware she was being chaffed, said, "Ja, ja," got up and led the procession of dogs and cats to the kitchen.

Left alone with his thoughts, Stephen asked himself what he knew about Mpho Mamela. A kind, hardworking young man, not short of initiative—he grew up poor but had put himself through university and had become a professional. Liked by everyone, particularly his boss; hadn't argued with anyone and no one argued with him. In line for a promotion to senior management in a year or two; received a good salary, his recent increase having been as good as anyone in the company got.

A shop steward, concerned for his fellow man, and popular among his coworkers; supporting his mother and putting his young brother through medical school. Religious and charitable, and adored by a priest Stephan had formed a high opinion of. Gay and in a relationship with another likeable young man; except that young man had tried to steal from the company and was now in prison.

Worried about something; and suddenly having extra money to spend. Possibly had an argument with Thuli, but possibly not—depending on whether Stephen should believe a man with a prize collection of bizarre psychoses.

And above all, dead. Dead in a way Stephen couldn't begin to understand. An accountant, way into the mining area where he absolutely should not have been, after-hours, and squashed by a moving conveyor belt that nobody in his right senses would have tried to interfere with while it was running. At night in the dark. Without first turning off his car.

That's all he knew, and it wasn't, he thought, a whole lot. Was he truly interested, though? Was this truly his concern? He'd promised the priest he'd take his story seriously; and if there was something that would help the company in court, he should try to find out what it was. But for the rest of it, was it his baby?

However he turned it over in his mind and from whichever angle he looked at it, he kept coming back to the same conclusion. There was a young man whose life had been lost too early, before he could get to his dreams, before he could live the life he'd prepared for so diligently. A young man who was no less entitled to a fair shake than Stephen's own son; and if this had, God forbid, happened to his son, Stephen would have turned the world upside down to find out every last detail.

He couldn't fix what happened, but he felt deeply saddened. It was all so wrong that one so young and so promising should be gone. No mother should ever have to watch her son lowered into a grave; and no lover should lose a soulmate so early. The unfairness of it, the bloody-mindedness of an uncaring world forced Stephen into a place where he could do no other: he had to try to find out what had happened. That much he and the world owed Mpho Mamela.

Chapter 12

"In my house there were no toys."

Stephen was in the passenger's seat of Thuli's red Ferrari. The car was much bigger than he'd imagined. In his mind's eye, before he'd been a passenger in this car for the first time, he'd thought he would have to squeeze in, and that his knees would be up around his ears all the way. More like wearing the car like a noisy red jacket, than riding in it. But it was large and flat, even though it was unreasonably loud. Bumpy too. And only a few inches off the ground. You had to put your butt in the seat first and then swivel your feet in. You couldn't just get in, like with a normal car. But size wasn't the issue: the seat was soft leather, deep and sculpted, and there was enough room for his feet.

When Thuli arrived to pick him up, Stephen wondered about the rules of Black Economic Empowerment that would make it okay to arrive at a funeral in a car that cost more than the combined net worth of all the other people at the graveside. But while he was still wondering, the next instalment of Thuli's Oliver Twist saga had begun. "When I was growing up, no toys. One year a guy who worked with our next-door neighbour said he'd take me to his work Christmas tree and I'd get a toy. But he came late and when we got there it was over. I just remember a worker kicking over a barrel of water and ice in which the cold drinks had been. It made a sound: *Woosh!* Like this. But I didn't ever get a toy."

As always, Stephen said nothing. The house he'd grown up in had had many toys; and when he'd gone with his brother to the annual Christmas tree, they always got there in time and had found a world of wonderful treats waiting for them. He'd grown up in Mandini, in northern Zululand, where the company his father worked for owned a paper mill. The village was small, new as a baby, and wild; and had been heaven for the kids who lived there and went to the little school where grade one to standard five, boys and girls, English and Afrikaans, filed into five classrooms. White kids only, of course.

The many treats for them were never better than on the Saturday morning shortly before Christmas when it was the children's party. They all arrived at the Rec to see Father Christmas. With a long white beard and red coat with snow white fur trimming at the edges, the old man sweated through the Zululand heat and humidity. Handing out colourfully wrapped presents passed to him by the Christmas fairy who wore a white ballerina's tutu and held in one hand a wand with a star on the end of it. Father Christmas always knew his name, how, he couldn't tell. "Yes, young Stephen," he said, "I know you've been a good boy. Now I don't want you and Alistair to fight next year, okay?" Astoundingly, the old guy knew his brother's name, too.

Stephen realised he'd been thinking about his own stuff and hadn't noticed that Thuli had stopped speaking. It wasn't that Stephen didn't care. It was just that Thuli's stories had the sound of a personalised mythology about them—the stylised retelling of when he'd been penniless and unknown. In all the time Stephen had known him, and in all the sound bites he'd heard in the long history of how the world had done Thuli wrong, they hadn't yet got to the part of how Thuli Mpongose, the man, had been made: the happy sequence of events that told how the now rich and famous CEO had come by his all-pervasive self-confidence. Hammering down the highway in a post-box-red Ferrari, the man still believed he was a poor boy, still wanted the world's apology for the deprivation of his childhood, still wanted that once-upon-a-time neglected kid to get an apology for how unfair things had been.

Stephen didn't ask for further details. Instead, he told Thuli about Mamela's case: that he'd been unable to find even a theory as to how the young man had been killed; about the new access point and how he thought that there may be a prosecution for a breach of a regulation. Whereas none of that was good news, he continued: "We have another, completely unrelated problem."

Thuli looked at him askance, braked hard, down-shifted into second and accelerated into a tight right-hander. Stephen braced, if not for impact, then for the centrifugal pull as the marvellously engineered machine sped through the corner, far too fast, but without as much as a squeal of its tyres.

"I think there may be a fraud in Accounts," he carried on; and then told Thuli why. "Can I call a meeting of the audit committee on Monday, and will you be there please? We must be as careful as possible. We don't want investors to hear a mangled story."

"Good thinking," Thuli agreed. "I'll be there."

"Did you know Mamela?" Stephen asked, watching Thuli's face carefully.

"Never met him," came the answer. The driver's concentration on the road didn't waver for a second.

"Trevor Hodges thought you knew him." Stephen still looked at the side of his companion's face.

"That man," Thuli shook his head. And that was all the answer Stephen got.

An old church building had appeared up ahead on the left. Thuli revved the pedigree engine and changed down to third and then to second, almost as if it were necessary to double-declutch as Stephen's father would've done in his Chevy in the fifties. The high-performance horses under the bonnet whinnied their enthusiastic agreement as Thuli wrenched the wheel hard and skidded the front wheels into the gravel of the driveway. The direct steering responded beautifully, as did the massive brake callipers, and a cloud of their own dust overtook them from behind. Thuli, foot on the clutch, revved the motor hard into a banshee scream ending in the sharp retort of a single backfire as he released the accelerator pedal. Then he crept forward at a snail's pace and into the VIP parking spot reserved for him. Every head had swivelled in their direction and several hands were pointing. The ego had landed.

They got out and Stephen looked around him. The building wasn't in good shape. The plaster had worn thin and fallen off in patches; the roof sat skew in rusted corrugations; the steps to the front door had been worn concave by generations of sinners' feet; and inside the floor was gritty with sand. The walls hadn't been painted in many a long decade. Row after row of unforgiving wooden benches brooded in the gloom, and were soon filled as the congregation drifted in, respectfully quiet in the presence of the Almighty.

There was no lofty pulpit, no ornate altar. God kept the stained-glass windows, the mighty organs, the magnificent tapestries, and shiny chalices for His other houses. This one was bare. Stephen had been in barren buildings like this before. In winter a bone-chilling cold would seep up from the bare cement floor, through the soles of your feet, slowly rising along the pipes of your legs. When it reached your heart, he knew, you would fall over dead without a sound.

As they settled down, the priest, Moruti Rikhotso came in. He was a tall stick of a man, his face set in dry disapproval and his robe shiny with age and use. In his wake followed the bold form of Ronald Ncube, spreading serenity around him like a cloud of Frangipani blossoms in the early evening.

The congregation stood for a prayer, and when they were back in their hard seats, the Moruti railed at them in a language Stephen didn't understand, conducting his outrage with a bony fist. Stephen, who had expected kind words and consolation, wondered what had made the priest so angry. God's representative went on and on and on, howling and shrieking in his holy echo chamber. The words didn't seem to matter; it was the cadence that did it. Sometimes it sounded like crying, sometimes like a bitter accusation, and sometimes like a desperate plea for forgiveness. The congregation sat together in the dock: guilty, mute, and appalled, suffering their expurgation, the forceful reminder that they deserved no better than their miserable lives. And at the end it appeared to Stephen that they were uplifted by their dejection.

Stephen sat next to Thuli, who kept his aviator sunglasses on throughout. The black lenses were as impenetrable as the man's expression.

Then it was Ronald's turn. He shuffled diffidently to the lectern, Friar Tuck impressively powerful in his dark robe. But his voice was deep and kind and he spoke to Mpho's mother as if she alone sat in this huge hall. Stephen still didn't understand what was being said, but the old lady, who had sat stoically throughout the Moruti's harangue, sniffed once, reached for a hanky in her sleeve, and started crying. After just a few of Ronald's sentences, she was shaking with sobs for the sadness of her loss. The deep timbre of Ronald's words sang of his grief for the friend he'd miss more than he could say. The liturgy of God and Heaven and Redemption was not in his brief this morning: He'd come to say sorry. Sorry for the world and how it was. Sorry for the boy who would never again see the morning sunshine on the land. Sorry for the golden promise his mother had been made on the day she first held the precious bundle in her arms; sorry for how her heart had been shattered.

Then he spoke a ray of hope, a tiny smile of consolation, the softest of farewells. When he'd said the last of his gentle words and silence once again hung heavily in the air, he went over to the front bench where Mpho's mother sat sobbing in sorrow. He knelt in front of her and wrapped her in a bear hug, his arms closing out the world and making her safe. Stephen watched in awe as little by little the torrent of her grief subsided.

The rest of the congregation sat silently watching, quiet except for the sounds of several ladies working their own hankies. Stephen, who hadn't understood a word the big priest had said, felt an itch behind his own eyes, knowing his tears weren't far.

Thank the Lord, he thought, he couldn't understand what Ronald had said. Because then he would've wept, for sure.

Stephen couldn't see how Thuli had taken it all behind his sunnies.

Later, at the open grave in a dusty yard, Moruti Rikhotso switched to English and seemed not to be so angry anymore. He told them that God would cherish and keep all his children from their first laughter in the cradle through summer's golden glow, from the tears of love's frustration through winter's icy blow. He stood back to let the big priest talk. Ronald looked at his congregants thoughtfully in complete silence for a long moment. Then he smiled sadly and told them: "There's a skipper in charge of the boat—your boat and mine, everyone's boat. Sometimes He allows us to sail on a pleasant, mirror-smooth sea; sometimes He sends us where the fishing is good; and sometimes He sends us into the storm."

After that he prayed, not saying much, for so much had been said already.

They sang one more hymn and the sad business was done.

Chapter 13

In Marshalltown, west of downtown Joburg, the grandest head office of them all commands its own precinct. Completed shortly before the Second World War on the sweat of thousands and the profits of gold and diamonds dragged from the deep, the monumental stone edifice reflects the sentiments and aspirations of a bygone era. Monolithic in design, it speaks of influence and capital. Broad shallow sandstone steps lead to the main entrance, as if this were Town Hall itself, not just one of the ratepayers. High above the towering entrance is a symbolic depiction of the southern African continent cleaving its way through the southern sea, forging through the turbulent waters on either side of its pointy prow. Straddling the landmass, a classically muscled figure pulls lightning bolts from the sky, clutching them in his fists. This is an African building, it seems to say, bonded to the roots of continental antiquity; Pallas Africana, to inspire all who enter to greater wisdom, courage, and shrewdness.

No one builds like that anymore, Stephen mused, because no one can afford to and, frankly, the heavy symbolism is a bit much. Corporate headquarters these days inhabit anonymous glass and granite complexes that can change identity as easily as the sign over the door can be taken down and the stick-on sandblasted logo can be scraped off the window. But the old impulse to claw your way to apparent importance by building wastefully ornate pavilions remains alive and well. There still is a direct correlation between the length of the rise from the floor to the ceiling in the reception area, and the length of the CEO's importance quotient. The greater the area of unused high-gloss granite floor, and the deeper the mausoleum silence that greets every visitor, the further up the chain of make-believe the company has positioned itself.

None of that applied to the Sethemba head office. A simple

rectangle on the ground and first floors of an ordinary building in Rosebank, sectioned into offices with dry-walling, was all it took. Stephen's office was nondescript, but so were all the others. The one concession to apparent style was in reception where Elsie, fat and friendly, waited for people to come see them. She sat behind a desk, the front of which was a slab of hollow white marble in which a light burned all day. It looked kind of fancy, but had been installed by the previous tenant and left behind when they moved.

Elsie presided over a room with its two coffee tables, two couches, and four easy chairs. On the walls of her kingdom were a map of the Middelburg coalfield, three metres by two-and-a-half, inside a thin dark frame; a sepia-coloured photo of old Johannesburg in the 1940s; and a poster celebrating South Africa's Soccer World Cup, a charcoal sketch of a player who is all arms and legs in mid-air, getting ready to kick a ball of twine over which the crosshairs of the artist's preparation are still clearly visible.

Stephen settled down to make his calls. He picked up the receiver and dialled.

"Dov, morning. Are you coming in today?" Dov Weinberg was sixty and a bit, getting readier by the day for retirement.

"I am. I'll be there in twenty minutes. Why?"

"We need an urgent meeting of the Audit Committee."

"That doesn't sound good. Can you tell me more?"

"Not on the phone. Two-thirty in the little committee room?"

"Sure," Dov said. "See you then."

Next Stephen rang Fatima Naidoo and Ernst Westcott, the nonexecutive members of the committee. Fatima was the chairman of the committee and insisted on being called the chairperson. Ernst grizzled about the time of the meeting but in the end agreed when Stephen repeated that it was urgent. With the meeting set up, Stephen looked in his wallet for the card, one of his own, on the back of which he'd written the number. He dialled, and it rang for a long time. He was about to hang up when a woman picked up and said in an uninflected voice: "Covenant."

Stephen wondered for a moment if he'd got the right number. "Who am I speaking to, please?"

"It's Therese," said the voice, flat as the Kalagadi salt pans.

"Good morning, Therese. I'm looking for Ronald Ncube please. Do I have the right number?"

"Hold on," Therese said, without changing her tone. There was a clunk as the receiver went down. Stephen held for an eternity until he heard sounds of someone coming back to the phone. More sounds as the instrument was picked up and Ronald's beautiful deep voice said: "Ronald speaking."

"Hey, hope I'm not interrupting? It's Stephen Wakefield."

"Stephen!" The priest sounded genuinely pleased to hear his voice. "I missed you on Saturday. I saw you but by the time I could get away you were gone."

"I waited a bit, but it looked as if you had to personally bless the whole congregation. So I skedaddled." On the other end of the line Ronald laughed his deep belly laugh. "Beautiful sermon, by the way," Stephen said. "Didn't understand a word, but you almost made me cry."

"I must try harder next time," Ronald chuckled. "Thanks for coming, it meant a lot to the old lady. And your car will be the talk of the township for years to come."

"Not my car, little brother. On my own watch I come and go without attracting attention." Ronald blew through his nose in amusement, and Stephen said: "I need your help though. I'm getting nowhere with trying to find out what happened to our boy. I don't even have a theory."

"How can I help?"

"I want to meet Mrs. Mamela and perhaps, if I can, Mpho's brother. And Ronald, is it possible for you to be there? They may be suspicious of me, or even scared. And, sad to say, I may need a translator I can trust."

"Of course I can arrange it and absolutely I'll be there. But they both speak perfect English so you won't need me to interpret for you."

"I'll really appreciate that. The inquiry starts on Wednesday, so this week isn't good timing. Can you try to arrange it for next week, please?"

Ronald promised to get back to Stephen, and they said goodbye. With that squared away Stephen had one call left to make.

"Stevie Wonder!" said the voice on the other end. It belonged to Shakes Hlongwane. His first name was Dikotso, Stephen had seen in official documents, but everybody called him Shakes. They met when Shakes had stopped being an MK general and had become a normal person. Normal with benefits. He played the world like a harpsichord: precise, never overbearing, but never without the perfect cadence of his choosing at the end. He was enormously influential without being in the limelight ever. Stephen had heard that the President would not lightly cross Shakes, and that the deepest pockets of the new order treaded lightly when he was around. Stephen had been in practice still, acting for a multinational, when Shakes found him at the signing ceremony of the deal they'd been busy with.

"Come work for me," he'd invited. The look in Stephen's eye had said *I'm a white man; you were a general in uMkhonto we Sizwe, the armed wing of the ANC*. But that mattered not a dot. Stephen had become Shakes's personal appointee at Sethemba, where he had the general's back.

"Got some things to tell you, Mon Generál. Have you got time for a quick coffee?"

"Sure. Tasha's, thirty minutes."

Stephen chose an outside table in the shade. He'd been sitting for a minute when he saw Shakes. The biggest thing about him was his smile. It never left him, never wavered; it never looked out of place, and you never saw him without it. He'd grown up as a cowherd on his father's farm in Zululand, and had worn his first pair of shoes when he was sixteen. When he finally got them, he found it impossible to get his feet into any of the stylishly narrow things the fashion houses produced for perfectly ordinary people to look foolish in. His preference ran to sports shoes that didn't hurt his toes and in which he could keep his feet firmly on the ground.

Shakes had come out of the war lean and fit, but the years since then had been good; and a combination of his jovial nature and many business lunches had given him a preference for elasticised waistbands. Today, he wore blue tracksuit trousers and a white T-shirt without a joke or an inspirational message on the chest. A tiny black label was folded over and sewn to the edge of the right sleeve. Stephen didn't recognise the brand.

"So what's up then, my man?" Shakes asked when the coffee cups stood before them and news of the family had been shared.

"There's something I have an odd feeling about. I don't know what, but something feels wrong to me." Then he told the story, leaving out nothing. When he finished, Shakes pulled at his chin, thinking. Eventually he asked:

"What are you telling me?"

"I'm not sure. I'm telling you that I don't get it, that the pieces don't fit. Something is wrong. But I don't know what."

"Have you told anyone? Other than me?"

"So now I'm stupid as well?"

Shakes laughed the tension away from the table. "Sorry, sorry," he said. Getting serious again he asked: "What do you think. Is there a fraud?"

"I don't know. We'll look, but Panico trusted this guy, and so did that priest. He thought him as straight as they come, and it's hard to fool a good priest. This priest is exceptional. Panico is efficient and dedicated. He has more checks and systems in place than I have seen ever. It's possible there's a fraud or a theft, but, if you ask me, I think it's unlikely."

"Then what is it?"

"I don't know. But something more complicated than that. Over-invoicing. Kickbacks from a supplier. That kind of thing. Or, of course, nothing."

"Let's assume there's money in it somehow. Who else is in it? Apart from Mamela and maybe his boyfriend?"

"Hell, Shakes. How can I tell? I don't even know for sure that there's anything at all. Just a feeling in my gut."

"How often is that gut of yours wrong?" Shakes frowned across the table. When Stephen made the not-that-often face, the general nodded. "Ja," is all he said.

The waitress came with the bill and a smile, and when that was squared away, Shakes pressed once more: "What about Thuli?"

"I really don't know. Hodges is a foolish man and loves stirring the pot. He's made up more stuff than Stephen King. Just for the hell of it. I don't know if there's anything in this story about Thuli and Mamela having had a scrap. Probably not. But when I asked Thuli in the car whether he knew Mamela, his answer didn't look right to me. It sounded okay, if you don't know what to listen for. But I was specifically watching for his reaction: He wouldn't look at me, and he answered too quickly. Also, Thuli prides himself on knowing everybody. He actively brags about it. That's the kind of CEO he is, he has told me often. Mamela was senior-middle management; when Dov retires he would have been senior management. He's been at the mine for eight years. And Thuli says he has never met him? That is an odd note in the symphony, if I've ever heard one. But, Generalissimo, those are small things. I wouldn't bet many shekels on a poker hand with only those few cards. It's very probably nothing at all."

"Maybe. But that's where the game is won and lost. Do you think there can be a connection between this fraud thing and the fatality?"

"I can't think how. Maybe Mamela had an attack of conscience and killed himself. But, as my big friend Jonny said, it's a hell of a way to do it, in the rollers of a conveyor belt."

The erstwhile general kept a stoic expression and a steady look in his eye. Then he pulled a face and said: "Thanks for telling me. Please have a full go at this. Don't stop before you're happy. And keep it between us."

"Sho' thang, Pardner," said Stephen.

Chapter 14

The N12 sweeps in four lanes past Emalahleni, the town that used to be Witbank. Place of Coal, it means. How the names have changed. Warmbaths has become Bela-Bela; Nylstroom is Modimolle; they call Lydenberg Mashishing; and Machadodorp rejoices in eNtokozweni. When Winston Churchill escaped from a Boer prison in Pretoria, he famously passed through Witbank on his way to Delagoa Bay, which later became Lourenco Marques, and now is Maputo. It happens elsewhere as well. There's an old Communist joke about a man who was born in St. Petersburg. Where did he grow up? Petrograd, is the answer. Where did he live now? In Leningrad, of course. But where would he like to live? In St. Petersburg.

Emalahleni, the Place of Coal, is not a good-looking *dorpie*. It has been around for a good long time, but still has that slightly defeated air of a wannabe mining town. Twenty-two collieries churn out coal within its municipal limits, and the Duvha power station is just over there. Tyre salesmen, diesel mechanics, and engineering works whirl in a flurry of commotion, yet the town's street plan remains the camel designed by a committee for the spatially challenged. And pretty the place is not. Except when it rains.

Stephen drove along at a stately 129 kilometres an hour with the sun sinking low on the horizon in his rear-view mirror. Driving into a thickening bank of low cloud as evening settled, he saw licks of lightning above the horizon, coming closer all the while. Then the rain swept down from the hills, spreading its wide dark poncho with both arms, painting the fields in deep brown and shiny wetness. When the first drops hit and the clever car turned on its own windscreen wipers, Stephen remembered Mrs. Smart on a long-ago morning, when the rain's tiny hands had patted on the windows of their English class, as she read from Milton: *And now the thickened sky like a dark ceiling stood.*

The dark ceiling stood coal-grey and moody over the stretch of highway. Gusts of wind butted his car around the shoulders, asking where it was going. Heavy round drops knocked at the windows, and before long Stephen was driving through sheets of sluicing rain. Thunder rumbled deeply around the hills, and the road became a mirror over which the wheels hissed. The outlines of things softened, the dust disappeared, and Emalahleni became the Place-of-Beautiful-Sunsets, suddenly wet and almost cold, smelling as only a million raindrops on the veld can smell.

Before the junction where the Pretoria highway joins from the left, the rain was over. The fields now lay wet on either side, and his headlights reflected off puddles and little streams trickling next to road, hoping to connect with a bigger stream, perhaps even a river, and who knows, maybe the sea. Stephen dialled, and listened to the ringtone on the car's speaker system.

"Jonny," answered a voice.

"Hey, young man. This is Clarence Darrow speaking."

"You've got the wrong number, sorry," said Jonny, without changing the flatness of his tone. He waited a second and then said, "Ja Omie." *Yes, Uncle.* "What's happening? Clarence is a place in the Free State. Why are you there?"

"I thought I'd take the scenic route."

"Don't get lost."

"I promise. I'm sleeping over in Crosby tonight. I'll be at the mine tomorrow morning early, probably at about seven-thirty."

"Make up your mind. Will you be there early, or will you be there at seven-thirty?"

Stephen chuckled. "The inquiry starts at nine o'clock, which means that's when everyone will drink tea. Get a good night's sleep. Tomorrow won't be a short day."

"Thanks, Meneer. I'll go to bed right away."

"See you in the morning."

Stephen rang off and thought about magistrates. The first ones were in Rome. The top-dog Magistratum was the Consul. There were two of them, and they were king for a year. Legal disputes were heard by another magistrate, who was called the Praetor. He was like the first Supreme Court judge ever. But as there were more and more people, and the American Dream taught them about litigation, the world needed more magistrates to listen to its fights, not all of which were about principles that govern the very fabric of society. A hierarchy of officials was established to deal with the corresponding hierarchy of issues. In the pyramid of appointments, each layer down-slope dealt with more mundane issues, until right at the bottom you got to Kraai Serfontein. His appointment came from delegated legislation, meaning the Minister appointed him. But in practical terms it was a secretary to the Minister who appointed the Inspectorate, and charged it and its members to investigate compliance with regulation of the auxiliary sludge pump at the tailings dam in Gamoep, which is sixty clicks from Platbakkies.

Because God has yet to teach those to whom He entrusted a little authority how best to use it, the Law of Indirect Proportionality of Importance and Self-Perception has led us to expect and to find that dealing with an Inspector can be trying at times. In Bloemfontein the Appeal Court judges treat those who appear before them with courtesy and respect. In the B traffic court in Kempton Park on a busy Thursday you can sometimes get short shrift from the Maggie; but in Kraai's court of inquiry there's only one guy who counts, and it's not you.

The boardroom had been cleared of its usual furniture, and instead a U formation of desks and chairs had been brought in. At the top of the room were three chairs. The middle one for Kraai, the other two for his assistants. Stephen and his team would sit on Kraai's left, and the witnesses who would give evidence, on the right. The place was wired for sound: in front of each chair was a microphone on a little silver tripod, and cables snaked like spaghetti to a central recording unit. In front of that sat Rita Swanepoel, a veteran at recording evidence at these enquiries. She wore an old-fashioned floral dress that looked homemade, she smiled at everyone who made eye contact with her, and she didn't say boo to a goose.

The team from Sethemba had been ready for a while when, shortly before nine o'clock, into the room swept Kraai and flanking him like pilot fish, his two assistants. Gugu Mabuza, short, with the plumpness of youth still in her cheeks, and although shy and retiring, ready to smile at anyone who took notice of her. She kept to her place; she took notes, wrote down the stuff that was said, and kept a handwritten record of what was happening.

The other assistant was Nesbitt Thwala, the real protégé. He, like Kraai, was tall and ascetically thin, with disdain imprinted in his DNA and etched permanently on his features. It was impossible to get into a polite exchange with him: he simply did not behave like an ordinary human. He refused to look at you, and in the middle of your sentence, would simply turn away and stop listening; or, if he had something to say, he'd speak over you. Unless you wanted to get into a ridiculous competition for airtime, you had to keep quiet. He was learning at the knee of the master, and clearly hoped one day to eclipse the achievements of his teacher.

Kraai's special way of underscoring his demand for obeisance was to disdain any attempt at friendliness. The deference he required ran within the borders of the prescribed regulations: his inquiries ran in strict formality, nothing excepted. Stephen had long ago given up trying to be nice to people like this. He cringed inwardly when he saw how brutally Kraai and Nesbitt rebuffed every approach. "Can I get you a cup of tea?" asked Lindiwe, the cheerful PA responsible for the boardroom, its furniture, and the timetable for who got to use it. The Terrible Two stared at her for an instant as if she were the shit on their shoes. Kraai said, "No," and Nesbitt simply turned away. The poor woman slunk out of the room as if she'd been slapped.

Stephen didn't try to establish eye contact with the panel, didn't try to speak to them, didn't pay overly much attention to what they were doing. He simply sat, waiting for the piano roll to start spinning.

The inspectors of inquiry unpacked their bags, pulling out reams of paper and files of many colours. They spent slow minutes adjusting and readjusting the layout of their paraphernalia, Stephen noticing in particular that Nesbitt lined up his quite startling collection of pens with OCD precision. For the entire time it took them, they ignored the rest of the room, as if it were empty. When eventually they were happy, Kraai looked quizzically at the microphone in front of him, and with a shaky hand flicked the switch behind it, turning it on.

The guy is actually nervous, Stephen realised with some astonishment.

"This"—Kraai said, and fumbled with his papers some more—"is an inquiry"—he looked first to his left and then to his right—"convened in terms of the Mine Health and Safety Act of 1996." He picked up a sheaf of papers, patted them into a perfect rectangle, put them down again. "Act 29 of 1996." For the first time he looked up, not at anyone in particular, but taking in the rest of the room, not just the desk in front of him. "As amended," he added.

"This," whispered big Jonny in Stephen's ear, "is going to be a very long day."

"The presiding officer," said Kraai in his snail's pace and with many pauses to think over the gravity of his words and their precise phrasing, "is Louis Christiaan Delarey Serfontein." He was appointed under Section 50 of the Act, so he said; and his assistants, Nesbitt Freedom Thwala and Gugulethu Pride Mabuza under Section 51. They were inquiring into the fatal injury and death of Joseph Mpho Mamela. They intended to call witnesses as per the list they'd sent to the mine, and they would consider the facts put before them and reach a conclusion on whether there had been any negligent act or omission on the part of Sethemba Limited or its managers appointed in terms of Section 3(1) of the Act.

That took him a time to get out. His list of intended witnesses was simply everyone mentioned in the report filed by the mine about Mamela's death.

"Please introduce yourselves, for the record," Kraai asked the room.

"Xoli Sibeko, General Manager, Sethemba," said Xoli. Jonny and Theuns followed suit, which left only Stephen.

"Stephen Wakefield, legal adviser, Sethemba," he tried. But LCD Serfontein was not happy.

"Are you here as a legal representative?" he asked.

"I'm a director of the company, and its internal legal adviser."

"But are you representing the company?"

"Yes, I represent the company."

"What's the name of your firm?" Kraai asked, getting agitated.

"I'm not in private legal practice. I'm a director of the company, and I'm authorised and instructed by it to represent its interests in this inquiry," said Stephen in an even voice.

"This is most unsatisfactory," the chairman said testily, looking at his dried-up colleague who nodded. The other colleague kept notes.

"How so?" asked Stephen.

Kraai reacted as if slapped. "*I'm* the chairman of this inquiry, and *I* ask the questions," he said.

"Very well, but I'm asking for clarification of a statement you made. Such is my entitlement. I'm sure you're familiar with the rules of legal procedure in that regard." Stephen spoke mildly, noticing that Kraai had no clue what rules Stephen referred to. His only rule was to bully, and he wanted to stamp his authority on the morning as soon as possible. Now this bloody lawyer was in the way.

"That's just it!" Kraai burst out. "If a legal point must be made, but it's not made by a lawyer, then what's its status in front of this tribunal?"

"Well, I am a lawyer. And the status of my submissions is identical to the status of any submission. The rules of law are unaffected by who relies on them, and are equally applicable if raised by lawyers and non-lawyers." Stephen deliberately held Kraai's gaze as he spoke. "That then is our first legal submission to you this morning, Mr. Chairman."

Stephen almost invariably spoke in a mild tone of voice, and had made no exception to that rule now. His only emphasis had been the slight raise of his left eyebrow and a tiny nod, almost as if he were saying to a toddler, "Now don't be silly, okay?" He'd known that this initial showdown must come, the first time when Kraai tried to undermine and shut him up, but he'd thought that the silly man would at least wait until there was a real issue.

Kraai and Nesbitt didn't really know what to do, even though they conferred for a long time in hushed tones. Gugu, however, knew exactly what was required of her: she kept notes, even when no one was speaking. *Perhaps she is writing a novel*, Stephen thought.

After a long deliberation, Kraai turned his microphone back on. Clearly out of sorts, he muttered: "It's most irregular, but in the interests of proceeding we'll allow it." He then went on a spiel about how important it was to prepare and keep a proper record of the incident, such record being the hallmark of a true democracy.

"Can't he just get on with it?" Xoli whispered to Stephen.

"He can, but he won't. He lives for days like today. And tomorrow, and Friday probably," Stephen whispered back.

"Three days! Are you serious?" the GM asked.

"I'd guess," Stephen said. "The world will end one day, and then there'll be bureaucrats like this lot to make sure the paperwork is done properly." Jonny had been listening to their whispered conversation and snorted a laugh. Which Kraai heard and pounced on.

"There is very little funny about the death of a worker, I assure you," he said icily, staring Jonny down.

"Our apologies, Mr. Chairman," said Stephen.

The morning dragged its torpid body around the clock, while nothing much happened. The Chairman called Jumpy Mashishi and Lebohang Duma to say where and when they'd found the body. Amos Hlongwane confirmed that he had called the medics, and then it was lunch. They stood, stretching the stiffness from their legs. Outside the room Lindiwe had set out sandwiches and coffee, but didn't make the mistake of offering them to the inspectors. The Sethemba crew piled lunch onto their plates and went to stand outside under a tree where the smokers puffed away.

"Is it going to go on like this all day?" Xoli asked, incredulous that so little had happened in such a long time.

"Pretty much. They'll call the ambulance drivers and the morgue staff next to establish the continuity from the scene to the coffin, so to speak," Stephen answered.

"In case they buried the wrong guy," Jonny said. Theuns huffed and Xoli just smiled. Stephen carried on: "I think they'll call it quits for the day after that. Tomorrow it hots up a bit. First they want Trevor Hodges."

"What for?" asked Xoli.

"I'm a smart guy, you're right," Stephen nodded. "But I sure don't know the answer to that question. My guess is they want to ask him about whether Mamela had been to safety training. It would be hearsay for Hodges to say, but I don't think I'll take that point, otherwise they have to call every training officer who ever had Mamela in one of his courses, and then we'll still be here next week this time. When they're done with him, they'll want Jozi, Theuns, and you, Xoli. In that order."

"Dan gaan die poppe dans," Jonny put in helpfully. *Then the fat is in the fire.*

"Yes." Stephen nodded. "The chairman will behave like a prick, as you have seen, and he will continue to do so. If it gets too much, I'll interfere. I have boxed with much heavier weights than him. And it will make no difference to the outcome. He's still cross that Hugh Kitchener fired him, and he came here to find someone guilty of something. Just remember, this is a sideshow. The real thing is in court where there are proper rules and a more sensible way of doing things. My home ground, so don't you worry. We'll be okay there, even though this inquiry probably won't end well."

The little circle of faces nodded, solemn but confident that Stephen was in charge. Jonny looked over Theuns's shoulder and pointed.

"Look," he said. In the room with the sandwiches the three inspectors were standing in one corner, away from everyone else. Trevor Hodges had come in the door, put a smirk from the top order of his sycophantic armoury on his face, and with charm oozing from every pore, oiled his way across the floor. To Kraai, who greeted him with genuine affection and his own improbable smile. Stephen noticed that Kraai had long yellow teeth, as if he usually ate grass for dinner. The two almost hugged, slapping each other on the back, and falling into conversation, like long-lost buddies.

"Well, I fucking never," mused Theuns.

Chapter 15

Stephen chose the same table at the open window. The memory of yesterday's rain made the afternoon no cooler, but the long shadows before sunset had now dropped the mercury back to its comfort setting. Hannes was behind the bar, serving a group of miners trying to quench the thirst only a long day at work can give you. They stood, laughing and joking, one of them telling a story: "I say to him, I say, get me the bolt cutters, man. And he just stands there looking at me."

His three companions laughed and sipped their drinks, waiting for the story to unfold. It took its time: "The bolt cutters, I say, pointing at them." He pointed a podgy finger away from the counter. "So he goes over and fetches me the big bobbejaan." *A monkey wrench.* His mates burst out laughing, yet still waiting for the punchline.

Stephen saw Panico in the doorway and waved him over to his table. "Hi. Glad you could make it. Thanks for coming," he said.

"Always a pleasure to find an excuse to have a drink with the Silver Fox," the young man smiled.

"What's your hooch, small fry?" Stephen listened and lifted a finger, catching Hannes's eye. "Can we please have a peach iced tea for my friend?" he asked. Settled and comfortable, they got down to business. "What can you tell me, please?" Stephen asked.

"Jonny got me the bank statements, and it's going to be very difficult. Up to the end of last year, it was just a normal account. There was one payment a month into it, his salary. And then little amounts went off, to his mother, to the university for his brother, for his rent, that kind of thing.

"But then it changed. In the middle of January this year one big payment came through. It was a foreign amount. My guess is it was $10,000, converted into South African Rands. The payment came from Zürich, from one of the Swiss banks. I have zero chance of being able to trace that one. And after that, around about the end of every month, there was a cash deposit of R25,000. He made the deposit personally.

"His expenses stayed about the same, except that he paid his mother and his brother more; but he hardly used any of the money that came into the account, other than for that. There were ten cash payments altogether. Most of the money is still in the account except for what he paid extra to his mother and brother. He used only a very little bit of it for himself. This was not a greedy man we are talking about."

Stephen frowned. "No, not a typical crook. But undoubtedly not doing anything frightfully legal either. So what do you make of it?"

"It's very hard to say. I really just don't know. The big payment from Switzerland really throws me. The mine doesn't deal with Switzerland. In fact, we don't deal with any regular offshore supplier. There just isn't anyone who should be paying a bribe from Europe. I can't make sense of that. And then, the monthly payments are even worse. It could be anything."

"Do you have a theory?"

"Stephen, I really don't. You know, in procurements when we have fraud it's almost always over-invoicing. The supplier sends a bigger invoice than he should, and the man on the inside gets the invoice cleared and paid through the system. For a cut. They always make mistakes, though: the cut is paid directly from the supplier's bank account. Or there's a deposit slip with information that leads us to a person or a company who made the payment. But Mpho didn't deal with suppliers. He didn't deal directly with their invoices, he had no contact with them. I can't see how he could've been involved in a fraudulent scheme like that. He had a purely accountancy function; I don't know what benefit anyone could get from bribing him."

"But you do think it's a bribe of sorts?" Stephen asked.

"Yes, clearly. Someone was paying him for something. But what, I can't tell. We've started with a full-scale forensic audit, but I must tell you upfront I don't think we'll find anything. This is outside our system. This isn't fraud in our accounts. This is a fraud outside the Accounts Department, which unfortunately seems to be administered by somebody who worked in the Accounts Department. But it's not in our system."

"Well, my friend. There is good news with the bad news then. Isn't there?"

Panico put a smile in the middle of his designer-stubble. "Yes. But then I have to see it entirely from my own point of view. My systems haven't been compromised."

"Only one way to see the world: from your own point of view. I heard even Mother Teresa saw it that way."

For a minute Panico wasn't sure whether he was being chided, ever so gently, but then he saw Stephen's crinkled smile and his nod.

"Thank you for coming by. We have to keep a lid on this. Very few people know about the audit: you, me, the audit committee, Thuli, Jonny, and the Chairman. And, again, well done. The guy worked for you and clearly knew he couldn't pull the wool over your eyes."

They stood, shook hands and, as the young man started toward the door, Stephen saw, through the open window, the form of his favourite priest shambling down the path to the front door. Hannes also saw him coming and greeted him with a smile: "Hey there, Preacher Man. Good to have a man of God in the house."

Ronald beamed back, as if they were in the finals of the Mister-Big-Smile Competition.

"I have come to bless your establishment, my son," he chuckled.

With that, Hannes put down the beer mug of Coke and ice he'd been pouring, sliding it across the counter top to the priest, who burst out laughing. Ronald picked up the mug in his huge hand and tilted it straight down his throat in one continuous draw. Hannes held a fist over his left breast pocket, like the rugby players do before a test match when they pretend to know some of the words of the National Anthem. The barkeep said: "Respect, man. Respect." And then he got busy refilling the preacher's mug. "I'll bring it over to your table." He nodded in Stephen's direction. Nothing much passed him by. That's why, in the movies, the detective always talks to the bartender, shows a picture of the dead girl and leaves his card with a number to call.

"Love your shirt," Ronald pointed at Stephen's chest. A simple black T-shirt with the word UMLUNGU written in white block capitals across the chest. *White Man*. "Absolutely perfect for where we have to go tonight."

"Where is that?"

"Kabela's Shebeen," answered Ronald.

"And where is that?"

"Rikhotso City," said Ronald, smug as a bug in a rug.

Stephen whistled a soft low note. "Are you that preacher from *The Cross and The Switchblade*?"

"Who's that?" asked Ronald, looking confused.

"Sorry. I keep forgetting I'm older than time." He shook his head ruefully. "When I was a young cowboy, in the sixties, there was a famous book about a priest who lived with the gangs in New York to convert them to Christianity. A movie too. His job was kinda scary, is all."

"No. No worries. It's nowhere near New York. It's about seven kays from here."

"And I must drive there at night in a Merc?"

"No, we'll go in my car. If we went in yours we'd come back without it."

Stephen couldn't help but laugh. Rikhotso City was the township that stood right next to Crosby. Well, not right next to, but in the close vicinity. He didn't know any white man who'd risk going to a shebeen there at night. In fact, he hardly knew a black man who would either. It was a labourers' village, and, by repute, the labourers didn't take kindly to any management types in their waterholes. They ate humble pie all day, round the seasons, round the years. When they drank, they liked to do it by themselves, without a boss in sight.

"Why would we go there?" was all he could think to ask.

"There's a man you must meet."

"He can't come here?"

"He can, but he won't." Ronald told him who it was and said: "You'll be okay with me. I know those boys. They like to pretend they're hard dangerous men, but they're like you and me. They just have more difficult lives and that makes them angry. No, you'll be fine."

"Shall we have dinner first?" Stephen suggested. Hannes took the order, nodding in approval when Ronald asked for the special again.

Ronald's car was a real *skorokoro*. It was a boxy little Datsun from the 1980s, a small four-door sedan without a single undented panel. It was impossible to tell its principal colour under the streetlamp, but Stephen saw that at least one door was very different from the rest. The inside was a tip. The passenger's seat had almost no upholstery, and the inside door panel on that side had no handles, either for the door or for the window. But the engine kicked into life with remarkable ease, and they rattled out of town toward Rikhotso City.

Down into the dip in the deserted veld outside town they drove, and there the wheels followed a rutted track to the left. There were no streetlights and not many road signs.

The older township, Clearyville, where the servants of Crosby used to live when the pioneers at the turn of the previous century were young and caroused in the saloons and dance halls on Saturday nights, was within walking distance of the centre of town. Rikhotso City was much further out. A separate development required a proper separation. Over the years Clearyville had become gentler, and its evil twin rougher. During the tumultuous 1960s and oppressive 1970s, and into the unkind 1980s, the people of the town lived without hope, squashed flat between poverty and desperation. The turmoil of the 1990s didn't help them much either. Nowadays there were signs of a trickle of capital into the hood: a few shops had opened and there was electricity. But it stayed a dismal place, unloved by any man or god Stephen knew of.

"They only serve beer. Sorghum beer and Black Label," Ronald had told him.

"Zamalek." Stephen nodded, giving the white man's beer its township name.

Ronald looked at him from the corner of his eye. "For an umlungu, you know some peculiar things."

Ronald lurched to a halt close to a house beside an open lot that evidently operated as a tavern. Music pumped into the cool November sky, and men stood in clumps near the open doors, licked by a tongue of harsh neon lolling into the dark from inside. Stephen got some odd looks on the way in, and one person away in the dark shouted: "Hey, umlungu!" Others laughed.

The room itself was packed, not as if this was midweek, but rather as if tomorrow would never come. Ronald shouldered his way through the crowd, everyone staring after the tall white man with snow white hair in the priest's slipstream. Those whose eyes he met, he smiled at and nodded; and mostly got a similar response. One or two people glowered at him in open hostility, until a tall man with obsidian eyes and a scar on his left cheek stepped directly into his way.

"What are you doing here?" he asked, beery breath in Stephen's face.

Ronald stepped in: "He's with me, Vusi. I brought him here."

"Why?" the man asked, not moving.

"He's here to try to help a woman who has lost a son, and a

boy who lost his brother."

"Mamela?" asked Vusi.

"Yes."

"How can he help him?"

"They have lost their support. If the umlungu gets the information he's looking for, he can try to get them support from the insurance." The man considered this, staying directly in Stephen's way. Then he said: "I don't like it that he's here," and stepped back, but only part of the way so that Stephen had to brush past him.

"He's here to help. I won't bring the wrong people here," Ronald assured Vusi before they pushed further into the room. Stephen didn't feel much comforted to hear that he was one of the right people. The glowering man let them go by, his head lowered like a prize-fighter waiting for the bell so he can rip into his opponent. Stephen's heart was in his mouth.

The priest threaded his way deeper into the shebeen, greeting just about everybody. Right at the back he found who he was looking for. At a table with an old Formica top, sat five people, each in earnest conversation with his own bottle. Nobody seemed to be saying anything. A slow silence hung over this lot, in stark contrast to the swell of noise elsewhere. In the corner sat a middle-age man, brooding in his personal bubble of solitude. He wore an old stretched-out work T-shirt and a battered knitted beanie. Both were a neutral brown, the type of colour that wouldn't show dirt easily. Ropey muscles defined his arms, promising uncompromising strength. His mouth was wide and thick, his look was strange, and his eye was odd. Ronald leaned over the table and spoke to him: "Bheka, I have brought someone to see you." The man raised lugubrious eyes off the table top. He looked first at Ronald and then at Stephen.

"Umlungu," he said, reading Stephen's shirt. Slowly he shook his head, a ghost of a smile on his lips. "You must have balls like coconuts coming in here in a shirt like that. I'm surprised you can walk."

"I'm a bit surprised myself but there's nothing I can do," Stephen answered.

Bheka considered his visitors in silence for a bit and then asked, "What are you doing here?"

"I've come to talk to you," Stephen said.

"Here?"

"I figured you wouldn't come to see me at the mine and you also wouldn't come to Crosby. So I had no choice."

"How do you know who I am?"

"Father Ronald told me."

"What do you want?"

Stephen told him. "A young man, Mpho Mamela was killed last week, and I'm trying to find out what happened to him."

"Why do you care? You're a white man."

"Do you have children?" Stephen asked.

"Six." The man nodded.

"I have two. One of them, my firstborn, is a young man now, just like Mpho Mamela. If my son was killed, I wouldn't stop looking until I found out what happened to him. This young man didn't have a father. So I'm looking as if I'm the father he didn't have."

Bheka regarded him in silence. Then he said, "What makes you think I can help you?"

"The Father," Stephen replied, and nodded at Ronald, "told me you saw something."

The man watched him with slow reptile eyes. Eventually he said, "Come stand outside."

He picked up his half-empty quart by the throat, and dangled it in his fingers as they made their way outside. It was cooler, quieter, and not nearly as achingly bright outside.

The man started talking haltingly. "I was coming off duty on Thursday evening at about seven. I'm a loader operator. I'm in the pit all day, loading the dump trucks. When I was walking to the bus depot to wait for transport, I saw a car with two men in it. I didn't recognise them." He told Stephen that the two in the car had just sat there, watching the front entrance of the Admin building, as if they were waiting for someone. Usually at that time Admin was deserted, so that seemed odd, too.

"Where were they?" Stephen asked.

"They were parked under a tree in the parking lot. It was empty except for them."

"What kind of a car was it?"

"A BMW. A black one. Shiny, polished up. A gangster's car."

"You look at its registration plates?"

"No."

"What happened?"

"Nothing. I walked past and they carried on waiting. But it looked out of place, and when I heard someone had been killed, I wondered whether they were involved."

"I wonder, too," Stephen said. "Do you know what they looked like?"

"Not really. They were inside the car and the lights reflected off the windows. One of them was wearing sunglasses, even though it was dark already."

"Were they black?"

"Both of them."

Bheka had nothing to add. Stephen said thanks for the help, and as he turned to go, the man said: "Mr. Wakefield," correctly identifying Stephen, somewhat to his surprise. "They say good things about you at the mine, and I can believe them, having met you tonight. But be careful. Coming here tonight like this was not a smart thing to do. You could easily walk into problems here, and no one would lift a finger to help you. And these men you're after, if they can put a young man through the rollers of a conveyor belt, then they can do bad things to you, too."

Stephen nodded. "Thank you," he said softly. "I know you're right."

He'd never been so glad in his life to get back into an old bashed-up banger. When the engine spluttered to life, he drew a long breath. But his companion was chipper, smiling like Baloo over the crunchy gear change to third, trying to make the old man feel best at ease.

"What do you think of that?" Stephen asked him.

"You're the policeman. I don't know," came the reply.

"I'm a lawyer. Big difference. Big. Difference."

"Heh, heh." Ronald laughed, but then he turned serious. "Well, if you ask me, I think those two were waiting for Mpho and they killed him."

"Jumping a bit to a very far conclusion there, Padre."

"Maybe, but you asked what I thought. Ask for an answer from me and I'll give you one. Priests do it with words. In any case, Bheka thinks so, too."

"Ja. That's true." Stephen nodded. "Nice approach you've got. My wife will approve. Ask for an answer from me, and I'll duck the question. Lawyers do it without committing to a version."

"Apart from that our jobs are identical." Ronald laughed.

"Exactly the same," agreed Stephen. "Are we seeing Mrs. Mamela next week?"

"Monday afternoon at two-thirty. And Bongani, his brother, will be there."

"Thanks, bro. And one more favour please. When you meet my wife, never tell her where you took me tonight."

"Deal."

Chapter 16

"Big Jon," Stephen greeted the security officer. Jonny was bent over his desk, reading a file that had spread into an untidy sprawl of loose sheets in front of him. His morning mug of coffee steamed at his elbow and the front page of a folded newspaper announced: "ANC, Corruption Allegations." *Why would that be news?* Stephen wondered as he stood in front of the desk, there being no chair for him to sit in.

"Hey, boss." Jonny jumped up, strode to the interconnecting door behind which his secretary sat. She was a cute, blonde *poppie* who wore coquettishly correct young Afrikaans fashion and radiated cleanliness as if she'd showered while her clothes were being washed and ironed; and that had happened less than three minutes ago. Her hair shone and bounced in a medium-length bob, her teeth were brilliant-white and her makeup was Pretoria-immaculate. Jonny called her Skapie, but her real name was Suné. Stephen hoped that the look in Jonny's eye when he gazed at her behind the typewriter twinkled with only professional admiration, but sometimes he wondered. Jonny plucked a chair from next door as if it were from a virtual reality, and put it down for Stephen to sit in.

"Thanks," Stephen nodded. "We've got some stuff to do."

"No rest for the soldiers," said Jonny.

"Yup. While you were sleeping last night, I went to a shebeen in Rikhotso City."

Jonny made big eyes at Stephen. "You're not serious?"

"The priest and I," Stephen answered, as Jonny whistled a long disbelieving note through his teeth, and shook his head. Stephen told the younger man about his meeting with Bheka and what the man had said. For once Jonny listened without a word.

When Stephen was done, big man said: "You're out of your mind going to a shebeen like that. Promise me you'll never do that again?"

"Easily given."

"Okay." Jonny nodded, though with a look that suggested he had much to add. He stared Stephen down, frowning, before he continued. "Well, it's a hell of a story and I really don't like it. There's a CCTV over the gate and I must go see if any of it's true. If it is, you know what we have here?"

"Yes, the implication is huge. Buddy, I want you to keep this between us until I speak to the General. This is above my and your paygrade. Do the investigation but don't tell anyone what you're doing. I'll get back to you as soon as I've had my chat with the Big Guy. But for now, it's just you and me, little bear."

"Net soos Groep Twee." *Just like "The Two of Us".*

"Exactly like that." Stephen got up to leave, but saw Jonny had something else to say. He waited, and out it popped.

"I've got stuff to do: if the BMW was there I have many people I have to talk to. Please boss, please. If I eat all my vegetables and never fight with the other kids ever again, can I miss the inquiry this morning? My arse is still lame from yesterday, and I can think of no good reason why I should be there." Stephen almost laughed out loud.

"Well, I don't know. What am I offered?"

"Everlasting respect."

"I thought I had that already."

"Advice on supporting the correct rugby side." Stephen was not a Blue Bulls man, as Jonny insisted everyone who understood the game should be.

"That's too much to ask."

Jonny thought for a second, raised his eyebrows twice and said: "I won't tell the chicks you don't eat biltong." He looked sideways at Stephen. Not liking biltong, which was true of the old man, was inconceivable to the retired player; and as he'd told Stephen often, was ever so slightly naff.

"Okay, it's a deal. See you later."

It didn't take long for Stephen to realise how big a favour he'd done Jonny. The first witness of the morning was Trevor Hodges, who played to perfection his part in the mutual admiration society he had going with Kraai.

"Before we start formally," Hodges simpered as he sat down in front of the mic, "I'd like to place on record how fortunate the mine and the company are that we have a panel of inquiry of such high calibre to assist us. We thank you for the excellent work you have done, and continue to do. If we can assist you in any way, in any way whatsoever, please don't hesitate to ask and we'll do our very utmost to assist."

Kraai smiled, actually smiled, showing his long yellows; and set about the most obscure line of questioning imaginable. What was the philosophy that underlay the training approach of the company? How best, in Mr. Hodges's opinion, should one adjust for the cognitive dissonance within the labour force that comes about from the tension between the desire to be safe and the unwillingness to comply with time-consuming safety regulations? What specific protocols of HR management had Mr. Hodges found to be most efficacious in establishing a platform for synergistic interaction between management and labour?

Talkative Trevor didn't disappoint. He gave full and detailed background information for each of his answers, on one occasion beginning with the position that pertained in the mid-1940s, before the introduction of the first labour regulation. He contextualised every response and fully explained every nicety and every subtle nuance of interpretation, lest important contradistinctions be lost in the byways of confusion. He shone like IK Pegasi B would shine, according to an article Stephen had read. The white dwarf, which is about 150 million light years away, is the same size as Earth but is one-and-a-half times heavier than the Sun. It's about to go supernova, and when it does it will burn brighter than all the other stars in the galaxy put together. But not for long.

Four hours later, Hodges was still before the microphone when the Inquisitor-in-Chief said that now it was lunch. Stephen had filled three pages of his notepad with the 3-D cube with windows on every side, Jozi had spent the morning sending emails on his phone under the desk, Xoli was quietly fuming, and Theuns was comatose. When they were gathered under their tree with plates of sandwiches and Theuns's cigarette, Trevor Hodges came bouncing over on happy heels, tripping the light fantastic.

"I think that went *very* well," he gushed.

"Yes, I think so too," confirmed Stephen. Theuns almost swallowed his cigarette, but managed to keep quiet. When Trevor, still grinning to himself, was gone, Stephen looked at Jozi.

"You're up next. Remember: don't speculate; don't say more than you actually know from your own personal experience. Don't repeat what anyone told you. Don't try to answer a question if you don't know the answer. Just say, 'Angazi.' That's the only right response."

"Sure. *I don't know.* I really don't know, actually." The young man shook his head. He looked depressed and nervous, and carried the look with him to the witness chair.

"State your name for the record," Nesbitt instructed him.

But before Jozi could say a word, the door burst open and in stormed three men in overalls and miners helmets shouting at the tops of their voices. Lindiwe was pulled along in their slipstream, still trying to stop them from going inside. The melee swirled about in raised voices and upset furniture until Xoli stood up from his seat and spoke to them in a strong voice that certainly wasn't a shout. Stephen hadn't understood what the threesome had been shouting, nor did he know what the GM had said, but the whip-crack of his voice was honed with anger; and the palpable force of his authority settled the intruders into griping silence: they had stuff to say but would wait until this scary man was ready to let them talk. Kraai and Nesbitt sat transfixed; Gugu took notes. Xoli swapped to English: "You have burst into this room and this inquiry because there's something you have to say. Start out by saying who you are."

"I'm Fanuel Dube," said the leader of the three. "I'm a Labour Representative, and I work in the engineering shop." He looked uncertainly around the room, raised his fist, and said, "Viva!"

Xoli stared at him until he lowered his hand, self-consciously folding it into his left. He stood with his hands clasped in front of him like a choir boy at Sunday morning mass. Xoli looked at the second man.

"Matthews Maroke," he muttered, looking timorously from under the lip of his helmet. He also tried a perfunctory raised fist, but lowered it before the salute got above shoulder height.

"Anokhosha Mokoena," slurred the third, barely audible.

"What do you have to say?" Xoli, still standing and still ignoring the panel, demanded. It didn't take the skill of a trained psychologist to see the man was properly pissed.

Fanuel answered. He clearly was the spokesman for and energy behind the troika. "You killed him. Killed him!" There was less vim in him now, but Stephen sensed that he was doing his best to muster his flagging vigour. He was an angry man: angry at the world and angry for the way things were. But the Big Boss was right here now.

"*I* did?" Xoli asked, pointing an accusing finger at his own chest and dipping his head with its deep frown toward his accuser. The flint in his eye matched the steel of his voice.

"Management did. Management killed him." Fanuel stuck to his point, but his conviction was starting to falter.

"What do you mean, man? I'm management. Did I kill him?"

"You all did. Look, here I have proof!" And with that Fanuel Dube Esq flung a file of papers on the desk in front of him. Some of the sheets stayed in the cover, but most of them fluttered out and ended up on the floor. Stephen didn't think he'd done it on purpose, but sometimes that's just how things happen.

Xoli kept dead quiet and stared the man down. After an

uneasy few moments, the three intruders bent over, picked up the papers, put them back in the file, and diffidently pushed it across the desk to the General Manager.

"This file says management killed Mpho Mamela?" Xoli asked.

"Yes, it does. Details are all in there. Management killed him for its own reasons. For money." The shop steward was trying for another pass at his previous moral outrage, pumping himself to find his stride again. "The workers want freedom!" he said, looking for support from his colleagues. Matthews did another half-hearted Black Power salute. But Xoli wasn't born yesterday.

"Were you there when he was killed?" Xoli asked, insisting that all three comrades reply separately. No, they weren't, all three confessed.

"Do you know who killed him?" No, they didn't know that either.

"Do you know how he was killed?" Unfortunately, they weren't too sure of that.

"Do you know when he was killed?" They didn't have full details.

"Do you know anything at all about his death?" No, not so much, they had to admit. Except that management did it. The file proves that.

"The information's in the file. His death is explained in the file," Fanuel maintained. But quietly now.

Stephen looked admiringly at the general manager. It would've taken the trio of stooges at the head of the table a week of questions to get to this point where Xoli had come to in exactly eleven minutes.

"We'll look at the papers and then we'll discuss this further," said the bossman. "Your conduct here this afternoon is most inappropriate, and we'll call you in to discuss that as well. In the meanwhile, you may leave."

The three would-be revolutionaries looked at one another

uneasily, shuffled their feet, and then traipsed out. They wore hangdog expressions that told of generations of oppression of the proletariat by the capitalist bourgeoisie. The spectre that haunted all of regional Middelburg was the spectre of scary general managers, like this cross man right here.

"Lindiwe, please make me seven copies of this file?" Xoli asked the hovering PA. "Bind them and bring them back in here with the original as soon as you're done."

"Yes, Mr. Sibeko." She curtsied and picked up the file. Kraai and Nesbitt hadn't twitched a muscle throughout the entire episode; and Gugu was still writing her novel.

"I think we can continue." Xoli nodded to Kraai, who had lost his thread altogether. He conferred with Nesbitt for a while with his mic off and then seemed to pull himself together.

"You're the responsible person for the area where the deceased was injured?" Kraai asked Jozi, who still looked like the principal accused.

"That's correct."

"Why did you not take steps to prevent the injury?"

Well, that's kinda direct, thought Stephen, nevertheless trusting the young engineer to get the answer right. And he wasn't disappointed.

"We did take steps. The conveyer complies with all technical specification, it's in a controlled area, and our personnel are trained in safety measures."

"But still this man was killed?"

"Yes."

"How do you explain that?"

"I have no explanation. The deceased wasn't authorised to be there, he had no business being there, and he disregarded several standing safety regulations by approaching and interfering with the conveyer. No one knew he was there, he was acting on his own and for reasons we don't understand."

"But it's your fault," hissed Kraai, catching Jozi off-guard.

"In what way?" he protested, holding supplicating hands wide, palms up.

"Look here, Mr. Moloi, don't think you can be like your lawyer. I ask the questions, not you. You answer. In this court of inquiry, you do as I say. You don't tell me what to do. Now answer my question and be aware that I'll hold you personally responsible for your answer and your actions." Kraai spat the words like poison bullets, trying to mow down this young man who now held the post that once upon a time had been the office of Mr. Serfontein.

"Now hang on a minute," said Stephen quietly, noticing how Jozi had blanched at Kraai's outburst.

"Don't you dare tell me to hang on in my own court! Hang on, he says! What an impertinence. I'll kick you out of this room!" Kraai seethed, flinging down his pen as flecks of spittle flew from the mean slit of his mouth.

Stephen waited for silence and then said in his quietest voice: "You'll try." When Kraai had no immediate rejoinder, Stephen continued: "You'll try to kick me out of this room, but not without consequences."

"What consequences?" Kraai emphasised the word with a shake of his head to maintain his control of the situation, but he knew it was slipping away fast. He'd suddenly become a fish on the end of this bloody lawyer's line, and had just asked exactly the question he had been tricked into. God, how he hated lawyers!

"There'll be several consequences," Stephen said softly. "The company will immediately stop cooperating with this inquiry and we'll ask the High Court on an urgent basis to set aside this entire process. The papers will be served on the Minister before you're back in Pretoria. In our application we'll ask not only for the inquiry to be reconvened from scratch, but also that you, Mr. Serfontein, be recused from taking any further part in it."

"On what basis?" croaked Kraai.

"On the basis of clear prejudice you have displayed against the company on an ongoing basis; and on the basis that you're conflicted by being a dismissed erstwhile employee of the company."

Stephen idly noted that Gugu wrote that down, while her boss struggled to swallow what he'd just heard. To his credit he managed. After a furious muttered conversation with Nesbitt, with the microphone off, he nodded and turned to Stephen.

"Very well, in the interests of getting things done as expeditiously as possible, you may remain, Mr. Wakefield. But the witness must answer the question." The man's stridency had dissolved and he now sounded as croaky as Willie Nelson after an all-night bender.

"You didn't ask him a question, Mr. Chairman. You said the fatality was Mr. Moloi's fault. That is a statement, not a question. If you have a question, then ask it of the witness and I'm sure he will answer."

Kraai stared daggers at Stephen and said, with sarcasm dripping off his fangs, "Was it your fault, Mr. Moloi?"

"No," replied Jozi, earning him a clear view of the slight smile that pulled at the corners of Stephen's mouth. His boy got that one right.

But Kraai wasn't finished. He'd seen other people do this and he wasn't about to go away without another try.

"I put it to you that it's your fault," he threw the words at Jozi.

"I deny that," the young man said quietly. A good coach can sometimes help you out in a sticky position.

"You're avoiding my questions," Kraai insisted.

"No, he's not," Stephen interrupted again, this time more rudely than he'd ordinarily do, but he wanted this silly man to stop. "You aren't really asking anything, and he has responded perfectly correctly and in full to what you have put to him."

Kraai sighed deeply and tried his last trick. "Mr. Wakefield, I'm minutes away from concluding this enquiry and making a finding of negligence against your company." Good news with the bad: Theuns looked up with twinkling expectation in his eyes, hearing that they may be minutes away from his being allowed to get out of this room, a day and a bit earlier than expected.

Kraai continued: "I'm giving you, the mine, and the witness, one last opportunity of convincing me otherwise. If you don't want to avail yourself of that chance to avoid the finding, then that's well and good. If there isn't a satisfactory answer from the witness, the inquiry will be terminated right here and now; and then you can deal with the fallout."

He sat back, smiling at his own masterstroke. But his pleasure with his own cleverness didn't last.

"Thank you, Mr. Chairman. The witness has given the only answer that will be given, and we understand that the inquiry is therefore terminated. We request to be given full written reasons supporting any finding you make against the company."

Kraai was surprised to hear that the inquiry was done. But he'd said that, hadn't he? Or had he not? He couldn't be sure; but he mustn't waver now, otherwise he would show weakness in front of this lawyer. He nodded in affirmation and smiled, sinister as a mafia hitman.

Stephen wasn't finished. "We reserve the right to apply to the High Court for a review of these proceedings on the basis of preconceived bias. The Chairman has told us what his finding will be, before having considered the evidence as a whole, and before having deliberated for an appropriate time. In addition, the Chairman has specifically required the company to establish its innocence, rather than the more usual position that the company would be presumed not guilty until the contrary is shown. Our submission is, of course, without prejudice to our other rights." Stephen kept his hands folded on the desk in front of him.

Kraai was lost for words. When he'd led his triumphant return to this boardroom on Wednesday morning, he'd wanted to spin the inquiry out for much longer. He'd relished the thought of shouting at Theuns and at Xoli. Oh, to shout at his former boss, Theuns, the man who thought Kraai Serfontein wasn't a force to reckon with!

But suddenly it was over, and somehow it turned out that *he* had made that decision. *He* had terminated the inquiry, he was sure; but when had he done that? He thought that he may have done that, and he certainly couldn't go back on his ruling: that would undermine his authority and he'd lose face here in the last place on Earth where he wanted to do that. To make matters worse, he was now staring down the barrel of a review. A review! On the basis that he was a bad inspector and bore a grudge because he'd been fired. God, he really hated lawyers. What else could he do? He settled for: "We note your statements and will give them due consideration. This inquiry is terminated at three forty-five on Thursday afternoon, LCD Serfontein presiding." Gugu wrote that down. Then he started packing up his many things.

Lindiwe chose that moment to hustle back into the room with the copies of the file, neatly bound in booklets. She looked around uncertainly and caught Stephen's eye. He winked and got up to meet her.

"Thanks, Lindi. I'll take those."

The original and three bound copies he gave to Gugu—the other two pretended to be in deep conversation and wouldn't look at him. Of the other four, he gave one to Xoli and one to Jozi; kept one for himself and one for Jonny. Theuns had started to hide when papers were being distributed and was overjoyed not to have to think up an excuse for not reading them.

They waited for the inspectors to bugger off, and then Stephen said: "Can we recap in your office in fifteen minutes please, Xoli? I want Jonny to be there if possible."

"Sure," said Xoli.

Their meeting was brief. Jonny, who had heard the story from Theuns with much guffawing, nodded at Stephen and said, "Nkosi." *You're the man.*

Stephen looked bashful. Shaking his head, he said: "I didn't really play fair." He looked around the room and continued, holding up the file Lindiwe had made.

"I'll look at this file carefully, but from glancing through it quickly, there seems to be nothing in it. Nothing relevant. But Jonny and I'll let you know if there's anything to it." He put the file down.

"I don't know what Kraai will do. He clearly wanted to find us guilty. He actually said so." Stephen shook his head at the man's stupidity. "But he is in a pinch now. He has behaved badly" — around the table there were nodded heads and murmurs of consent — "and I think he may just look after Numero Uno. It's just possible that his report will be that the mine is not at fault. He missed the point about access. Didn't even raise it. Theuns, get your new checkpoint up as soon as possible."

The Chief Engineer nodded.

"If the report finds the mine guilty, we'll look at it carefully, because they must give reasons. We'll decide later, but we could ask for a review. I think Kraai will be hard pressed to explain what he did. If we don't go for a review, we'll speak to the prosecutor; and if that doesn't work, we'll go to court. There isn't anything to panic about. As I say, though, with a bit of luck, it's all over."

Chapter 17

"Elsobe de Ruiter works with mixed media," Lisa said, in response to Stephen's question. He'd pulled up on the left where the car guard showed him, just a few paces short of the ancient plane tree that Hugh, his well-heeled friend, had told him was a heritage tree. That means, so Hugh said, that you can't chop it down—it was protected by the force of law. The force of law. *That sounds like greater protection than it is,* Stephen had thought.

"She is a photographer and a painter," his wife prattled on. "Well, she is more than that: she is a mixed-medium artist. Her stuff is beautiful and thought-provoking. She lives here in Johannesburg, but has exhibited in New York."

Stephen nodded thanks to the guard, and together he and Lisa strolled down the sidewalk to the gallery. It was Friday early evening, opening night of the joint exhibition: Elsobe de Ruiter, the mixed-medium artist, and Dikeledi Ngwenya, about whom even Lisa didn't know much. Art was her passion, not Stephen's. Actually, art was one of her several passions, along with looking after anyone who needed looking after; being devoted to her private menagerie; traveling to places around the world that look good in magazine articles; reading more books than seemed possible for one person; watching celebrity chefs and trying out new recipes from Ottolenghi to Kossie Sikilela; and watching soapies on TV. She knew the entire neighbourhood and all its issues and all its *skinner,* its gossip; and was friends with an unlikely number of people. She was a much more interesting person than he was, Stephen knew, and he still couldn't believe his luck that she'd picked him out of all the young men who had been after her.

"Dikeledi worked with Norman Catherine in the Young Artists' Workshop," Lisa said. She was endearingly proud of herself for having met Catherine at an exhibition, and having told him that her children, when they were small, had been scared of his stuff—three odd-looking creatures with spiky ears, bristly stubble, and short fangs, riding a skateboard built somewhere in an exotic *Star Wars* galaxy. The old man had laughed proudly, so Lisa said.

"I know nothing about Dikeledi's work, but he is highly regarded."

At the door an improbably beautiful girl met them, tall on spiky high heels, in a matt-black figure-hugging mini. She wore her midnight-black hair like Nefertiti, in a straight short bob. The teeth in her smile had cost someone a fortune to look that perfect, and her lips were cosmetic-ad red and full. She passed Stephen a register in which he wrote his name and telephone number. Art is for the soul, art is the barometer of civilisation, and art leavens even the most turgid of personalities. But art also is a branch of the stock exchange with a derivative market too complicated for any calculus formula on this Earth. The register then was to keep track of the potential of all those cheque books.

Behind a marble counter two young men in black suits and white shirts poured flutes of champagne. Checked-in and drinks in hand, Stephen and Lisa stood in toward the crowd.

Stephen had, once upon a time, seen something in this very gallery that had fascinated him: an old tree had been cut down to just above the ground, and uprooted. Some enterprising person had washed all the dirt out of a three-metre circle of its roots, and then varnished the whole lot to a shiny light yellow. To Stephen's eye it was magnificent, the complexity of twists and turns, the wooden knots of interlacing Gorgon-head tendrils. The thing had stood at the main entrance for many months; and Stephen hoped it was classified as art. So he too could say he liked art.

The crowd tonight was no different from the usual. A short, overly confident man in his late fifties with long grey hair in greasy curls hooked nonchalant thumbs into the pockets of jeans that were more torn white fibre than actual denim. In his unlaced sneakers and fingerless weightlifting gloves he looked like a teenager in an old man's body. A bookish scholar balanced thick black horn-rimmed spectacles on a nose like the one Cyrano de Bergerac was sensitive about. Despite the summer's evening, he wore a full length coat made for the chic front rooms of European fashion. A huge woman with heroic hair wafted around the room in a mauve kaftan large enough to hide Demis Roussos. A man with the face of a claims clerk at the Auto and Accident Insurance Company wore a conservative dark suit and formal leather office shoes, but the trousers had been cut down to shorts. Stephen wore Woolworths jeans and a golf shirt, the only one in the gallery this evening.

"Darling!" someone behind them said in a deep androgynous voice. Even before they turned, Stephen knew he wasn't "darling." Before them stood a tall person with hair shaved to a stubble, a leathery smile, orange glasses like Ali G's, and more bangles than the Rosebank flea market.

"Rose!" Lisa exclaimed, giving the apparition a name. "You remember Stephen?" she asked, pulling him by the arm as if sensing he was about to scarper. Stephen couldn't remember Rose, but equally didn't think he could ever forget such a sight. Perhaps last time he'd seen her she'd been in human form.

"Hi," he said politely, and shook the bony hand extended in his direction. And then he did scarper.

On the wall to his right was one of the display pieces: a square no bigger than fifteen centimetres across, painted completely black in what looked like a slurry of sand and fine gravel. Perhaps there was a stick or two in it as well, but it was difficult to tell. When he looked at it carefully, he saw it wasn't completely black: There was the slightest hint of non-blackness in it, a subtle nuance of not-completely-uniform black. *Interesting*, is what he'd have said if Lisa had asked what he thought. Retracting from his close inspection of it, he noticed on the wall to his left there were another two just like this one, but about twice the size. They appeared to be identical, but when he looked carefully he saw that they were not-quite-black in slightly different ways. *Interesting*, he'd have said again.

Behind him Lisa and Rose weren't nearly done with their conversation, so he took the first turn to the right, into a large room with many people and on the walls another eight blacknesses. But these were big and rectangular, easily a metre by a metre and a half. If Stephen had been asked what thought he of those, he wouldn't have known what to say. He turned left into another large room with even more art people milling about, and on the walls were four really big rectangular black slurry smudges. Really big, four meters by three. *Jesus!* Stephen thought.

In the middle of the room, laughing and swirling a champagne glass stood General Shakes. Even as Stephen saw him, he was saying goodbye to his companions, who moved along to look for deeper meaning in the huge black smears.

"What's an apparently normal person like you doing here?" Stephen asked the man. Shakes laughed and tilted the remains of his champagne down his throat.

"Supporting the up-and-coming artists. Keeping my finger on the pulse of culture." He laughed again, and, pointing the stem of his flute at the large canvas closest to him, asked, "What do you make of this?"

"Well, if he can sell any of these, I think he's a genius."

"Just what I thought. My art adviser says the artist is really hot and these will double in value in no time at all. How do you tell which side is up?"

"You look for the signature: that will be the bottom right-hand corner," Stephen advised with the assurance of an art critic. Both of them leaned in toward the canvas but found no signature disturbing the uniform very-nearly-blackness.

"Subtle," mused Stephen. "Then you must look for which corner the artist would've signed, if he hadn't minded disturbing the integrity of his work with his actual name."

Shakes laughed again.

"Let's get another drink," he said, and together they moved to the counter for a refill. "I've had enough of this shit, but I can't leave yet. Come outside and tell me how it went."

They made their way into a tiny courtyard where a large metal block of irregular proportions stood with Zen dignity in a bed of precisely raked snow-white pebbles. Shakes looked at the thing and sighed. "This one's so good it's not even for sale." He shook his head.

Stephen sipped his drink.

"Shakes, we had a busy week. I'm in your diary first thing Monday morning, but it's better we chat here." He told the Chairman of his visit to the shebeen and the story about the black beamer. "I asked Jonny to check it out, and bad news. It's true. The car came in with two occupants at about six o'clock on Thursday evening. I've seen the CCTV footage. The guard checks their ID and lets them through. Jonny hasn't spoken to him because we wanted to tell you first and ask what you thought. But I don't think the guard will remember: he saw two ID cards that looked right and he let them go in.

"You can't make out the registration number unfortunately. Jonny's installing an extra camera so that doesn't happen again. Anyway, maybe they were employees, but maybe they had forged cards. And the cards are easy to forge. Look here."

Stephen pulled his Sethemba ID card from his wallet. Against a blue background with the name of the company and its double-shadowed Cheetah head logo, were his photo and his name. On the back were his signature and his employee details. The whole thing was encased in a credit card-sized laminated plastic folder, sealed at the edges by the machine on the desk in the security hut. Everyone at the mine, all 1,650 people who came and went daily, had one of these.

"The car shows up again on the camera when it leaves at ten

past nine. There's no ID check; they just open the boot to see if anything is being taken out, lift the boom, and out goes the car. It's impossible to see from the footage who is in the car."

"What do you think all of that means?" Shakes asked.

"I don't know. Personally I don't think it adds up to a row of beans. We don't know who these people are, or what they did. Or even if they did anything at all. We really need to look into this further. I think it's too early to draw any conclusions."

"Is it possible this may have something to do with the fatality? Or the fraud?"

"It's possible. But how probable it is, I'm not sure."

Shakes listened solemnly. "Who knows about this?" he asked.

"You, me, and Jonny," said Stephen. "That brings me to the next thing. Who can I trust in this? I need to know."

Shakes thought carefully before answering. "I don't know who you can't trust, but Jonny is on our side. He's like you, handpicked. Our man. You can trust Jonny. Until we know more, keep it between us."

"Okay. That means no police? Even if we think there's been something more than simply an accident. Not that I think so at the moment."

Shakes snorted derisively. "The South African police, you mean? No, Stephen, they'll fuck this thing up for sure. You and Jonny keep looking. Maybe you don't find anything, but you can't do any worse than the thin blue line, Middleburg branch."

Stephen moved on with the report, telling Shakes about the fraud and the audit. "We're going to draw a blank." He told Shakes about the foreign payment and the cash deposits and the balance left in the account.

"Last time you spoke to me about this, you didn't think the fatality and the fraud were connected. Do you still not think so?"

Stephen thought carefully before answering. "I don't know. It's possible that they're linked, but I can't see how. The mystery BMW and the fraud and the accident may not be connected at all.

But maybe there's a connection. I don't know."

"Do you think the mystery men killed Mamela?" Shakes asked.

"I have no reason to think so. I don't know what the two in the car did while they were on the property. It's possible they did nothing at all. I just don't know enough to say." The General nodded.

"But I'm not finished yet," Stephen continued.

"Oh?" Shakes looked him straight in the eye.

Stephen told him what had happened at the inquiry. The relevant bits only, which happily shortened the story considerably. When he got to the episode where the trade unionists burst in, Shakes shook his head and looked at his shoes, but offered no comment. He wore black leather shoes tonight, but with broad round toes.

"That's the interesting part of the story," Stephen continued. "The file they threw at Xoli, and he made them pick up again, was mostly about nothing. The rules of the Share Incentive Scheme, the Trust Deed of the Community Trust, some correspondence about bursaries for people going on various courses, some trade union suggestions about how a transport subsidy should be introduced."

"So nothing interesting?" asked Shakes.

"I said *mostly* about nothing. In the middle of all sorts of other stuff, about nothing really, there's an email that, if you read the whole thing, is decidedly weird. Extremely weird, in fact. One of those mails that bounce back and forth between a group of senders and recipients, and keeps getting longer and longer.

"But the sender and recipients aren't always the same people. The last mail is from the Minister, and isn't part of the chain. It says the Minister has signed the official letter consenting to the acquisition of the business of Biesiesfontein; and it will be delivered to the company the next day. I have, of course, seen that before, but without what went before it.

"I almost didn't read the rest of the e-mail chain, assuming it was just admin. But as it turns out, the exchange taken as a whole tells a different story."

Stephen took a sip of bubbles and remembered how Sethemba had bought the business of Biesiesfontein. The price had been agreed when coal on the international market sold for sixty-five dollars a tonne. In the many months it had taken for the banking documents to be put in place and for the Competition Tribunal to approve the deal, the coal price had increased to a hundred and ten dollars a tonne, making the colliery the buy of the century. The last condition for the transaction was the written consent of the Minister. That had come through twelve hours before the deal would've failed, giving many of the Sethemba people indigestion and extra grey hair. It was clear that if the Minister did not agree in time, the seller would pull the plug and keep Biesiesfontein, which suddenly was worth much more than Sethemba was paying.

"As I said," Stephen went on, "the email bounced around a few times. The interesting part I hadn't seen before was an exchange between only the Minister and Thuli. The Minister wrote to Thuli only, saying quite clearly he wouldn't approve the deal. This was three days before the deadline. Thuli wrote back, two days later, saying thanks for the chat and look forward to hearing from you. Only that. And, on the same day, immediately after Thuli's mail, the Minister says, tomorrow the formal letter arrives. Complete about-face from one letter to the next." Stephen stopped talking while the General thought in silence.

"Who knows about this?" he asked eventually.

"You and me," Stephen said quietly. "Except for a few things. Someone put that letter in the file, perhaps for a good reason, perhaps not. We know the Trade Union has it, but has said nothing. They don't strike me as careful chess players, so I think we can assume they don't know what it is. Apart from them there are seven copies of the file. The inspectors have the original and three copies, but, necessary respect and so on, they're too stupid to understand anything as subtle as this. Nor will they even read it. They like the idea of lots of paper because it makes what they do look important. But actually they read nothing, this I have seen many times.

"Xoli and Jozi each have a copy, but they're busy people and will wait for me to report back to them on whether they need to bother with the file or not. And Jonny has the other copy. He will read it, but probably won't pick up on the anomaly. I only saw it because I was involved in the transaction and know what was supposed to have happened."

Shakes nodded. "The Minister and Thuli are big mates," he said to Stephen, frowning as he churned through his thoughts. "They live in the same suburb. You know what happened here, don't you?" He raised his eyebrows at Stephen.

"I can guess. You think the Minister took a golden handshake?"

"Something like that." Shakes nodded. "My consortium and I had agreed to buy in if the deal went unconditional. We stood in for forty-five percent of the company on the basis of the letter the Minister wrote. The second one, the formal consent letter. Not the first one. Thuli stood to gain lots from the deal: he'd be paid a success fee, he'd be the CEO and he'd get a substantial allocation in the share incentive scheme. But only if the deal went ahead."

"That's right. I remember; I did the agreement."

"Yes. Now it turns out we bought in after the Minister did an abrupt U-turn." The General was silent for a few moments. "Stephen?" Shakes looked at the older man. "Here is your fraud. This is what you're looking for. Your man Mamela found out about this. Someone first paid him to keep quiet, and then they made sure his mouth stayed shut forever."

He spoke like an old soldier, matter-of-fact life-and-death stuff. No hype, no high emotion; equally no guessing.

Stephen thought there were some unwarranted assumptions

in the General's logic. Maybe he was right, but there were many other possible explanations.

"Shakes, we have to do more work before we can draw any conclusions. I'm going to have to tell Jonny about this. Otherwise he can't help me properly in trying to find out more."

"Yes, I think that's right. As I've said, you can trust him. I do."

Stephen put on his most serious face: "And I can't tell your CEO. I don't know what he is involved in and what not."

"Yes." Shakes sighed heavily. "Fuck, this is a mess."

Behind them there was a knock on the window. Stephen turned to see Lisa smiling at him and beckoning. Rose was fortunately no longer with her.

"Time to go," he said to his companion. "I'll keep at it and let you know. I'm seeing the Mamela family on Monday. They probably can't tell me anything, but you never know."

He left Shakes brooding in the courtyard, and joined Lisa and the other culture vultures.

Chapter 18

Monday morning took a tenuous hold of the day, settling grumpily from a rainy sky. The sun, packed away in grey layers of sodden cotton wool, strained to see through the window into the kitchen where Stephen and Lisa sat down to breakfast. The dogs had tracked in mud from outside, and lay steaming under the table. Lisa was strict with her dogs: if their feet were muddy, they could mess up only the kitchen, not the carpets and the rest of the house as well. Except for Cindy—she was old and could do as she pleased. It's good to have a firm hand when dealing with animals. The cats watched from their fastidious perch on the countertop. They wouldn't go outside when it rained, and disapproved of dirty paws.

Lisa had made a bowl of fruit salad: apple, mango, papino, grapes, banana, and a squeeze of orange juice. If she put granadillas in as well, Stephen complained that bits got stuck in his teeth. His job was to man the toaster, and he was also in charge of coffee.

"Michelle and Lexy and I are having tea this morning to pick what we want to see in Salzburg. There are so many things. We have to agree on a list, otherwise there'll be chaos." The organisation of the Austrian trip was moving with the momentum of the Anaconda roller-coaster at Gold Reef City, heading for the loop-the-loop; and with the precision of an actuarial calculation.

"In Tyrol, we've booked a show called *Zigeuner Lieder*. Lexy says she and Braam saw it in Vienna when they were there last, and it's fantastic."

"Isn't it a Brahms composition?" Stephen asked, because, of the many things his wife liked, classical music wasn't one. Two hours of Brahms would put a dampener on even her enthusiasm.

"No, I don't think so. It's a show of folk songs, gypsy music. Lexy says its old-fashioned acoustic guitars and concertinas, and someone who does tricks on a violin. They play the percussion with wooden spoons and washboards and tins. It's great fun, so she says."

Fun like an oompah band, thought Stephen, relieved not to have to sit through it. "You excited?" He smiled at his wife.

"Yup." She nodded, smug with her cup of coffee and slice of toast. "What are you doing this morning?"

"I'm seeing Thuli first thing. And then Jonny and I are still working on some loose ends in the fatal accident case. We're going to see the young man's mother this afternoon."

"Shame," Lisa said with real feeling, spoken like a true South African.

When the coffee cups were empty and cold, they headed off in their separate directions. In his office, Stephen fired up his laptop and glanced at the headlines: "Violent crime upswing affects police leadership." The police were in turmoil, the report said, and without proper leadership, because there was so much violent crime, the generals couldn't cope. *I know a general who wouldn't say such a thing*, Stephen thought. He put down the paper and headed down the passage for his meeting.

Thuli's office wasn't much bigger than anybody else's, and was sparsely furnished. An ordinary desk out of a catalogue of office furniture, a high-backed swivel chair behind it, and a round conference table with four seats. The floor was carpet tile and the ceiling ordinary rectangles of white regulation pressed board. On the side wall a whiteboard carried a collection of coloured board markers, and on it was written RBCT 28/11 440Kt. Behind the desk one photo only, in a simple black frame, showed Thuli and his wife in a stiff photo-studio pose: he is seated and she is standing behind him with her hand on his right shoulder. They are formally dressed; soberly, as if on their way to buy expensive new furniture from Bakos Brothers; and neither of them has found anything to smile about.

The only other thing on the almost bare desk was a laptop, its cradle, screen, and cables; and a management-motivational-type slogan printed on an upside-down T of brown leather: "INNOVATION distinguishes a LEADER from a FOLLOWER."

Stephen thought of the sign as borderline nonsensical, even in this modern era of management advisory consultants and motivational speakers. He supposed it meant something like—*the ability to see things in a new and improved way, coupled with the ability to introduce sustainable ways in which previous inefficiencies in a system would be eliminated, is the ability of someone who would likely be a successful coordinator of a collaborative effort.* Even then, Stephen wasn't sure he agreed. The guy who thought up a new way of accounting for fluctuations of value in a marked-to-market asset pool was likely not to be the person best suited to tell a unionised workforce to work overtime for no additional money. Nor, probably, was he the right guy to keep peace in a boardroom where tempers were flaring.

Thuli thought of himself as a leader of men. Followers, people like Stephen, were two-and-a-half steps behind. The essence of being a leader was hard to pin down. Stephen thought it took three things: an immediate answer to every question; not remembering how often you were wrong; and knowing that all the money in the world belonged in your pocket. Those three rounded out your Atlas complex: You alone had to carry the world. And because the job you did was so important, you could tell everyone else what to do and think.

The leader was late. Stephen sat at the round table and waited, wishing his phone was as interesting as everybody else's. People in restaurants hauled out their phones and stared at the screen in rapt attention. Eventually they'd drift back from the land of tele-make-believe, only to be whisked away again if that rectangle of plastic so much as let out a peep. Even as he toyed with idea of staring at his phone to pass the time, he heard Thuli in the passage, coming closer. The CEO was telling an unseen companion a part of his life story.

"It was tough in the townships. One of my cousins was mugged. In Zulu they called it an *Inkunzi*. A violent mugging. They hit him with a brick in his face and took his money. We thought he'd die but after a long time he came home from hospital. Now the whole side of his face is misshapen."

"Wow," said his audience, a male voice Stephen identified as Kabelo, a young graduate in Investor Relations. He was a cool young dude who had been in nappies when Nelson Mandela had stepped on to the balcony to make his first speech as President. *"Out of the experience of an extraordinary human disaster that lasted too long must be born a society of which all humanity will be proud. Never, never and never again shall it be that this beautiful land will experience the oppression of one by another."* Kabelo had grown up in Houghton and had gone to St. Johns College and UCT. Of the deprivations of apartheid townships, he knew not a thing; and Thuli was fixing that for him.

Thuli left Kabelo in the passage and came into the office. "Stephen," he said, by way of greeting, apparently unaware that he'd made his colleague wait.

"Morning," said Stephen. Thuli put down his notepad and pen and sat down in the seat opposite. He looked at his phone, scrolled down to see all his messages, and read them in silence. Then he typed a long SMS to someone, read it carefully, frowned at the screen, and pressed *send*. When he was done, he clicked off the instrument and looked at Stephen, who was just beginning to feel aggrieved by the man's unquestioning belief that he was entitled to behave like this. Stephen looked back at Thuli, who eventually broke the silence.

"Do you have a report for me?"

"Are you finished?" Stephen asked.

"With what?"

"Your phone."

"Yes. What's your point?"

Stephen held his gaze steady. "Simple point. Our meeting was at nine-thirty, that's twenty minutes before you arrived. And if you want to send SMSs to your mates, don't do it while I'm waiting to speak to you." Thuli blanched.

"Stephen, you treat me like you're a white man and I'm just another black man. You're a white boss and I'm your darkie servant. You're a racist." He jumped up in agitation. "A racist! That's what you are."

"No. You're simply rude. My saying as much has nothing to do with race."

"I'm the boss and I won't have you telling me how to behave."

"Very well. Then you'll continue to behave badly." Stephen nodded and said evenly: "Shall we start then with what we are here to discuss?"

Thuli sat down again, still fuming. "My grandmother taught me what I know and I never forget an insult. Never. It's who I am." Thuli said, shaking his head emphatically. "I'll never forget this."

"Okay," said Stephen, already regretting his spat with this unreasonable man. He'd known it was coming. It had been building for months, block by block like a wall of Lego: Thuli making and taking telephone calls while Stephen was trying to speak to him; Thuli not listening to what Stephen said, preferring to read whatever appeared on his phone screen; Thuli being late for every arrangement.

"Remember for always then that when I'm in your office, I'm more important than your phone. So, do you want to know what happened?"

Thuli sat in his chair sulking. He didn't answer, but had the good grace to turn his phone over so he couldn't see it.

Stephen gave him a report of the previous week's events as if nothing had happened. He didn't often have the CEO's undivided attention, but he did have it now; and he rather enjoyed it. He told Thuli about the inquiry and the union's inter-ruption of it. Of the file of papers, he said only that it didn't hold anything significant. The new checkpoint would be in place already, he said, and in his view and with a bit of luck the incident was done and dusted—he doubted that anything more would come of it.

Then he told Thuli, who was increasingly forgetting the mortal insult he'd vowed always to remember, about the audit, the foreign transfer of money into Mamela's account, and the monthly cash payments.

"I don't think we'll find anything. We'll go through all the steps and complete the audit, but I expect it to be inconclusive." Thuli by this time had perked up considerably.

"Well, that worked out nicely. So you think it could all be over?"

"Yes, I do. As I say, I think it's unlikely the inspectors will recommend a prosecution. And if they do, we have a good shot at a successful review. Not that I think it will get there. And the forensic audit seems to me hopeless. We won't find anything, mostly because it isn't in our books. I'm sure there's a fraud of sorts, but it's extraneous to our records. We'll be able to tell the Audit Committee that we have an all-clear."

"Well, that's good news." Thuli nodded, as if he and Stephen had never had a scrap in their lives. "Thank you very much. I appreciate your efforts."

"Thanks for your time. I'll keep you posted of any developments, even if it's nothing." Stephen stood, smiled at the man who liked to think he was everybody's boss, and walked out of the office.

He didn't really like not having told Thuli the rest of it, about the letter, the black BMW, and the fight Trevor Hodges alleges he witnessed; but he saw and agreed with Shakes's point that to tell everything would be to destroy any hope of ever finding out what really had happened. Stephen understood the need to be secretive, but couldn't yet convince himself that the CEO was involved in anything untoward. Something had happened, for sure. But they probably wouldn't ever know what. The men in the black BMW could have been doing anything at all. The theory of their having killed Mamela seemed a bit too much like Hollywood. Stephen had no idea how he could find out more; and if he did, he was sure that it would emerge that Mamela was taking payments from a supplier. The black beamer, he thought, very likely had nothing to do with the story. How Mamela got himself killed, though, remained a mystery.

Chapter 19

To get onto the N17, Stephen turned off the M2 at Rissik Street and headed south under the bridge in the direction of Wemmer Pan. His whole adult life in the Golden City hadn't taken him south of the racecourse at Turffontein except when he'd dated a girl who lived in a flat in Rosettenville. On Friday evenings he'd parked his boy racer in the street and together they'd walked a few blocks to Geno's, where the Portuguese owner provided plastic chairs and tables and red-checked plastic tablecloths. They ate espetadas impaled on young shoots cut from a Bay tree, grilled on an open fire and rolled in coarse salt crystals. Afterward the girl made Irish coffees in V-shaped tumblers with a foot like a wine glass but without a stem. Between the green four-leaf clovers and the golden rim were written the words *Irish Coffee* in curly leprechaun script. Instant coffee with a shot of scotch and squirty cream on top; but the glasses were authentic.

The highway swept east, threading between the rump of Johannesburg and the shoulder of Alberton, through the tollgate to Alrode, where Elizabethan mills belched evil clouds and heavy machinery ground the silence into a viscous paste of tensile stress and smoky days. A short hop past the brightly colourful tents of Carnival City, the casino that looked like the playground for the Sheik of Araby and his extended retinue. From there the veld was empty to the Springs turnoff and the street Stephen was looking for: Tonk Meter Way. He got there ten minutes early, but on the verge in the shade of a row of gums, Ronald's banger already stood waiting.

"Hey, young man," Stephen greeted him fondly. "I don't think you should leave your Barouche here. Someone may just think to redistribute it from your ability to his need. I have a GPS that should get us there. Follow me?"

Stephen did a slow U-turn and set off in the direction of Kwa-

Thema, where Mpho Mamela's mother lived. The road stayed out of town, dipped down into a vlei with reeds and bulrushes, and then the faintly Teutonic woman's voice on the car's speaker system instructed Stephen, "In three hundred metres turn right." He slowed down and saw in the mirror that Ronald's indicator was on. "Turn right now," said the woman; and he did.

They drove first through the oldest section, Tornado, named after the storms that had struck during the forced removals that had established Kwa-Thema—which, at the time, people said was an evil portent, a sign of heaven's displeasure. Unless you took a long view, that had just been wishful thinking. Down potholed Thema Street they made their way to Phomolo and then Overline. Shabangu Street led them further in among the shacks, scrunched together by lean years and hardship. At the stop in Kgaswane Street in Masimini, Stephen turned left and drew up in front of number sixteen. The house stood almost against the fence, one window on either side of a front door behind a security gate. The roof had been red at one time but had faded to russet and was speckled with age. Old-fashioned lace curtains kept strangers from looking through the windows. The narrow strip of yard had been swept that morning, and the door stood slightly ajar.

Ronald opened a garden gate and padded to the door. "Ko, Ko," he called softly, imitating the sound of knocking. Sounds of someone getting up in the room on the right were followed by footsteps coming to the door. A young man stood before them, thin and gangly as only youth can make you. He wore his white short-sleeved shirt tucked into navy-blue chinos, and his black shoes gleamed with polish and attention. His smile was nervous and his eyes were bright. The hand he held out to them was long and thin, the fingers bony and big-knuckled.

"Bongani Mamela," he said, nervous but not overwhelmed. "Thank you for coming. Won't you please come inside?"

He stood back from the door to let them in. To the right was the lounge, not a large room, but immaculate. Two two-seater couches and one single chair in the same style filled the room. Framed in worked mahogany with ball-and-claw feet, the seats were light brown velvet, brushed to perfection. Against the wall furthest from the door the TV stood silent and dark on a trolley with brass wheels; and on the wall away from the window were framed family photographs, and Psalm 23 embroidered in cross-stich. *The Lord is my Shepherd, I shall not want.* On the coffee table in the middle of the room cups, a milk jug and sugar bowl waited only for the steaming teapot to join them.

On one of the couches sat an old lady. She started getting up when Stephen and Ronald came into the room. She was dressed formally in a long dark skirt and a floral top, and on her head she wore an orange-brown beret. The open friendliness of her face was overlain with lines of sadness. Her hands were as delicate as a sparrow's wing, but had the strength of someone who had never shirked from heavy lifting.

"Blandina Mamela," she said, smiling in turn at Stephen and Ronald. She held the elbow of her right arm respectfully in her left hand while she shook hands with them. When she started talking, Stephen was delighted with her. She was from a generation that had never been to school. In her day the masters of apartheid had made it their policy that black children should be allowed to gaze on the green fields of education, but never play on them. Despite that deficit, Blandina was confident and her sense of humour irrepressible.

"I think you're the first white man ever to come into this house." She chuckled, looking at Stephen. "Welcome. I hope it's a new trend."

"I hope so, too." Stephen smiled. "Next time I'll bring my wife. You'll like her, I'm sure. Everybody does."

The old lady liked that. "Men must never be allowed too far away from female supervision. That way they get ideas, and all the problems in the world come from when men get ideas."

She'd sent her son into the kitchen to boil the kettle, and when he returned with the teapot, she scolded him: "Where is the cosy? Silly boy."

The fond look she gave him told that in her eye he was an apple. Embarrassed, he jumped back into the kitchen and came back with a red, yellow, and green knitted teapot-sized beanie. His mother pulled it over the teapot, musing: "Rastafarian tea for everybody?"

With his teacup in hand, Stephen started on the sad stuff. "Mrs. Mamela," he began.

"Blandina, please," she interrupted him.

"On condition only that you call me Stephen," he replied. "I'm dreadfully sorry for your loss. I couldn't speak to you at the funeral, there were so many people. But you're in both my and my wife's thoughts and prayers." Blandina said nothing; she just looked sad.

"Father Ronald and I want to understand what happened to Mpho, and I'd be most grateful if you could tell me anything, anything at all, that could give us some idea as to what might've happened."

"You don't just think it was an accident?" the old lady asked. The most difficult question right up front.

"We don't know, honestly. I just can't understand how the accident could have happened, or why. Mpho was well liked at work, and he had such a bright future ahead of him. I don't understand why he was at the conveyor belt at night, or how any of this happened, really."

Ronald frowned in sympathy from his couch. Stephen sat in the single seat, Blandina and Bongani on one of the couches, Ronald almost filling the other.

"You know we weren't there, and all we can do is guess. But there was something wrong in the weeks before my boy died." One traitorous tear escaped from the old lady's eye. She wiped it away almost without noticing. She was thinking deeply about something she wanted to ask.

"Mr. Wakefield. Stephen. You're not a judgemental person, are you? I know Father Ronald isn't."

"I try to take the log out of my own eye so that I can see the splinter in yours better. No, I'm not particularly judgemental," Stephen answered.

"You know my son liked other boys?"

"Yes, I do. But, truly, that makes no difference to me. I don't mean to be forward, but I know that your son was in a relationship with Frankie Mabena, and all I'm sad about is that they didn't have a longer opportunity to be happy together."

Mrs. Mamela looked for a minute as if she'd start crying again. But she made up her mind not to.

"When I was bringing up my boy, I tried to make him know that money wasn't all-important. It was very difficult to do, because we had none. You can only afford to be nonchalant about money if you have enough of it in your pocket. The devil dances in empty pockets, you know." She smiled experimentally at Stephen, checking how far she'd managed to push back her tears.

"I used to tell him that we are conceived in sin and come into the world in sin; and we leave it the same way, with or without forgiveness. How much money you get to spend in the middle makes no difference. Everyone knows that." She suddenly looked so defeated, Stephen wanted to reach out and squeeze her hand. But he didn't interrupt.

"Mpho was determined to make enough money not just for him, but also for the two of us. He sent just about his entire salary home. It paid for me, look how much I've got." Her gesture took in the whole room. "And it paid for Bongani's classes."

"Father Ronald has told me that. Truly amazing boy, that one of yours," Stephen said.

"But something was wrong with my son. It wasn't work, because he was doing so well, and he liked his boss so much. It had something to do with Frankie. He thought that the company had treated Frankie very badly, and he thought also that the magistrate who sentenced Frankie had been harsh. Mpho said Frankie's sentence was longer than it should've been, because the magistrate was anti-gay. I think Mpho was right. But that still wasn't the issue.

"Mpho was a private person, but one night when he was very sad, he told me something. He said: *Steal a few cents and they put you in jail; steal a few million and they put you in charge.* That was what was bugging him. I don't know exactly what the details were, but he thought the company, or someone at the company, should try to help Frankie. To get him out of prison earlier."

Blandina looked away for a moment, searching for the right words.

"Stephen, this may shock you, but I agree with my son. I really like Frankie and I feel so, so sorry for him. He didn't steal because he was a bad boy. He stole because he couldn't think what else to do."

"Are you in contact with Frankie still?" Stephen asked.

"I am. Why?"

"I'd like to see him." Stephen had decided this on the spur of the moment. "Father Ronald, will you come with me?"

Of course, the kindly priest said yes.

"But, Blandina, what you have told me isn't specific enough for me to follow up on. I need you to tell me more than that, if you can. Please." Mrs. Mamela shook her head sadly.

Just then Bongani piped up: "I really don't know what happened either, but can't you have a look at his tablet? He always carried that around with him as if the secrets of the world were written in it. Have you had a look at that?"

"I'm an old man. What exactly is a tablet?" Stephen asked, feeling at least a little foolish.

"Oh, it's like a fancy new laptop. Mpho was so proud of his— he had a new tablet someone from the company had bought for him in Singapore. One of his bosses. It was a Surface Pro 3. He used to brag that although it was as light as a feather, it had the processing capacity of a sophisticated massive old laptop. He carried it with him everywhere. He really liked the idea that you could pull the keyboard off the tablet. It attached magnetically. And when you took the keyboard off, the tablet was a touch screen. It's quite a machine. And I'm pretty sure all his secrets were on it."

"Nobody at the mine has said anything about a computer. Do you think it could be at his digs, where he was living?"

"No, Mr. Wakefield. I specifically looked for it. Because I wanted to see if there were any clues to what happened to my brother. Also, if no one else was using it, I would've liked it for myself."

"We'll start looking for it right away," Stephen told them. "And I'll let you know when it turns up. It can't have gone anywhere."

Mother and son nodded, doubt darting like swallows into their eyes. In their experience, when things like laptops and telephones went missing, they stayed that way.

They chatted for a while—Stephen taking the opportunity to confirm that the company had been in touch about Mpho's pension and insurance benefits; which it had—but that really was the end of the conversation. Privately, Stephen couldn't stop wondering why no one had mentioned the laptop, the tablet, to him. It could only be that neither Panico nor Jonny knew about it. For the first time he felt that perhaps there was more to Mpho Mamela's death than met the eye. And then it struck him: the two workers who found Mpho's body and the vehicle must have found the laptop, too. They must have taken it. And that's where he'd start. He'd send Jonny over to retrieve the thing. It would be simple enough. There was no need to panic, then.

Except. Except, he had one nagging doubt: what were the chances that a young man who worked at Biesies and lived in the single quarters in Crosby would know anyone who could get him high-end electronics from Singapore? And Thuli had spent ten days in Singapore in February, meeting investors. Stephen pushed his thoughts to the back of his mind and focused instead, too late to get the gist of it, on Ronald's story about what one of his parishioners had done the week before. They all laughed when the story was done. After his second cup of tea it was time to go.

They said goodbye at the door, leaving Mrs. Mamela and her son in the room Mpho had paid for. "I'll let you know when I find something," he reassured them.

In his wallet were the details for contacting Frankie Mabena. At the car he stood talking to Ronald.

"These are such nice people, Ronald. Why do things like this happen only to nice people?"

The priest lay a heavy hand on his shoulder. "They don't, little brother. They happen to horrible people as well. You just don't feel sorry for them, is all."

"I suppose. Listen, Captain, it's a long way for you to come and Frankie is in Diepkloof. When I go see him, I don't think it's necessary for you to come along."

"Thanks," said Ronald. "But if you need me, I'll be there."

On the way back, Stephen listened to Classic FM. He was deep in thought, humming along subconsciously to the music. "That was Johann Nepomuk Hummel," announced the DJ in his preposterously affected tones. "'Oh du Lieber Augustin', played for us there by the Vienna Philharmonic under the baton of Josef Krips." Stephen had quietly been singing: *Did you ever see a lassie, a lassie, a lassie; Did you ever see a lassie gae this way and that.* Good thing no one had heard him.

Chapter 20

The waitress wore a red-and-white striped skirt, a white blouse, a white apron with a frilly red border, and a scowl that looked as if it hadn't left her face in a decade. She'd used hairpins to attach a tiny red cap with a frilly white border to her unruly mop. She put down her red plastic tray on the red Formica table top, and unpacked its contents in front of Stephen, who sat on red leatherette in his window-side booth. Through it he saw the busy forecourt of the service station, cars and trucks pulling in and out, pump attendants jumping to refill empty tanks. The waitress unloaded a cup of coffee, a toasted sandwich, a knife and fork rolled tightly in a white paper napkin, and three sachets of tomato sauce.

"Thank you, angel," Stephen said kindly. She rewarded him with a smile that was like a starburst on carnival night.

Negligent toast, thought Stephen, looking at his plate. His toast had been made with neglect and apathy, not with care and skill; certainly with no concern for wholesomeness. The coffee looked as if it had been scooped directly from the Vaal River and heated up some of the way to boiling, and its only taste would be the packet of sugar he stirred into it. Every time Stephen left home in the dark to drive to the mine, he stopped at the Ultra City for breakfast. Every time it was the same. When he'd ordered his meal, the waitress, who hadn't yet treated him to a smile, had asked, "Small or large chips?" Stephen had read that French fries were hopping with acrylamide, a carcinogen found in fried food. The chips he'd been offered, according to the article, had three hundred times more acrylamide than was allowable in drinking water. There would come a time, the writer had predicted, when French fries would be the villain of a health campaign, just as cigarettes now were.

"Why do you stop there, then?" Lisa had asked when he'd

complained. The answer was banal for the predictability of human behaviour: the rest stop was just far enough away from Johannesburg to make it feel as if you had been travelling long enough to deserve breakfast; it was right on the side of the road; and it was immediately after the tollgate, which acted as a natural caesura in the journey. His decision was founded in behavioural psychology, not in any expectation of the restaurant or its fare. Predictably irrational. When he travelled with Lisa, she had a basket with definitely-not-negligent sandwiches and a flask of real coffee. They whizzed past these roadside attractions without a second thought.

While he was chewing on the thick toasted slices of his negligent sandwich, his phone rang. It was Jonny on the line.

"Morning, Sergeant," Stephen answered. "This is an early time of day for idlers and slackers to be awake."

"Good morning to you as well. Did I wake you up? Did I get you out of bed?"

"That's more than one question. Which should I answer first?"

"Answer them in the order I asked them."

"Very well. You did wake me up," Stephen said, "because I have been on automatic pilot since I got out of bed several hours ago, and started driving to Middelburg to see my favourite safety officer. I'm right now drinking the best coffee on offer in your district, at an entertaining venue on the side of the road. It specialises in petrol and coffee, but sometimes they mix the two up."

"Nee Stephen, man," Jonny said in Afrikaans. "How can you stop there for coffee? It will poison your whole outlook on life. Come here, and I'll give you a proper cup."

"I'll be there in forty-five minutes. Can I have a chair as well?"

"I'll get one just for you. And I'll get Skapie to sit in it to warm up the seat. Don't linger, I've got lots to tell you."

Stephen left a generous tip for the waitress who had smiled at him so prettily. He hoped it might relieve a smidgeon of the tedium of working in a place like this.

The slipway from the parking area joined the highway from the left, and almost immediately Stephen moved into the right-hand lane, the robust German machine accelerating whisper-quiet to his usual cruising speed of 129 kilometres an hour. On either side of the road corn stood in regimented ranks, looking good. Too early in the year for it to tassel, but already making early promises of a bumper crop. Every few kilometres, on the corner of a planted field, an enterprising marketing man had put a large white sign with the picture of three ultra-healthy cobs smiling yellow rows of kernels from behind thick green leaves. The logo under the picture said: "Mielies. Dis Mos Kos!" *Maize. That's food for you.*

He found Jonny behind his desk, trying his hand at the art of Sudoku.

"Hey, boss." The young man grinned and pointed an outstretched hand at an empty chair standing out of place in front of his desk.

"Skapie not in today?" Stephen asked.

"She is. But she pulled out a copy of her job description and threatened me with the CCMA when I told her to warm up the seat."

"How are you getting on with that puzzle?" Stephen asked, seeing that Jonny had filled in about four or five squares.

"These things are bloody impossible." The tall man threw down the newspaper and his pencil. Stephen noticed the puzzle he'd been working on was rated "very easy."

"You can't do it by trial and error, you know? Each puzzle has trillions of possible solutions."

"These ancient Chinese people were so smart." Jonny shook his head.

"These ancient Chinese people were Japanese. And they made up the age-old game in the late 1980s," Stephen replied.

"Like I said," Jonny agreed. "Let me get you a proper cup of coffee." He got up from behind his desk and stuck his head into his secretary's office. Stephen heard him say: "Skapie, kan jy vir ons twee koffies organise, 'seblief?" *Can you organise two cups of coffee for us, please?*

When he was back behind his desk, he lifted his eyebrows twice, making deliberately big eyes, and asked: "What would be the most astonishing thing I could tell you this morning?"

"That the NG Synod has decided all Afrikaners must wear shoes in church?"

"Baie snaaks, ja." *Yes, very funny.* "Nope. The most astonishing thing is that I found your black BMW; and the driver and his passenger are in the little boardroom."

"Big Jon, that *is* amazing! How did you do that?"

"I got lucky. I put in an extra camera at the gate to record registration numbers as well. And while I was looking through the footage this morning, Bang! There she was. But, Mr. Columbo, this isn't going to solve your big mystery. The car comes here every day, with the same two guys in it. They work in the engineering shop. They didn't need forged ID cards. They have real ones. Do you want to chat to them?"

"I certainly would. But you already have?"

"Yup. But let's hear the story again," the big man said, getting up from behind the desk.

The small committee room hadn't changed since the last time he was there. The files were still on the floor and the window blinds were still violet. At the table sat two men in workers' overalls, looking apprehensive but not scared.

"Gentlemen," said Jonny, "this is Mr. Wakefield from Head Office. He's a director of the company and he wants to ask you some questions. Please introduce yourselves."

"Andile Nzima," said the man on the left. He looked to be in his mid-thirties, sinewy and muscular, and six inches shorter than Stephen. His expression was serious and his eyes gave nothing away.

"Chips Radebe," said the other. He was the yin to Nzima's yang. He filled his overall to capacity and good humour exuded from the chubbiness of his cheeks. He looked young in the way well-fed people look prosperous. For a minute Stephen thought the man had winked at him, but it was just the engaging manner in which he smiled and pulled his eyes into slits when he said: "We are both from the engineering shop. We both live at Three Shaft." Which was a hostel.

Stephen liked him on impulse. "Chips," he said, "you have a car?"

"A beauty, Mr. Wakefield"—he shook his head in wonder— "she is as black as an African queen at midnight, and she runs on low profiles. Every weekend I polish her spokes and her pipes, and she never gives me a minute's trouble." He'd spoken with reverence and added with a grin, "Not like the other ladies in my life. They're full of problems."

Stephen laughed. "I must get me one of those. She is a BMW?"

"Oh, yes. She is a 2006 model 335i. Turbocharged with an N54 straight-six. That baby doesn't wait around." He made as if his right hand were holding the wheel, shaking it from side-to-side to keep control of all those skittish horses. Stephen liked him even more.

"Chips, Andile, you were here at the mine two Thursdays ago between about six and nine in the evening. Is that right?" Both men nodded. "Were you on duty?"

Chips answered: "We were on standby. The engineering shop has a list for emergencies and they can phone you anytime to come out. It's a sadness when you're on and it's the weekend. You have to be sober in case."

Stephen noticed how *Phuza-Thursday*, Drinks-Thursday-Evening, had casually been included as part of the weekend.

"Were you called out?"

"Yes, Apie phoned Andi at about five-thirty. I was just kicking off my boots and we had to come back."

"That's right," confirmed Andile.

"Who is Apie?"

"Apie de Waal," said Jonny. "He's a foreman in the shop."

"So what did you do then?" Stephen asked.

"We came in. We parked close to the Admin block because Apie had to get the paperwork sorted. There was hardly anyone around so it was easy to find a parking." Chips looked at Andile who nodded his confirmation. "When he came, we went to the shop. There was a pump with a bearing assembly problem. The housing was fine, but the impeller wasn't moving properly. It had a leaking seal as well. I don't know why they didn't spot it during the day, but that turned into our Thursday night's entertainment."

Andile took over: "We serviced the pump and took it to the spiral to reinstall. That took us about three hours."

Stephen nodded as if he understood what they'd done. "Did you see anyone while you were waiting?"

"Like who?" Chips asked.

"Anyone. Someone you didn't know?" The men looked at each other, trying to remember the details from two and a half weeks ago. They started shaking their heads slowly when Andile said: "There was that big guy . . ."

"Yes, that's right!" Chips' face brightened. "A huge man went in the front door just before Apie came out. We didn't know him and still said to each other that he must be a weightlifter or a bodybuilder or something."

"Tell me more?" Stephen asked.

"I don't know much more. He was taller than you, but not as tall as the Police." Chips tilted his head in Jonny's direction. "And he was built like an ox. Not fat"—he gripped his gut with both hands and shook it, grinning like a lunatic—"no, he was just muscle."

"A white man?" Stephen asked. He knew that in South Africa you're not supposed to ask such a thing, but it helped so with identification.

"No, he was a real person." Chips spluttered with laughter. Even Andile cracked a smile. Stephen chuckled and Jonny waved an admonishing finger across the table.

"Pasop vir jou!" he said. *Watch your step!* And that made Chips laugh even more.

"Hey, hey, Thaba." He chuckled, wiping tears of mirth from his eyes.

"Can you remember what he was wearing?" Stephen asked, keen to strike while the iron was hot.

"Actually, I can. He was wearing a black leather jacket that looked really expensive. It was so hot that I couldn't understand why he'd wear such a thing. But if I had spent so much money on a jacket, I probably would wear it all the time as well." Chips was enjoying himself. "I'm not sure what else he was wearing. Black jeans, I think."

"He was wearing sunglasses," Andile said.

"I didn't see." Chips shook his head.

"And you don't know who he was?" Jonny asked. Both shook their heads.

"I've never seen him before. I would've remembered him, because he is so big." Chips looked at his mate, who nodded to agree.

"Well, gents. You have been very helpful. Thank you very much for your time." Stephen stood and shook their hands. "Drive that sweet chariot of yours carefully, okay?"

"Now, Mr. Wakefield, what would be the good of having a car like that if I must drive it carefully?" Chips asked.

On the way back to Jonny's office, Stephen mused: "The Lord taketh away, and the Lord giveth." Jonny laughed.

"It looks like it. Apie should be waiting for us in my office."

And so he was. Jonny pushed the door open, and a short man in blue overalls and a white safety helmet was standing at Jonny's desk, there being no chair for visitors. Skapie had taken it away as soon as Stephen left. Apie stood no taller than five foot four, his legs short and bandy as if he spent his life on a horse. His arms were improbably long and simian, and his forehead was broad and flat. He had the cauliflower ears of a retired boxer. It was obvious where his nickname came from.

"Apie, thanks for coming. This is Mr. Wakefield, a director from Head Office. He wants to ask you about that Thursday night, about two weeks ago. Please tell us what happened?"

Apie nodded apologetically to Stephen, turned to Jonny and said: "Ja, I remember. It was six o' clock when they phoned me and said the fokking pump on the spiral feed was fucked."

"Whoa, whoa!" Jonny stopped him with an open palm. "Mr. Wakefield is an old man, and you must speak respectfully."

"Sorrie, Meneer," Apie dipped his head in apology. *Sorry, Sir.* "There was this pump on the spiral that was broken. It had to be serviced, otherwise we'd be off-line for the whole night. I phoned two engineers, Chips and Andile. We started at about six, fixed the pump, and reinstalled it. We were done by about nine o'clock."

"And those two were with you all the time?"

"Yes, sir."

When Apie was gone and Jonny had retrieved the chair for his visitor, Stephen looked at him evenly. "Mr. Wakefield is an old man?" he asked from under furrowed brows.

"Heh, heh." Jonny grinned. "Do you have another version?"

"No, you got that right." Stephen shook his head, smiling. "Okay, let's start off with this morning. There can be no doubt these three people are telling the same story, and that it's true?" Jonny nodded. "But now we have a mystery man in an expensive leather jacket and dark glasses. Big, but not as big as the Police."

"Die Boere is groot bliksems," Jonny agreed. *The Boers are big bastards.*

"Do you have any idea who he could be?"

"I don't know who he is. Someone like that would stand out.

Certainly there isn't anyone in the Admin block who fits that description. I'll ask at Security. If he works here, they'll know him. If he doesn't work here, they may remember him."

"You think they may know him if he works here?"

"For sure. The head of the front office is a chap called Dumisani Mabasa. He used to be a sergeant with the SAPS. Everybody still calls him Sarge. He stands in that office all day, and he sees who comes in and goes out. And I swear to you, Stephen, he has the closest thing to a photographic memory I've ever come across. He remembers everybody, knows their names, knows which department they're with. Hell, he can tell you when they went on leave, and how long they were gone for. If this guy works here, Sarge will know him for sure. If he doesn't know him, we are off on another wild goose chase. But let me start with Sarge."

"You want me to come with you?"

"Old Timer, you'll get in the way. When the Silver Fox from Head Office is with me, everyone says less than they usually do. Let me go on my own."

"Before you go, I've got something else to tell you," Stephen said.

"Fire away."

"I know a man in his sixties who got up very early this morning to visit someone who lives a long way off, and that person could spare only one cup of coffee to say thanks. What do you think about that?"

Jonny considered this, shaking his head sadly. "What's the world coming to?"

He got up, stuck his head through into the next door office, and asked: "Skapie, is die koffie alles klaar?" *Is all the coffee finished?* When she brought in the two mugs, one of them Jonny's California Highway mug, his eyes followed her with greater appreciation than a simple round of coffees justified.

"Jonny." Stephen sipped his coffee, "I went to see Mamela's

family yesterday," Stephen began. "They don't know that he was taking a payoff from anybody, but his brother told me something that we didn't know. Mamela had his own laptop that he carried around like a prayer book. Do you know anything about it?"

"Haven't heard of it. I thought his only machine was the one on his desk. Shall we go ask Panico?"

"Let's split up. You go to Security and I'll go to Accounts. If they do have his laptop, I'm going to spend a long time looking through it. Meet you back here later?"

Chapter 21

Stephen drove back the same evening. Three hours there in the morning and three hours back again in the late afternoon, with all the action in the middle, made it seem a full day. He used the time alone in his car to think over what to do next.

First thing, he must see Frankie Mabena, just to have a chat. What for, Stephen didn't have clear in his head.

Second, he should find the missing tablet. It wasn't in Accounts and they didn't know where it could be. How he'd find it, he didn't know; and what for, also wasn't clear.

Third, he must try to find the big man in the leather jacket and shades. Again, how and why were difficult questions.

He sighed, knowing he didn't know much and his plan wasn't great. Mpho Mamela had probably whisked his secrets with him into his early grave. And, come to think of it, if he never found out how the young man had died, would it matter? The company would be unaffected, and so would Stephen.

And yet. A young man was off the bus long before his appointed stop, long before getting to his plans and his dreams. He left a heartbroken mother and brother, and a young lover who would miss him for all eternity. That was sad enough, but it wasn't all that bothered Stephen. He seldom worked on instinct, but he couldn't shake the thought that somebody, somewhere had done this for profit. For money. Somebody killed Mpho Mamela for money. That's what really got Stephen down. That, nobody was allowed to do. The least he had to do for his own peace of mind was make sure that wasn't what had happened.

He made two calls on the way home. The first to Lisa, as soon as he hit the highway. The phone rang for a while before she answered.

"Hey, chum. It's me. Have you had a good day?"

"Not bad, thanks, and you?" she asked, happy to hear his

voice.

"Long. I'm on the way back. If the traffic is good, I'll be home at about eight or just after. Tell you all about it then."

"Perfect," she said. "I'll wait for you with dinner. Drive carefully."

The second call was to Shakes, and it was even shorter: "General. We've been busy and I have things to tell you. Can I see you tomorrow?"

"Does ten sound okay?'

"It does."

"See you then."

A crescent moon rose way off to his right, with Venus beckoning brightly above and to the east. It was the beginning of the lunar month; the moon, so said the Muslims, was like a smile of hope to light up the darkness. He went back to his musing. Why did he care about someone he hadn't ever met? The best answer was that he cared because that's what humans do. They look out for each other and they care.

He felt himself slipping over a maudlin edge, thinking broad shapes of how things were long ago: the late-afternoon sun peeking through a slit in red velvet curtains in a house his family had left when he was six; his mother bending over his single bed in the room he shared with his brother, turning out the bedside lamp and saying softly to him, "Sleep with the angels." The tyres hissed and the wind hummed, and Stephen's thoughts sank further into a deep pond where everything was quiet and nothing called him away. And all the while the big car dealt with the road, mile after mile.

From the Springs turnoff, yellow lights on a row of pylons down the center of the highway pushed the darkness to either side, and slowly brought Stephen back out of the cave of his introspection. He was sweeping through the curves between Brakpan and Benoni, past the lake and the building that was supposed to look like a paddle steamer, when the car phone rang.

He thumbed the switch on the steering wheel.

"It's Thuli. Where have you been?"

Stephen was taken aback by the abruptness of the question, and the peremptory rudeness of the tone. *Don't overreact,* he thought. *Just play it cool.* He simply said: "I was at the mine. I'm just getting back now. I'm at Brakpan."

"When I was growing up, I had an aunt who lived in Brakpan," Thuli said. "One day her husband didn't come home. He had a bakkie. They found him three days later. His bakkie had been stolen and his throat had been cut."

"Goodness," said Stephen. There was silence on the line for a while and then Thuli asked, "What were you doing today?"

"I met with Jonny and Panico, chasing down loose ends in case the inquiry comes back with a recommendation to prosecute."

"I thought you said it was all over."

"I said I thought it probably was all over. But if I'm wrong, it would be a good idea to be properly prepared."

"What did you speak to Panico about?"

"The fraud inquiry. The forensic team isn't done yet."

"And?"

"They haven't found a thing."

"Okay. Keep me informed."

"Sure. Will do. Thanks for phoning," and then the line went dead.

Stephen brooded over the call. It still irked him the next morning when he parked in the basement of Shakes's building. He signed the book, gave his telephone number, and ticked the boxes to say he had no gun and no laptop. Then he took the lift to the ground floor, where hard-edged granite merged seamlessly with glass and chrome, sweeping up to the distant ceiling, five floors above. Over the white-noise tranquillity of an angular water feature in which several colourful koi drifted lazily, Stephen told the pretty receptionist he had an appointment to see Mr. Hlongwane.

"Please have a seat. Zondi will be down to fetch you in a minute," she told him with a conspiratorial smile.

Stephen perched in a chair designed more for a style magazine than for the human anatomy. Idly he picked up an out-of-date current-affairs magazine, the cover of which featured a long-view black-and-white photo of a power station under construction with the discouraging headline: "ESKOM WOES CONTINUE." The article spelled out details of a R23 billion bailout announced by the finance ministry. A spokesman for Eskom blamed the crisis on a lack of diesel and water, and bad weather conditions. The writer of the article disagreed. He said the problems were indecision and incompetence.

"Mr. Wakefield?"

Stephen looked up. Zondi was almost as tall as he was, but she was cheating—her stiletto heels were taller than the tallest martini glass. She wore a smile and a pinstripe skirt that was so tight her longest stride was as short as the staccato click of her heels on the high-gloss floor. Her teeth were as bright as the brilliant white of her blouse. "Will you follow me, please?"

Stephen followed her through a double glass door she opened by swiping the security card she carried on a lanyard around her neck. She ushered him to a cosy room that was not a meeting room with a table, chairs, and a whiteboard as he'd expected, but had instead a dark brown two-seater leather couch and two armchairs surrounding a sturdy glass-topped coffee table. The leather was soft as dusk at a quiet waterhole in Singita, and the room spoke of confidence and power. Zondi left him with the promise of returning with a cup of coffee, and he sat down in the chair facing the door.

On the walls were pencil drawings of indigenous birds in various poses: clinging to reeds, sitting in thorn trees, nestling on a branch. The sketches were exquisitely detailed, on big sheets of thick-gauge high-quality white paper, each in a simple black wooden frame. In the corner of the room stood a Swedish LED standard lamp; the rug was Afghan; the colour of the walls muted; and the air was thick with the quiet assurance of money.

Shakes got there before the coffee. "Stephen," he said, as he followed his hand on the doorknob into the room. "So glad you could come. Are you well?"

"I'm just fine, thanks. Good to see you, too. Hard at it still?"

"We do what we can do," Shakes laughed a deep-throated chuckle.

The coffee came on a tray in small white cups and with sugar cubes in a bowl with tiny silver tongs. Shakes took three and Stephen none.

"Mon Generál," Stephen began, "we found the drivers of the BMW, but they weren't who we thought they may be." He told Shakes about Chips and Andile, and ended with the description of the big man in the expensive leather jacket.

"We have no idea who that is. Jonny is certain he doesn't work at the mine, and there's no record of him coming or going on the day. He's a real mystery man. He doesn't show up as a pedestrian on the CCTV, and there's no record of him coming in in his own vehicle. We don't know who he is or what he was doing."

"How could he have got in?" Shakes frowned.

"Jonny says it's easy. There's such a volume of traffic through the gate, he could have come in in any number of different ways. The easiest would've been to hide in the back of a truck."

"Why are our access systems so lax?"

"Because they aren't set up to keep infiltrators out. If you get onto the premises, then so what? You couldn't get to anywhere important without attracting much closer scrutiny, and you can't do a whole lot by just getting inside the gate. The system is not designed to keep secrets; it's really only the first in a series of filters. Which is why I asked them to put up the new access control to the mining area."

"I see."

"Anyway, we don't really know how to look for this guy or even if it's worth doing. But Jonny will do his best. He's resourceful."

"Yes, thanks."

"We are also looking for a lost laptop."

Stephen told Shakes about the tablet, and Mamela's brother's theory that if there were any secrets, they would've been stored electronically.

"Panico knew about the tablet when I asked him. He'd been quite envious of it, and knew that somebody had bought the thing for Mamela in Singapore. Who, he didn't know. He imagined the tablet must have been at home, among Mamela's things. Which, of course, it wasn't. It's not in Accounts either, and the men who found Mamela's body swear blind there wasn't a laptop or tablet on the scene, either where they found the body or in the vehicle."

The general nodded.

"Nor, by the way," Stephen continued, "was there a telephone. His mobile is also missing, and the two of them say they didn't see that either; nor did they take it. According to Jonny, that is either true or not, but there isn't anything we can do about it, unless the laptop or the phone turns up again somehow."

Jonny had put out word among his contacts in town, dealers in electronics who may be offered the equipment for resale. The laptop was such a specialised unit, so unusual in Crosby or even Middelburg, it would stick out like a red flag on St. Patrick's Day. All they could do now was to wait for further developments.

"So, General, we have many loose ends, but we don't have a whole lot to go on," Stephen concluded.

"Are you planning to do anything else? I mean, do you have any other ideas, perhaps?"

"Yes, I intend to visit Frankie Mabena in prison. He was Mamela's lover. He may be able to tell me something, although what, I don't know." Stephen pulled a Charlie Brown face, the one with big eyes and a squiggly mouth, when Charlie didn't know what to do next.

"Tricky," said Shakes.

"Shakes, there's one extra thing I want to talk to you about." Stephen leaned forward in his seat, uneasy about what he needed to say. His companion kept his face neutral, waiting for his friend to speak.

"It's this: although I try not to say it to myself, I think that Thuli is involved in this somehow. I don't know exactly what this is yet, nor do I have any concrete reasons for thinking that, but he is behaving so oddly. I think he has something to hide."

Shakes nodded, he thought so too.

"But this is the problem: it feels like a vendetta to me. With the best will in the world, I can't manage to like Thuli at the moment. I think he behaves like a proper little prick. He's arrogant and self-important. And he's as rude as hell. He keeps on telling everyone, specifically including me, that he's the boss, and that if we don't hop to his every whim, there'll be a bill to pay. He truly believes he's untouchable and entitled to behave this way." Stephen stopped talking, feeling deeply uncomfortable. He didn't like talking about anyone like this.

"I think so too, Stephen," Shakes said. "Don't worry about this."

"Well, there's more. Thuli and I had a spat yesterday, about a silly thing. He can't leave his telephone alone when I try to talk to him, and it irritates me beyond measure. I ticked him off about it, and he reacted like a scalded cat. He said that I behave like a white boss and treat him like a black servant. He says I'm a racist."

"Yes, he would say that. You know, Stephen, it's the last resort of the unimaginative. If you don't know what else to say to a white man, you say he's a racist." Shakes smiled slyly. "I wouldn't worry about that either, if I were you."

"But you know how it is. It's like being accused of being a child molester. You're presumed guilty just because the allegation is made." Stephen sighed, sitting back in his deeply comfortable chair.

The man opposite him chuckled with real amusement.

"So, what you're telling me is that you aren't a racist?" Shakes grinned some more. "I know you aren't, Stephen. You have chosen to be my friend, and I'm an MK general. Not many white supremacists have done that. I think Thuli is a fool. I share your views about him entirely. Don't feel badly about what he said to you. He has to deal with you somehow, because he knows you are on his case, even though you haven't told him so. The only thing he can find to say in his own defence is that you're a racist. It's irrational but understandable. So don't worry about it."

The General held Stephen's eye, making sure the older man knew he was being sincere. Stephen nodded, thankful for the sentiments. Shakes was done with that conversation. He made that clear:

"Moving on, would it be possible for you to have dinner with me tomorrow evening. I want you to meet two of my associates who are interested in what you and I have been talking about. Our discussion will be confidential, as will be the dinner itself. I want them to hear directly from you what we are dealing with."

"Shakes, of course I'll have dinner with you and your friends. But, honestly, I'm still dealing in speculation. I can't substantiate any of my theories. I really am operating on gut feel, and that is a most imprecise science."

"It's more than that, Stephen. And I trust your intuition. So, please meet with us? I'll get Zondi to book a table, and she'll let you know the arrangements."

The two men chatted for a while after that. Stephen told Shakes about Lisa's trip to Austria. "She and her mates leave next week. She is so pumped, it's wonderful to watch. Just like a kid before Christmas." The General listened and smiled.

"Wish her well for me, in case I don't see her. I'm sure she'll have a blast," he replied with a chuckle.

Chapter 22

In the space where the older folk of Johannesburg remember the roadhouse at Uncle Charlie's, there now is a spaghetti junction of multi-lane highways where only a GPS can keep the irregular visitor from driving to the wrong province. The junction is still called Uncle Charlie's, but the roadhouse is long gone. For many years cars pulled up in the parking lot where waiters trotted out with trays of milkshakes and toasted sandwiches. They hooked the tray onto the half-open driver's window and balanced it over the support leg with its rubber foot, just so, against the door. When the feast was done you flicked your lights and they fetched the dishes again. Another roadhouse close by had an actual Dakota aeroplane on its roof, and there too you could sip cider through a straw.

The De Villiers Graaff Motorway every morning carries a heavy load of traffic north through Uncle Charlie's and into the city. In the afternoon it groans under its Sisyphean burden going south again. From the southern tip of the double decker M1 near the Old Market edge of the city, the motorway points southwest, in the direction of the Gold Reef City skyline with its Big Dipper and Ferris wheel. The street names recall a time when the world was more martial than it is now: The Fair is in Alamein Road, named after El Alamein where Monty turned the tide of the German campaign in North Africa in late 1942. After the battle the General said: *Give me two divisions of those marvellous fighting Boers, and I'll remove Germany from the face of the Earth.*

If you stay on the motorway heading out of town, Riflerange Road slips past the window before you know it, and it was there that Stephen took the slipway onto the Golden Highway, famous for its having been the main road to Vereeniging, where the Second Boer war ended. The road in many lanes sweeps past the Southgate Shopping Centre, which provides the people of

Soweto with the mall they didn't have for so long. The South Western Townships under apartheid first got lumped together under its now famous name in 1963, and current estimates are that two million people live there, very nearly half of whom are Zulu.

Stephen saw, coming up on his right, the sign for Johannesburg Correctional Facility, the prison called Diepkloof by the public and Sun City by its inmates. An unusually high and robust wire fence enclosed a complex of buildings with the actual jail right in the middle. It looked even grimmer than Stephen had imagined. An ungainly impenetrable iron gate into the prison was the compound's Bridge of Sighs: It slammed closed on all hope, showing you one last glimpse of freedom in the sunshine of a beautiful Highveld morning. Nothing that Stephen had read or heard or thought prepared him for the shock realisation that actual humans were locked up in there, like so many animals in a cage.

Jonny was there to meet him, waiting at the gate.

"Stephen," Jonny had said on the phone, "let me come with you. If you go on your own, they'll stuff you around all morning. I know people there, and they'll help us." Stephen had been thankful then; and was even more so this morning when confronted with the stark reality of the place.

"Morning, boss," the big man greeted Stephen.

"Hi, Jonny. Man, I'm glad you're with me. This place gives me the creeps."

"Wait till you get inside."

And Jonny was right. In the building were more people than he'd expected. They stood in long queues, waiting to be processed by bureaucrats in prison-guard uniforms, who dealt with the visitors officiously, rudely, and dismissively, as if they too had committed a crime simply by knowing someone in jail. It was even worse if you were related to one of the inmates: that earned you an extra helping of disdain.

The visitors, on the other hand, were depressed and humble, doing their best to please; and, with few exceptions, had dressed up for the occasion. Mothers in long Shweshwe dresses as if on their way to a funeral; wives and lovers in Sunday-go-to-meeting outfits; young kids with fearful expressions, clinging to an adult hand, shining from a thorough scrubbing and uncomfortable in formal going-out clothes. A trendy young lady in jeans sported hair extensions that doubled the width of her face and added eight inches to her height; a plump lass wore a lacy see-through top, showing more flesh than Stephen was used to seeing; another young sweetheart wore sunglasses that swept up past her eyebrows like the tailfins on a '58 Chevy.

Jonny bored his way through the crowd, getting to a window with brass bars in front of it, where no one else had dared go.

"I'm here for Colonel Maluleka. Please tell him Jonny van Straten is here for him."

Behind the desk, the uniformed woman's expression suggested she hadn't heard a word he'd said. She looked straight through him without any reaction. Then, her eyes fixed on the middle-distance, she reached for the phone, dialled, and deadpanned something on the phone to the person who answered. All Stephen heard was the name *Maluleka*; and then a carefully enunciated response to a question from the other side: *van Staden*.

"Close enough," murmured Jonny.

While they waited, Stephen looked around the building. It was hard-edged in a way that cannot be faked. This was a penitentiary, and there were no concessions, none at all, to either style or grace, or to basic creature comforts. If you wanted to come here, then you put up with how it looked and how it was and what they said and did to you. Otherwise, don't come.

On the wall there were many rules about how long you were allowed to stay, how close to the person you were visiting you were allowed to be—not very—and what you may and may not give him: two kilograms of cookies; two kilograms of apples; five pieces of chicken and five pieces of beef, which had to be cooked and were not to have any sauce on them. Toothpaste, soap, and cigarettes. Everything had to be in a see-through plastic bag, said the notice. Like at an airline check-in counter.

A door opened next to the window at which they were standing, and a short, stout prison guard in uniform glared at them both.

"You can go through," she said.

She turned on her heel, and they followed her down a passage that smelled of official buildings and government-issue soap. Halfway down the passage their guide took a left onto a stairwell, taking the bare concrete steps one at a time to the next floor up. There she turned left again, down to the end of the passage, around the corner to the right, and pushed open a door to an office. She motioned with her head for them to go inside, and left them there.

Behind the desk sat a man with greying temples and a substantial stomach. His smile was as wide as the Lord's mercy as he scrambled to his feet and grabbed Jonny by the hand. "My man!" he said, pumping away enthusiastically.

"Lindani, man, it's good to see you," Jonny said. "How have you been? I see you've had a few decent meals!"

"Prosperous," said the man, patting his belly affectionately.

"This is the old man I told you about," Jonny said, introducing Stephen; and set about explaining why they wanted to see Frankie Mabena.

"Mr. Wakefield is a lawyer, and we're investigating an incident that took place on the mine. There's a lot we don't know about it, and it may just be that your permanent visitor down in the cells can help us with the details of a fraud investigation we are busy with. It's mighty fine of you to help us like this."

According to Jonny, ordinary visitors saw their friends and family in a crowded room where they sat on benches facing each other. There were guards who made a nuisance of themselves, enforcing the rules about no contact and all the other rules they made up from time to time. Also, you were only allowed to see the prisoner for a short while, so you had to say your bit and get out again. But Stephen and Jonny were allowed to see Frankie in a private room, with no guard in sight. The room had a raw concrete floor and walls of unpainted face brick. There were no windows, only a massive steel door with thick iron bars like the gate on the tigers' enclosure at the zoo. The guard locked it with a key at least five inches long. The only furniture in the room was a steel table that was fixed to the floor, and three plastic chairs.

Frankie shuffled into the room wearing an orange jumpsuit and a pair of ancient shoes that may at one time have been brown. He was thinner than just about anyone Stephen had ever seen. At five foot nine he couldn't have weighed more than fifty kilograms. His eyes were fearful and he brought an air of palpable despair into the room with him.

"How long have you been here, Frankie?" Stephen asked.

"Almost four months now," the boy said.

"And how long is your sentence?"

"Three years. I can apply for parole in eighteen months."

Stephen regarded him in silence, finding it difficult not to try to console the young man. Jonny, eminently more prepared to deal with this type of thing, did it for him.

"Here, eat this." He pushed a packet of fatty biltong slices across the table. Frankie's eyes darted between the two men and down to the food on the table.

"Thank you," he whispered. He fell on the biltong like a wolf.

While he was chewing, he started talking again, like an automaton, as if his every emotion had been cauterised.

"This place. I don't think I can make it for another fourteen months. I'm in a cell made for twenty people but we are fifty-six in there. Some of the people are career criminals, murderers and robbers and rapists. They decide what happens in the cell. Thirty of us sleep on the floor and there are no blankets. I'm attacked several times every day, some days five or six times. If you resist they beat you. Two weeks ago a boy died after they beat him. We are fed once a day but not enough food. There's only one toilet and no paper. You have to wipe with your fingers and rinse in the left-hand bowl. I can't survive this. I'll die in here." He hung his head low, stared at the tabletop, kept all feeling out of his voice.

Stephen didn't know what to say. This young man had been sentenced to death for trying to steal a few hundred Rand. Into the brooding silence he asked: "You heard about Mpho?"

"Yes, I did." Frankie shook his head sadly and added: "He was my only hope."

"I need you to tell me exactly what you mean. I want to find out what happened to your friend. There's a lot I don't know and even more I don't understand." Stephen spoke quietly.

"I'm in here because I was stupid," Frankie began. "Mr. Wakefield, you may condemn me for having tried to steal money from the company, but it wasn't easy for me. I'll save you all the dreary details, but I grew up poor. Very poor. My whole family made sacrifices for me—there really wasn't enough money to send anyone to high school, let alone university. But they all clubbed together, and we managed. It wasn't easy, this I can tell you." Frankie's eye drifted away to the corner, remembering his family. He looked back at Stephen.

"When I qualified, there were so many people I owed. And they asked. Boy, did they ask." He shook his head miserably. "My mother is old and sick. There were her medical costs to be paid. My sister was at school, and she needed books and school fees. My uncles and my aunts and my cousins needed food; and every month there was another special expense." His shoulders slumped with sadness.

"Just before I did my really stupid thing, my aunt died. In black culture a funeral is an important thing. The whole family was looking at me to pay for the funeral, because they'd helped me, and now it was my time to help them. But I had no money. I had been living off Mpho so much that I felt embarrassed to ask him again. And so I tried to pinch money from the company. I know it was wrong, but I didn't know what else to do at the time." Frankie hung his head inches above the unforgiving steel table top.

Stephen looked at him in silence, feeling awful and helpless. "What about Mpho, Frankie? What happened to Mpho?" he asked eventually.

"I don't know. He used to come visit me here every weekend, and he brought me food. He said he was trying to get someone at the company to reopen my case, and to see if they could have my sentence reduced. I don't know who that was, but I got the impression it was someone important. Mpho wouldn't tell me."

"Do you know if it was a lawyer? What was that person going to do?"

"I don't really know, unfortunately. But from what Mpho said, I think he was doing that person a favour or doing something for him. I'm not sure. And he was going to ask that person to reopen my case. Mpho said to me: *Steal a few cents and they put you in jail; steal a few million and they put you in charge.* I may be wrong about this, but I think Mpho knew about someone in the company who was in a powerful position, and who had stolen a lot of money. I think he was helping that person in some way, and he was going to ask that person to help me. At least, that is my speculation. I have no real way of knowing."

The young man looked away, and murmured: "And now he is dead."

Stephen wanted to get up and hug this young man and tell him everything would be fine; and then take him away from here and fix all his problems. Instead, he kept to what he could realistically do and what he wanted to know: "Frankie, tell me about Mpho's tablet?"

"He was so proud of it. The same person he was helping had

gone to Singapore for some or other reason. On company business, I think. And he'd bought Mpho the tablet, so that he could keep track of the things he was doing. Oh, I don't know"—Frankie shook his head—"I'm just guessing. But I think that the tablet was meant as some sort of a secret system, on which they kept the details of whatever Mpho was doing for that person. I wish I knew. But he didn't ever show me, and wouldn't allow me to see."

"Did that that person pay Mpho?"

Frankie shifted his gaze guiltily, looking at Jonny. He didn't know who Stephen was, but Jonny was the Law at the company. He clearly came to a decision that his position could get no worse, no matter what. He said: "Yes, he did. You may think that makes what I did all the more stupid; but look at it from my point of view. I was living like a parasite off the person I really loved; and he was doing something or other, I don't know what, to earn extra money. And I was asking him to give that to me as well. I didn't want to do that anymore."

"I want you to guess who the other person was," Jonny said.

"I can't." Frankie shook his head slightly, and looked away again.

But something in his eye made Stephen wonder. After a long silence, Stephen asked in a deliberately impassive tone: "Was it Mr. Mpongose, Frankie?"

The young man pooled the hurt and despair in his eyes and said, so quietly Stephen could almost not hear, "Yes." He nodded; and repeated: "Yes, Mr. Wakefield. Mpho didn't ever say. But it was the CEO, Thuli Mpongose."

Chapter 23

Cindy, the long-haired German shepherd, lay directly in front of the fridge, listening to their conversation, the triangles of her furry ears standing tall and straight. Angus, the male Labrador, had annexed as his own the space in front of the countertop where Lisa had set up her workstation. Findlay, the fattest of the three dogs, lay in her basket snoring with the sound of a percussion drill in a wall. Lisa stepped carefully over Cindy, opened the top door of the fridge and took out a bottle of milk. She stepped back over the first dog, put her feet on either side of the second, taking care not to disturb him, and added a splash to her mixing bowl.

"You spoil these mutts," Stephen commented dryly, not for the first time in his life. Lisa took it as a compliment.

"Ahu, my Gussy!" she said playfully, looking down at the black dog under her feet. Angus *thwocked* the floor twice with his sturdy tail. The ginger kitten watched from the windowsill, not approving, but not saying a word.

"So, did Thuli tell you another story?" Lisa asked, cracking two eggs into the mixture.

Stephen sat at the table watching his wife. She was fantastically dexterous around the kitchen. Things he battled over she did effortlessly while speaking on the portable phone pinched between shoulder and cheek. It was nice that he was in the kitchen, but if he didn't sit down he got in her way.

"Yes, he did." Stephen nodded. He told her the instalments of Thuli's life as he heard them. "One day, he said, one of his uncles who lived in the house with them argued with his girlfriend about food. He said the food that the women, including his girlfriend, cooked was tasteless. *Knock yourself out*, she apparently said, *cook your own meals*. But he took offence and knocked her out instead. With a beauty of a punch that caught her under the left eye. He was a labourer and she was a slip of a thing, recently out of school. She was concussed for days, he says."

Lisa shook her head and said, "Sorry for the noise," and turned on the eggbeater. She twirled it this way and that, just as if it were a lassie. When her bowl looked as she wanted it, she switched off and asked: "Are all these stories true?"

"I can't think why not. They were poor, and poverty is the best fertiliser for domestic violence. Mrs. Mamela, when I went to see her, told me the devil dances inside empty pockets."

"I thought he finds work for idle hands."

"He multitasks," Stephen said.

"Just like me." His wife smiled smugly, stepping over another dog to check the temperature of the oven. "Hey, my Angus?" she asked again; and again the thick black tail bashed three beats on the floor.

"He was so defensive about my having gone to prison to talk to Frankie. Attack has always been his best defence. But he painted a picture of that poor boy in prison that just doesn't sit right. Thuli describes him as a callous no-goodnik, a hardened thief. He said I don't understand how it is in the townships. If you give your pinkie, they grab your whole body, arms, legs, and all. He couldn't forgive someone, so he says, who stole from him; because that's what his grandmother taught him. He's always going on about his bloody grandmother. Anyway, that's why he insisted the company prosecute, and he's glad the kid is in prison. His grandmother would apparently approve."

"Some grandmother. She sounds like the fat old granny in Giles. What did you say?"

"I said I think it's harsh and we must try to intervene to get him an early parole." Stephen toyed with a serrated paring knife with a bright green plastic handle. He'd picked it out of the fruit bowl.

"And?"

"And Thuli almost peed into his shoes. Not while he was the

CEO, he said. Over-his-dead-body kind of stuff. Then he reminded me of his many sacrifices for the company and his fiduciary duty to its shareholders." Stephen put down the knife. "He's a real prick."

Lisa poured the mixture into a baking tray and asked, "What will you do?" Stephen thought about her question for a while. He didn't have a ready answer.

"I'm not sure," he said. "I'll talk to Shakes about it."

"Won't Thuli think you've gone over his head?"

Stephen laughed. "He won't think it. He'll know it. But that's just tough. There isn't much he can do about it."

Lisa closed the oven door on her cake and looked at the clock on the wall, making a mental calculation when to open it again.

"I see you've started packing," Stephen said.

She chortled. "Only the winter stuff. It'll be cold in Austria and I'm not wearing any of my woollies around here at the moment."

"And it pays to be prepared?" he teased.

"Yup. I'm one of the wise virgins. I take extra oil to the wedding feast." She'd been schooled at a convent, and the stories from the Bible were still vivid in her memory. Stephen wondered what women's' lib would think of that parable: Ten virgins went to meet the bridegroom who arrived at midnight. To light their way in the dark, they took oil lamps with them. The five smart ones took extra oil in case the wait was long, but the other five were foolish and didn't take extra oil. So they missed the party. Bad, disobedient virgins. The girls of Stephen's ken were as likely to pour oil over the bridegroom and set him on fire, as they were to wait respectfully until he eventually pitched. To add insult to injury, the man of the moment then picked himself a companion for the night. Run that by the Northern Suburbs girls in modern-day Jozi, and see how it goes for you.

"We're going to Tartufo d'Oro tonight. Have you heard of it?"

"I saw a review," Lisa said, stacking the bowls and spoons

she'd been using, and stepping over Angus to put them in the sink. Then she stepped over Cindy to put the milk back in the fridge. If there had been a review of the restaurant, of course she would have read it. She knew more-or-less everything, Stephen had concluded long ago.

"It's top-end fancy and expensive. The chef is Tertia Terreblanche who used to run The Snoek Shack in Cape Town. Apparently it's very good, if you have a deep pocket."

"Well, I'm not paying," Stephen said. "What do you have planned for tonight?"

"I'll watch *Downton Abbey* and go to bed early." Both things she would've had to do without Stephen in any event.

The restaurant was in a side street in Parkmore. To get there, Stephen drove down Sandton Drive, past the neon-outlined landmark in which Norton Rose Fulbright had made its eagles' nest. The firm, when the world was less complicated and Stephen's hair was dark brown, had been called Deneys Reitz, after the man who was another one for multitasking. He was a statesman, lawyer, soldier, journalist, and writer, and an all-round Boy's Own adventurer. He described Paul Kruger, whom he met when he was a boy, as the ugliest man he ever saw. The two halves of the new building for the old-but-now-international firm stood like a dancing couple on the Sandton skyline: Dali's rendition of a fifteen-story handsome man leading his shorter partner though the steps of an everlasting tango. Attorneys in the twenty-first century stepping lightly.

A guard in paramilitary uniform motioned Stephen into off-street parking behind a tall gate. The lot was full of top-of-the-range German automotive engineering, except for a canary-yellow Maserati and, over in one corner, a steel-grey Aston Martin. This wasn't a fast-food outlet where you arrived slowly and ate quickly. The fawning maitre d' with foppish hair and limp wrists showed Stephen to the salon privé where he'd be dining in splendour and discretion.

Shakes met him at the door. "Hey, Stephen. Good to see you. Come in and meet the others."

I got here after the VIPs. That's a first, thought Stephen. And what VIPs they were. Although he hadn't met them before, their faces were hardly new: they were in the papers and financial weeklies, and on television, all the time.

"Zola Nkabinde," said the first, holding out his hand to Stephen. The man was an inch shorter than Stephen, but slightly broader. His glasses were old-fashioned dark frames and his complexion was light, almost as if he were Malay. The mouth that smiled at Stephen was full and underlined by a downy black beard, just long enough to be rather than not to be. Stephen noted that the navy sports jacket Zola wore would be an exclusive line item at one of the mystically expensive boutiques of which Mr. Nkabinde himself was the major shareholder. Stephen introduced himself to the man, who was soft-spoken and appeared to be mild-mannered. Close up he looked the same as in the pictures Stephen had seen of him. He'd been the CEO of a massively successful multinational that expanded its network, under Zola's leadership, into Africa, particularly Nigeria. His own company had resisted a listing so far, so that Nkabinde remained autonomously in charge.

The other man was the real heavyweight. "Ernst," he said, thrusting an open jovial palm in Stephen's direction. Minister Khuzwayo, thought by many to be the Crown Prince for the presidency. He looked and presented like a man used to being in charge, in this case in charge of an entire country. The demands of his social obligations had thickened his middle and filled out his cheeks, but the easy assumption of power sat comfortably on his shoulders. He was a handsome devil, the square jaw of a Hollywood romantic hero underlining a constantly smiling mouth, and an irrepressible twinkle glittering in his eye. He wore an open-necked soft white cotton shirt, pleated at the wrists—as Lisa always wanted Stephen's shirts to be, so far without success.

Stephen had seen so many pictures of Ernst and had heard him on television so often that it felt eerily as if he'd known him for years.

"Well, hi." Stephen beamed, somewhat celebrity-struck. He felt like a vervet monkey in a cage of silverbacks.

"Drink?" Shakes asked.

"Yeah, thanks. Buffalo Trace on ice, please." Stephen nodded to the waiter in the white tux.

"Single or double?" the man asked. Only this waiter wore a white jacket and a white bow tie—the other waiters, of whom there were many, wore black jackets and black bow ties.

The wallpaper in the room was dark grey and the downlighters subtle. The walls were lined with black-and-white photographs of people Stephen didn't recognise. The furniture was dark and heavy, and the air-conditioning whisper-quiet and almost cold.

"Shakes tells me you like jazz," Stephen said to Zola. "What are you listening to?" If you pay close enough attention to what's on your hi-fi, that question means: *What's your current playlist?*

"Roy Hargrove," Zola replied, curious to see if Stephen knew who that was. Of course he did and soon they were talking about Chucho Valdes and the video both of them had seen of the bony old Cuban in his eighties playing a long-fingered upright as if he'd been in musical isolation for most of his life. Which of course he had been. When it was time to sit down, Stephen faced Shakes and had the Minister on his right.

"You happy with the Storm Valley Chenin?" Shakes asked the table before nodding to the white-coated waiter. Stephen read on the wine list Shakes showed him that the wine was characterised by crisp acid and linear fruit, slightly oxidative in character, that come together in barrel-fermented elegance with an underlying complexity of judicious focus and balanced finish. If it was good enough for them, it was good enough for him.

Stephen ordered, as a starter, the chef's choice of herb-infused seasonal succulent spinach and onion compote, hand-glazed with Japanese tamari and manuka reduction, topped with a spring-garden puree of luscious local flavours, drizzled in a dainty delectation of imported oils; and lamb chops as a main. When the waiter had written an essay on his notepad and left them alone, Shakes set about the business of the evening.

"Gents, you know who Stephen is and what reports he's made to me. I need you to hear the story from the horse's mouth. Stephen, if you'll be so kind?"

Stephen nodded and started speaking, delivering his report in uninflected language and tone, *nec clam nec vi*, which is how lawyers say, "without hiding anything and without being forceful."

"We've discovered a fraud in our company and we think it involves a bribe to a Minister, to get him to approve a transaction. There isn't anything wrong with the deal. The consent should've been a formality. But it seems as if the bribe has been paid to get the consent."

Minister Ernst, Zola, and Shakes nodded; this wasn't the first time they'd heard a story like this.

"Problem is, I think it's possible that one of the Accounts Department employees found out about it, and it may be that he's been murdered to keep him quiet. I'm speculating to a substantial degree, but Shakes doesn't want me to be careful and hedge my bets when it's just us four."

"Damn right," Shakes confirmed.

"I have reasons for thinking what I do, as you'll hear. But before I tell you any of that, it's important that you know something: I feel as if I have a personal axe to grind and it may have clouded my judgement. The person whom I think paid the bribe is Thuli Mpongose. The CEO of the company. But here's the problem: I don't like him and he doesn't like me, and increasingly we are at loggerheads. He says I criticise him because I'm a racist; whereas I feel I criticise him because he behaves like a prick. But our mutual dislike for each other predisposes me to want to find him guilty. So, when you listen to my story, you must be careful not to make the same mistakes as I may be making. Please keep a balanced perspective."

"Stephen," Ernst interrupted. "Don't be too apologetic here. Shakes has told us about how the two of you feel about each other. I for one share your view that this guy is a prick. But what we are dealing with here is a legacy issue: Apartheid was what it was," the Minister summarised with commendable brevity. "It has left us with a complicated set-up. There are many white racists left, to be sure. But black people have also been left with a ready excuse whenever they don't like what a white man says or does. They say he is a racist. The three of us don't use that line, except of course when it's true. But black chauvinists exist, and Thuli is one of them."

Stephen nodded at Ernst, at which point the door behind him opened and in came three waiters in black jackets, two of whom were carrying two plates each. They slipped the food onto the table, as a fourth waiter, in the white jacket, walked into the room. He filled their wine and water glasses, and all four of them left again, closing the door. Stephen looked at his plate. He couldn't easily identify any of the bits on it, but it looked very pretty. The type of plate people photograph and post on Facebook. He'd have to eat slowly, though, otherwise he'd be finished very soon.

Stephen recapped the main events of the story for his companions. "There are many reasons I think Thuli is involved in the bribe. Apart from that, there are odd circumstances about the death of the young accountant. I can't say for sure what happened, but his death is peculiar. I don't know if the two incidents are related, but let me tell you why it's strange."

Stephen ticked the reasons off one by one: Thuli saying he didn't know who Mamela was; Trevor Hodges overhearing them argue a day before Mamela was killed; the missing laptop and phone; the fact that the laptop had been bought in Singapore at about the same time as Thuli spent two weeks there; the suspicion of Mamela's mother that there was something amiss between her son and a senior manager of the company; the fact that Thuli so hated Frankie; that Frankie said Thuli was the one who was paying Mamela to do stuff for him; but most of all, the suspicion and aggression Thuli showed whenever he asked Stephen about his investigation. During those conversations, Stephen got a palpable sense of Thuli's unease and his visceral desire to see Stephen stop asking questions.

"It's not a lot to go on, but I'm convinced he's involved on some basis, and I'm increasingly less able to think that Mamela simply died by accident. The details are just too bizarre, and the coincidences are just too big."

The door opened again and in waltzed two black-coated waiters and one in white, whisking away the plates and filling the glasses, and disappearing again.

"What are you going to do next?" Ernst asked.

"We're waiting for possible leads from Jonny van Straten's mates, who could lead us to the missing laptop. But I'm also seeing an IT specialist tomorrow because Mamela's brother thinks he backed up the laptop to a cloud. That would mean we can see what was on it without having the actual machine. But we need to guess which cloud it was backed up on, and we need a username and a password. I'm looking through Mamela's personal papers in the hope that I can find it, and Panico, his boss in Accountancy, and his brother are doing the same with some other documents and papers he left behind. Maybe we get lucky. And, we are hoping that maybe we find the mystery muscleman in the expensive leather jacket and shades. Maybe that can give us an extra steer. It's not a whole lot," Stephen conceded.

Shakes, whose glass was empty again, nodded and said: "Well, maybe we can help you there."

He pulled out the leather folder he carried with him always

instead of a briefcase, unzipped it, and produced three glossy black-and-white jumbo-sized photographs. Just like in the spy movies. Pushing them across the table to Stephen, he said: "We think this is the guy you're looking for."

The pictures were grainy and indistinct, as if they'd been taken from a long way off. The three shots were taken in sequence at close intervals. All three showed the same man, from slightly different angles. He was enormous, at least six foot four or five, with the powerful build of a professional athlete. He was wearing a dark jacket, probably leather, stretched tightly across massive shoulders; his arms thick and chunky, bulging in the sleeves. He looked not completely different to O.J. Simpson, with fine features and a strongly handsome face. Stephen couldn't see his eyes—they were hidden behind dark glasses. The man was standing next to the open door of a car, looking over the roof at the second man in the picture: Thuli Mpongose. Stephen stared at the pictures, noting that Thuli was eight inches shorter than his companion, and looked scrawny by comparison. What they had in common was perfect skin and a very dark complexion, almost as if they were from up north, somewhere equatorial.

"Who is this?" Stephen asked.

"His real name is Gobevu. Tuesday Gobevu. But if you call him that he'd snap your spine. He likes to be called Ikubu. It's short for *Ikubulala*, which means murder. Not very subtle, our man. In the townships, where he is legendary and people are petrified of him, they call him Ruby Tuesday. Because where he goes, the blood flows ruby red. He has quite a record, according to our friend General Maduna." Stephen recognised the name of the sky-high ranking policeman. "He's been a foot soldier and assassin in the taxi wars, a gun for hire. He's linked to at least fifteen shootings, but stays a step ahead of the police. If Thuli has hired him, he's playing with fire. A man like this is impossible to control."

Silence settled around the table, until Stephen said: "Well, it looks as if he may have done exactly that."

Ernst sighed. "Yes. It does look that way. Mr. Mpongose now has his own private army, it appears."

Just then the three black-jacketed waiters were back with more plates of food; and the white jacket followed on their heels to refresh the glasses. The four of them bowed and scraped their way back out of the room, and the men at the table tucked in. Stephen was thankful to find three recognisable lamb chops on his plate, with potatoes on one side, and, on the other side, sticks of carrot and long green beans cut to exactly the same length. They were tied into a parcel by something green, a leaf of sorts.

Ernst took the word: "The ANC is in trouble and we and several of our friends want to save it from itself. So that we can run this place properly. Run it efficiently. Our president is a twit, as you know; and the government is riddled with dishonesty and corruption. This is something we must stop or else we'll lose control. In order to change things, we need to start at the top. Thuli and his pal the Minister are a pocket of corruption and ruthless dishonesty. They have teamed up with a bunch of unsavoury businessmen and politicians, and they're becoming more powerful by the day. We used to trust Thuli, because we thought his heart was in the right place. But money and power have run away with his soul. And now we have to stop him. If he is involved in this bribe and murder, we'll bury him and his Minister friend forever; and that will break the back of their cabal. And that, Stephen, would suit us all very well. We would like to ask you to help us with this. We want to ask that you continue investigating, and that you let us know everything you find out. And we'll help you in every way we can."

Stephen chewed while he thought. His food was as good as Lisa had predicted. Then he nodded. "Gents, I would've wanted to continue with the investigation in any event, because I think that a great wrong has been done. What has happened is grossly unfair and should never have been permitted. I can't tell you how sorry I feel for that young man and his family. So I'll carry on scratching around and I'll tell you what I find."

The other three nodded.

"But there's something I want to ask you to help me with, whether I succeed or not."

"What would that be?" Zola spoke for the first time in half-an-hour.

"I want you to help me get Frankie Mabena out of prison. His life is a shambles already, and I have no doubt that by now he is HIV-positive. He won't survive another fourteen months until he can apply for parole. And what he did, or what he tried to do, is just not serious enough to deserve a death sentence."

His three companions looked at each other and nodded. "Sure," they said.

Chapter 24

When he left legal practice after a quarter of a century, Stephen had accumulated a gargantuan paper filing system. Eight grey steel filing cabinets, four drawers each, heavy with files. Against one entire wall of his office were wooden pigeonholes, groaning with more. That was just the current and recently finished stuff.

Now he kept no paper at all. After more than a decade in a mining house where paper flowed with no restraint, he had a laptop; and on it was everything he'd done or read in that time. He literally never discarded a thing. The little gadget also carried all his family photographs and all the music he'd ever bought. And here's the thing: if he lost that little box of tricks, he'd still have every bit of information he'd ever stored on it. It sounded like magic to him when Cleo, the IT consultant, explained it. But he believed Asimov who said any sufficiently advanced technology is indistinguishable from magic.

Stephen waited for Jonny downstairs in the lobby. He was early, ten to nine, for their appointment with Cleo White, who headed his own outfit called *WhyTee*. Cleo had dropped out of a BSc in Computer Science because, according to him, the lecturers spent all day belabouring the obvious. Finding how remarkably stupid people with personal computers were, he was soon in business, now with a wide-ranging network doing the types of things Stephen nodded about when Cleo listed them all. While Cleo's enthusiasm spun out the explanation, Stephen remembered about Chaim Weizmann who had travelled across the Atlantic on a boat with Einstein, and every morning as they strolled on deck, Einstein told him about his theories. Weizmann, when they got to New York, said he was fully convinced that Einstein understood what he had been talking about. But Cleo was a nerd in the truest sense and had cross-examined Stephen on the business machines of his early career. He was astonished that the man was ancient enough to have worked with a golf ball typewriter; he was incredulous that the first memory machines displayed one line of text only; he grinned that the first electronic printer Stephen used printed one line at a time, one forwards and the next backwards; and fell out of his shoes when he heard Stephen's first memory storage device had had a capacity of sixty-four kilobytes.

Stephen stood next to the revolving door in which, against all three partitions inside, there were three signs proscribing various activities. There was a picture of a cigarette with a diagonal line through it, a gun similarly crossed out, and a soccer player with the same line of prohibition across him. Inside this revolving door, don't smoke, don't shoot anyone, and don't play soccer. Just then he saw the huge form of the safety officer on the pavement outside, heading for the restricted-activities door.

"Morning, young man." Stephen shook his hand.

"Howzit boss," Jonny responded. He had a hand the size of a baseball glove with fingers like courgettes. But he never showed how manly he was by squashing Stephen's fingers to a pulp, as was the custom in much of the mining industry. He either didn't think Stephen warranted such a display of strength, or he thought he was too old to be tortured. Either way, Stephen was grateful.

"Shall we go see the man?" Jonny suggested.

They rode a pokey lift to the third floor, where there was no sign to identify which of the many offices belonged to WhyTee. They found it by asking at the reception desk of ExquisiTravel. Behind the desk were posters of sunny idylls, fit for a king, on tropical islands with pineapples and coconut trees; and a happy receptionist who told them, "Around the corner, first left."

WhyTee was not a paperless office. The floors were stacked with manuals, directories, invoices and take-away menus, and every desk was cluttered with more stuff: paper, plastic containers, ashtrays, empty food cartons, electronic bits and bobs, long straight things that may have one function, short curly things that may have another. In the only clear space on each desk stood a laptop, and behind it the type of person who usually only comes out at night. Some nerds go for cardigans and neat hair; this lot went for punk hairstyles, aggressive T-shirts and tats.

"Gentlemen!" drawled a voice from a corner half hidden by a screen onto which photographs of customised motorbikes had been pinned. Cleo shuffled to his feet and did that obscure trendy handshake with them where you first palm-slap the other fellow's hand and after several squeezes and readjustments, you hooked your new friend's fingers in yours and pulled till your hands snapped apart. Stephen didn't get it even approximately right, and secretly hoped Jonny would grab the programmer's hand and squeeze it like real men do.

"Hey, Cleo." Stephen grinned. "Eccentric workspace you keep here."

Cleo couldn't have been more highly complimented. If you go for a look, it's always good when the world acknowledges your work.

"Thanks, bro," he mused. Cleo was tall, and thin at both ends although thick in the middle, as if he'd been designed in a wind tunnel. His T-shirt was black with a picture in silver of a dog's head, a satanic hell-hound, with a steel collar studded with sharp spikes and a snarling maw of evil fangs. Under it, in Gothic capitals, it said: *MANIFESTO*.

"Something to drink?" he asked.

Stephen, who had read much about waterborne disease, declined. "Cleo, we need your help," he said, when Jonny had also chickened out. "We want to know what's on a laptop without knowing where it is."

"Piece of pie," said the man and moved his feet on to a corner of his desk, in the process tipping a thick printout onto the floor. He left it there. "What kind of machine?"

"A Surface Pro 3."

"Fancy." Cleo whistled admiringly. "And you two muggles know nothing else?"

"That's about the size of it," admitted Stephen.

"We have to guess a few things. But really, people are predictable when it comes to IT. They're scared of it and never get out of first gear." He smiled at his audience, who noticed that IT and dental health didn't necessarily go together like love and marriage.

"We must decide which cloud the machine is backed up to. Word provides a free cloud for Surface tablets. It's called OneDrive. It's the high exception where somebody has a free cloud and uses another one. So right there is our first box ticked, with 99.9 percent accuracy."

Cleo took time to look smug before he told them the bad news. "We also need the username and password. They can be anything under the sun. But believe me, most people are easy to guess if you know a bit about them. Very often the username will just be an email address. So, for example, *Jonny@Sethemba*. And often people have one password they use for everything. Otherwise they forget it. So if we can find out what other passwords this guy used, we'll try them."

"And if we don't find the username and password?" Jonny asked.

"Then you're pretty much stuffed." Cleo nodded, without a hint of grief.

"Can we approach the cloud administrator and ask for access?" Stephen ventured.

"Dunno. You're the lawyer. They'll probably want a court order and they're in California. Good luck with that," the computer man replied with a grin.

"You know how to log on to the cloud if we can get the access codes?" Stephen asked.

For the first time Cleo looked offended. "Of course," he said, without trying to hide his incredulity that someone would ask him such a thing.

Stephen and Jonny said their thank-yous and goodbyes, and shuffled through the mess back out to the lift. On the ground floor they made it out into the street, where Stephen suggested breakfast.

"Never too late for breakfast," Jonny agreed.

At Patisserie they found a table outside under an umbrella. A steady stream of people flowed down the walkway from the Zone to the Firs, looking in the windows on the left at flamboyantly colourful sneakers and in the windows on the right at artfully distressed denim jackets and jeans. Three young suits sat at the next table discussing their strategy with self-confidence and financial jargon.

"We'll tweak in a sliver of mezz. The cash flow is robust and when the bullet is due we'll roll the facility." The beefy one with a thatch of fringe over his eye stopped speaking to watch the progress of a pair of shapely legs between the hem of a tiny skirt and the tops of spiky-heeled shoes, and his mates watched too.

"Five Roses for me, please, and my big friend wants a cappuccino," Stephen told the waiter.

"Are you going to eat?" Jonny wanted to know.

"No, but you're a growing lad. And they do only healthy stuff here."

"In that case I'll have the Classic." It came with eggs, bacon, sausages, mushrooms, tomato, and toast.

While Jonny was hoovering up the plate, Stephen asked, "Any sign of the laptop?"

"Nope." Jonny was monosyllabic now that he had more important things to do.

"And the mobile?" When they'd belatedly started looking for the laptop, they'd started looking for the missing phone, too. When you rang the number it was disconnected. The electronic woman told you: "The subscriber you have dialled is not available."

Jonny swallowed a mouthful, and as he swung the next loaded fork from plate to face, he replied: "Nothing."

"I'm not sure we'll find anything," Stephen shook his head. "I have gone through a bunch of his papers and there's nothing in them. Nothing out of place. No letters, no notes, no record of secret passwords. Panico has done the same, and he also hasn't found a thing. Mamela's brother found an old telephone book in which Mpho had written a few numbers, but he didn't keep it up to date. He probably just kept all his contacts on his phone. Even I do."

Jonny nodded, almost done now.

"Panico has sent me a note of Mamela's log-on details for his work computer," Stephen went on, "and they look like our best bet. The mine IT department sets them for all company machines. I hope Cleo is right that people are predictable. I haven't given him the details yet because I haven't decided if he should see whatever is on the cloud. It may be sensitive, you know, for the company."

Jonny put down his knife and fork, wiped his mouth, and looked at Stephen.

"Boss, because you read everything you get, you make the wrong assumption about other people. If Cleo found a few dirty pictures, he'd take a good look, for sure. But if he found words or figures he'd call it *text*, and give it to you on a stick. He reads nothing—he just pecks away at his keyboard. The stuff on his screen is like a game to him. He must move it around and make it change shape; but what it is, he couldn't care less."

"You think?"

"For sure. Give him the codes and let him do his thing."

"Okay." Stephen nodded. "Now," he said, sliding an A4-size envelope across the table top, "have a look at these." Jonny drew out the grainy black-and-white photographs and frowned at them attentively.

"You think this is the big stranger in the leather jacket and shades?" he asked.

"Shakes thinks so; and so does his mate General Maduna. He's head of the CID, Special Branch."

"Special for not being able to find their arse with both hands," Jonny muttered.

"Maybe. But Shakes thinks the man knows what he's doing. One of the things he's doing is looking for the man in said picture."

"Told you they can't find a thing," Jonny said, but a ghost of a smile on the young man's face told Stephen that this was part of the obligatory ribbing Jonny always gave SAP. He was full of statistics to back up his point of view: the average violent crook in the country commits a hundred offences before he is arrested for the first time; the conviction rate for murder is four percent; and a good third of all crime goes unreported because people think the police don't care, won't put themselves out for you, and will rob you if they can. The brave boys in blue are less likely to help you than they are to help themselves.

"His name is Tuesday Gobevu," Stephen said, "but he operates under the stage name *Ikubulala*. Ikubu, for short."

"Subtle," Jonny said. He was fluent in Zulu.

"In the townships he has a Robin Hood cult status, but without the giving-to-the-poor part. What he takes, he keeps himself. They call him Ruby Tuesday."

"Why?"

"Because wherever he goes, the blood flows ruby red. Like Mack the Knife."

"*Wie's dit?*" *Who's that?* Jonny asked, but just to get Stephen down.

"He's wanted for at least fifteen murders and a bunch of other things as well. They say he's a mercenary assassin. You can hire him to kill people for you. At least, so says General Maduna."

"Useful service." Jonny was thinking. "You want me to ask the two from the black BMW if they recognise him?"

"Good idea. But take Thuli out of the picture before you show them."

"Yes, what the fuck is he doing with this guy?"

"Jonny, I don't know. But it doesn't look good, does it? And it's probably dangerous, so be careful who you speak to and what you do."

Together they wandered back through the new section of the Mall toward where they'd both parked. On the way they ambled past a flashy shop that sold new televisions. Central in the display were three huge screens, bent like bananas, together making up one picture, like the Cinerama of Stephen's youth. The name had been invented in the 1950s as a cross between *cinema* and *panorama*; and the only place he ever saw one had been in Doornfontein.

Jonny stopped and stared at the high-definition picture. A cricketer was giving a post-match interview.

"Well, ja, HD. We went back to the drawing board, and the bowlers came to the party. A lot of the youngsters put up their hand. And, ja, we took our chances and we executed the game plan." HD smiled encouragingly.

"Look at the size of this thing," Jonny marvelled.

"That's what she said." Stephen grinned, playing the game his son had loved so well during his middle years at high school.

A hopeful salesman had sidled up to them, smiling like Uriah Heep at a flea market. "Can I show you gentlemen the special features?"

"Nee dankie. We're just having a look," Jonny said. To Stephen alone he added: "In Crosby we've got bigger shops than this one."

"Time you get yourself back there then. I'll get onto Cleo and let him know those codes. You chat to the witnesses and see if Murder Gobevu is the man we're looking for. Keep in touch." Stephen headed for the lower level where his car was.

Chapter 25

A kind soul had put a saucer on Stephen's desk. In it were two cold sausage rolls and a slice of chocolate cake with many twirls of artificial cream, chocolate sprinkles, and one red maraschino cherry. He put down his bag and went next door to Pauline's office. She was nominally his secretary, but also worked for Julian de Andrade, the head of logistics. Julian kept her whirling like a dervish in Istanbul, which suited Stephen fine. He did his own typing—it was faster, more accurate, and less public that way. He made his own travel arrangements and fetched his own dry cleaning. Sometimes he asked her to get him stationery; and she fetched him cake from the tea trolley when someone was a year older. Their working relationship was perfect.

"Hi, Pauline. Whose birthday is it?" Pauline was, as usual, flustered. Her life was one never-ending emergency. She'd complained to him once that she didn't ever feel she had enough time for a bathroom break. *TMI*, thought Stephen; and remembered the story of Tycho Brahe who needed to pee at a royal banquet, but it was really bad manners. So he held it until his bladder burst and he died, but without the social disgrace of having left the King's table.

Pauline stopped typing, looked frantically to her left, picking up and immediately dumping a sheaf of papers, and blew a frustrated breath that lifted her fringe in the updraft. Her dress sense was from the sensible 1950s and her hairstyle from no discernible period.

"What? Oh, it's Nomhla," she said. Stephen saw again the butterfly tattoo on her shoulder and wondered, not for the first time, how that had happened.

"Thank you for getting me cake," Stephen murmured, but Pauline had set off again, tearing up the QWERTY under her impatient fingers. He left her to keep the world safe from late trains to Richards Bay, and ambled downstairs to Nomhla's domain of files and formal notices. They often worked together when there were board meetings, he writing the text for the resolutions as he wanted them, and she doing the rest. Which was a lot: she drafted the formal notices, prepared the board packs, nannied the directors, kept minutes, and filed what needed to be filed at the company's office. The recordkeeping of official documents was also her baby.

She was behind her desk, cheerful, loud and colourful. Thirteen inches shorter than Stephen, she shared her jokes with the world from just above counter-top height. He loved her enthusiasm and open straightforward honesty.

"Hey, chicken." He grinned at her. "You aren't allowed to get old, you hear? We like you just the way you are."

Nomhla beamed like the princess of the fiesta. "I'm getting younger," she said, getting out of her chair to receive a congratulatory hug; and left Stephen thinking that all people should be this hyped about something as simple as their birthday. The world would be a happier place.

Wandering back upstairs he bumped into Thuli on the half-landing. The man was in a froth.

"Where have you been?" he snapped.

"Good morning. Have we met? The name is Wakefield," Stephen replied, cooler than he felt.

"Answer me. Where have you been?"

"I've been to say Happy Birthday to Nomhla. Where have you been?"

"Don't try to be funny with me," Thuli seethed. "I'm the CEO. Answer me!"

Adrenalin spurred Stephen's heart into a gallop. Doing his best to control his voice, for suddenly he felt breathless, he answered: "I can't deal with you on this basis. If you remember how to behave, come see me in my office. You know where it is."

He brushed past the man and carried on up the stairs, willing himself not to rush. The hand he put on the bannister had developed a slight but definite tremble: *Fight or flight?* His body wanted to know. His head rang with questions as his heart raced with anger.

As soon as he reached his office he sat down and immediately connected his Dictaphone to the conference microphone that stood permanently on his desk. It was so much more efficient to record a conversation and listen again later to the bits you needed to remember, than to take notes on a pad. No sooner was he done than the door burst open and Thuli stormed in, now with a proper head of steam. Stephen turned the Dictaphone to record, and fingered the *on* switch. He saw the tell-tale red light wink at him, a co-conspirator in his stealth.

"Don't fucking think you can turn your back on me. I'm not your gardener. I'm not your servant. You're not my white boss."

"Yes, I know," Stephen replied evenly.

"I asked you a question and I'll have you answer me properly or I'll chase you out of here like a dog. Like a dog!"

"Do you mean you'll fire me?"

"I'll fire you. And you'll never work in this town again. I'm the CEO. I'm in charge. I'm not your nigger, you hear? I'll chase you like a dog."

Stephen waited in silence for a few beats. His heart hammered in his chest. "Sit down," he said in a deliberately mild tone. Thuli reacted as if he'd been slapped.

"Don't you fucking tell *me* what to do. I'm *your* boss and *you* will do what *I* tell you. You think you can order me around: Do this! Do that! But I'm not your servant. I'm in charge and you'll listen."

Stephen said nothing, just gazed at the fuming man.

"And yes. Yes! I'll fire your arse. I'll throw you out of here," Mpongose ranted on.

Stephen sighed, looked down at his desk, and then back up at Thuli. "You aren't my boss and you can't fire me. You know that."

"I'll run you out of here. You treat me like your servant. A black servant boy and you're this mighty white man. Well, fuck you, you hear me, fuck you." Thuli spoke with such venom Stephen thought he might lunge over the desk and attack him physically. But he made certain his face betrayed nothing of his thoughts.

Working hard at keeping his voice steady, Stephen said: "What's got into you? Why are you so cross?"

"I asked you a question and you refuse to answer me. You *will* respect me. You'll *show* your respect!"

"Sure, but stop with the white-man black-man stuff, okay? I'll tell you where I've been. When exactly are you interested in? This morning?"

"You know exactly. Don't play games."

"I'm not playing a game. So let me tell you. This morning Jonny van Straten and I went to an IT company to ask them to help us with our investigation."

"What investigation?" Thuli asked, seeming to settle down a little.

"Thuli, we are investigating the fraud case that involves Mamela. You know that. I gave you a copy of the Audit Committee's preliminary report, and we've spoken about it several times since."

"Who authorised you to speak to outside consultants?"

Stephen so nearly made the mistake of saying the chairman had authorised it. Instead he said, "I don't need specific permission. I'm investigating on behalf of a board committee and I have plenary powers to do what's necessary."

He was prepared to stake a month's salary on a combination of things: that Thuli didn't know what *plenary* meant, and that he wouldn't ask.

"You do things you don't understand. You compromise the company and you hide behind your fancy legal terms."

Thuli spoke now in cold hatred, no longer in raging fury.

Stephen idly thought that Thuli had nearly proved him wrong and had been about to ask what he'd meant by "plenary powers." Not that he'd have been able to win that round. If he'd asked what the lawyer meant, he would've lost face; not asking meant he didn't know what had been said. An old trick.

Stephen looked at the man steadily. "What do you mean?"

"You tell people outside the company and that is a breach of confidentiality. What do you think investors will say if they find out about this? That's what I mean. You don't understand politics or investor relations. You think the world is still run by whites and apartheid."

"I don't know what you're talking about, to be honest." Stephen had got his breath back under control. The conversation had turned from a direct man-on-man confrontation to a discussion in which he was trying to make sense of what was being said. He was on home ground now.

"The people, and the Minister will say, what's this? And the ANC won't take us seriously. The trade unions will ignore us. That's what I mean."

"Because I'm investigating a fraud in our Accounts Department?" As he spoke, he allowed ridicule to creep into his eyes. Thuli saw that.

"You see! That's what I mean. You think you're so smart, but you understand nothing. You're like a dinosaur, still operating under a different system. Well, wake up, it's long gone."

"Okay. I get it. You're cross with me because I'm a white man," Stephen replied in a flinty voice. As he spoke he saw Thuli blanche. "And you're smart and apartheid is done." He looked steadily at his accuser, who had pointedly refused to sit. "But you make no sense. I'm investigating a fraud which may involve the company. Somebody may be stealing from the company. I don't know yet. And here's the crime you accuse me of: I'm trying to find out who's doing the stealing. So, let me ask you, then, do you want me to stop? Don't you want me to find out who's behind the fraud?"

"I'm the boss here," Thuli spat at him. "You don't ask the questions, I do."

"You're not my boss. We're on the same level. And you're avoiding the question. Do you want me to carry on investigating? Simple question, yes or no?"

"I won't have you speak to me like this. You're not my *wit baas*, I'm not your—" But Stephen interrupted, steel in his courtroom voice:

"Cut the crap. Are you telling me not to investigate? Because if you are, I want to know why."

"I'm not accountable to you."

"Fair enough. And I'm not accountable to you. We both report directly to the board. If you insist, I'll take your point of view, whatever it may be, to the board for its decision and instruction. Do you want me to tell the board you want to discontinue the investigation?"

Thuli sulked, staring at his feet. Belatedly he pulled out a chair and sat down. "How far have you got?"

"Not as far as I would've liked. I have given the IT consultants information from which they may reconstruct Mamela's access codes so we can see what is on his laptop. But so far they haven't been able to break into the files." While Stephen spoke, Thuli's head jerked back in surprise. Stephen noticed because he was watching for it.

"But his laptop is missing. What are you working on?"

Jesus, it really is him, Stephen realised with a jolt. Up until now he'd still been doubtful. He had retained a lawyer's point of view that nothing had been proved. But the CEO had stumbled into another trap, set for what it may hopefully reveal. And the revelation he just received made all the difference in the world.

Stephen had deliberately not told this man, or anyone else outside a very tight circle, about the missing laptop. On the contrary, he'd been very careful to tell everybody who knew about it to keep dead quiet: the fact that the machine was missing, their search for it, the attempt to recover it or its contents. And he'd told them why: if he found out that anyone else knew the machine was missing, he'd be a mile closer to knowing who had taken it in the first place.

Stephen tried his luck, pushed for one bridge further: "It's not actually a laptop," he said. And the fish took the hook, the line, and the sinker:

"Well, it's a tablet. But it's the same thing."

"So I'm told." Stephen didn't miss a beat. "We are working on the theory that Mamela backed up the tablet on a cloud storage facility." Again he watched carefully, like a poker player looking for a bluff. Thuli would've lost his boots around the green baize of five-card stud.

"Huh?" he started. "Is that possible?"

"Theoretically."

Thuli slumped in his chair, looking miserable, and Stephen could almost hear the cogs behind those eyes spinning.

"Who else knows what you're doing?" his CEO asked at last.

There was a new quality to his voice: He'd given up on the line of attack; now he was trying another approach, this one defensive. With the change came a greater calmness. Thuli had throttled back on his rage, and now spoke as if he were discussing the detail of an everyday occurrence.

"Specifically? I know. Jonny knows I'm looking to find out what's on the computer, but he doesn't know why. And now you know."

"The IT people haven't cracked it yet?"

"No. They say they're unlikely to get further with what I've given them. They have tried all the permutations they can think of, without success. Either they can't crack the code or there isn't a backup. They're not sure."

"Well," Thuli said. "In that case, carry on with the investigation. Keep me informed. Let me know immediately if something happens." He pushed back his chair and got up; turned to the door and left without further comment.

Stephen watched him go; then turned off the Dictaphone. *A sociopath,* he remembered his daughter telling him when she was brimming with new knowledge from the course she liked most in second year at UCT, *was someone with a psychopathic personality, who behaves antisocially, and who has no sense of moral responsibility.* "Bingo; Mpongose gets a full-house," he muttered to himself.

He tried to order his thoughts about the encounter. He'd long known that the CEO was prone to wild outbursts, but hadn't expected ever to be on the receiving end of one. Certainly not one as venomous and personal as the one he'd just endured. He'd been taken by surprise: Attack surely is the best defence; but what an attack! The unpleasantness of the whole thing, however, paled into insignificance next to his newfound conviction that Thuli Mpongose was somehow connected to both the fraud and the murder. There, he'd said it to himself: The murder. Mpho Mamela had been murdered for what he knew and, possibly, for what was on his laptop.

Stephen took out his mobile phone and dialled. "Shakes?" he said, when the chairman answered. "We need to talk."

"I'm on my way to the airport. Is it urgent?"

"Yes, I think it is."

"Would you mind driving with me? We'll talk in the car, and Terence will bring you back."

Seventeen minutes later the big white Rolls glided to a halt beside Stephen, who had walked five-and-a-half blocks from his office to wait in the shade of the jacarandas on the corner of Blandford and Wantage Roads, where no one would see even this car. It was pearl white, except for the brushed stainless steel bonnet that always reminded Stephen of a large butter dish. That bonnet was the only loud thing about the vehicle. The engine, notwithstanding the brute force of its twelve cylinders, was as quiet as a Hitachi Quiet Mark tumble drier; the back door through which Stephen got in, and which opened in the wrong direction—backward—opened noiselessly and snickered closed behind him; and the passengers' cabin where he settled into the soft leather of a seat pinched from first class on an Emirates A380, was as the grave.

A thick, soundproof partition separated them from the imposingly wide and thick shoulders of Terence, the quietly spoken driver who doubled as a bodyguard. Terence had served in Shakes's battalion during the war and had done things, Shakes once told Stephen, not many people are capable of. After Stephen had said hello to Terence over the intercom, Shakes turned it off and opaqued the screen at the touch of a button.

"What's up?" he asked.

"I had a major run-in with Thuli this afternoon. He had a go at me like a bolt of lightning from a clear blue sky. The outcome is that I no longer have any doubt that he's involved up to his neck in the fraud." Stephen shook his head. "Also, I'm becoming convinced that there was a murder, and that he's in that as well."

Shakes raised his eyebrows, but didn't interrupt.

"I threw out a line to see what I might catch, and he was on the hook when I reeled it in."

Stephen told the General of the laptop and how Thuli knew more about it than he possibly could have without another source of close and accurate information. Then he said, "I know how you say it's more helpful to be at a meeting than to be told of it. Here, listen to what he said."

Stephen slipped the SD card he brought with him into the slot in the console between the seats, turned the volume up and heard his and Thuli's conversation reproduced over the hidden speakers of the big vehicle: A door slammed and Thuli's voice was in the compartment with them: "Don't fucking think you can turn your back on me. I'm not your gardener. I'm not your servant . . ."

Shakes listened to the end without comment. Then he turned

off the sound system, sighed, and said: "If I've ever heard a guilty man, it's that one." He thought for a minute and continued, "Stephen, there's enough on there for me to move against him at board level. I can fire him for this; and I will, if that's all we can get. But there isn't anything that definitely ties him to anything yet. A smart lawyer, like any of your pals," he smiled, "will run rings around a prosecutor on this."

Stephen nodded. He was right.

"I want to bury him deep. I don't want him coming back and saying he's innocent and just the victim of a smear campaign. That's a politically dangerous position for me, because we live in a country where plausibility has a low threshold. And, unfortunately, where public corruption and dishonesty simply earmark you as a potential bedfellow for any number of crooks who want to pool skills with you. Dishonesty undoes nobody in South Africa. But if I can tie him to murder, that's a different kettle of fish. I'll move on this alone"—the man gestured toward the console—"if we reach a dead end and this is all we have. But I don't get the impression you're quite finished with what you're doing yet?"

"No, I'm not. I truthfully don't know what I'm going to do next, but things have a way of turning up. Jonny is still doing things, and I may yet find something in Mamela's papers. It's clear, by the way, that it was Mamela who slipped the letter from the Minister to Thuli into the trade unionists' file. He kept a note saying so. They didn't know what it was, but he meant it as his insurance policy. He told them the file was a smoking gun. Quite subtle as a tactic, and it almost didn't work. But here we are: Mamela was trying to finger someone, and I think he meant Thuli Mpongose. Give me a week or so? If I don't get anywhere I'll let you know and we'll formulate a plan on what we have."

Shakes nodded. "Can I keep this?" He gestured at the card in the slot. "I want to let the others hear what the trustee of their funds sounds like in his unguarded moments."

"Sure." Stephen nodded, as they drew up outside domestic departures on the upper level of the drop-off zone at OR Thambo. "I'll let you know if anything happens. When are you back?"

"Tomorrow morning," Shakes said, lifting the expensive-looking leather overnight bag from the seat next to him, opening the door, and stepping out onto the pavement.

On the way back Stephen tried the fridge between the seats. It hinged open like an old-fashioned jewellery box, a little tray of glasses sliding out with the lid and coming to rest above and away from the contents of the cool-box below. In the hold there was Coke instead of Bollinger, but that suited him fine: He wasn't thirsty, he was after the obscure thrill of having a chilled drink in the back seat of a chauffeur-driven Rolls-Royce. He spooned ice into the bubbling liquid with the silver tongs he found there, and sipped from his glass, feeling like Richie Rich.

Chapter 26

"Shall we take the dogs for a walk?" Lisa asked, as he stepped into the house.

When he'd been younger, Stephen had resented the immediacy with which he was expected to adjust between the world of papers and people who demanded his exhaustive attention all day to the world of children, chores, dogs, and domesticity that flooded over him as he stepped through the door. His day job was way more important, so he thought, and what happened at home was derivative, had to wait until he'd cleared the space behind his eyes and was ready to engage with it. Engage he always did, eagerly and without limit. *But give me a minute or two*, he used to think.

Without his noticing, the sinews of time had tied and retied their knots, until his sails were set for a different wind: his worlds traded places. If one of the dogs wasn't well, it was more real to him than the quarterly results at the office; if his wife wanted him to walk a circuit with her around the pavements of his burb, the CEO and his idiocy must wait. If one of his children needed him, he upped anchor and set sail while the shadows of their words still whispered down the telephone line.

Only Findlay walked without a leash. She remembered the heady excitement of her days as a young dog when an hour's walk was heaven: the smells, the sounds, the things to see, the neighbourhood dogs imprisoned behind their own gates to bark at. Now she lagged behind, smiling around her lolling tongue, trotting along at a dainty matronly pace, only just ahead of her forever wagging tail. The smells and sounds were no less, but now she took her time not to miss the detail. Cindy stayed on a leash at Lisa's heels, mostly for the peace of mind of the walking couples and singletons they met. Humans haven't quite got over their primordial fear of a lean prairie wolf, and the old girl still looked the part. Angus ran on the end of a four metre retractable lead that ratchetted in and out of the spring-loaded handle in Stephen's hand. If left to his own devices, he'd follow the lonesome call of the wandering star he'd been born under. And he'd wee on every tree he came across.

"How was the day?" she asked, when they'd negotiated the thrill of getting out the gate. They left through the pedestrian entrance set in the motor gate and all three dogs surged through the minute it opened a fraction. Angus barked excitedly and, every once in a while, Cindy bared her wolf's fangs at him: Let this puppy settle down.

"I sipped a glass of bubbles in the back of a chauffeur-driven limousine today," he bragged.

"Champagne?"

"No. It was Coke and ice, but it had bubbles."

Lisa laughed. "How did you get that lucky?"

"I had to chat to Shakes and he had to get to the airport. I rode with him in the back of the Rolls, and swiped a Coke on the way home." Lisa didn't ask what he spoke to Shakes about. She knew Stephen wouldn't say.

"And you?" he asked.

"We had our last meeting to plan the trip. We leave tomorrow night! Isn't that exciting?" The plans and the bookings were set and the schedules confirmed. "Austria, here we come!" she said, managing to sound a little nervous and a lot excited. "Hello there," she added, confusing Stephen somewhat until he noticed her waving at an old man in a gardener's uniform. The old guy smiled and waved back. Stephen also waved lest he felt left out.

"Who's that?" he asked when they were out of earshot.

"Stephen! It's Shadrack, the Baileys' gardener. You've seen him lots. He has just been home to Zim. He says things are looking better there."

"Oh," Stephen said. He had no memory for faces, and where his library of first names, surnames, and job descriptions should've been, there was only a smoking ruin. Lisa, by contrast, remembered everyone she met, and the things they told her. *Hell, I wish I could do that*, Stephen had often thought.

"You'll be okay while I'm gone?" Lisa frowned enquiringly.

"I'll miss you," he said truthfully, "but I'll certainly cope. If I don't, I'll ask a woman to help." Lisa's network consisted of competent women who kept the world wobbling on its axis and the moon skidding through the clouds. They and the tides waited for no one; and Stephen had their telephone numbers—Lisa had written them down for him on the blackboard in the kitchen where she usually kept the list of out-of-stock groceries. Stephen's reply had been only half-flippant.

They walked around the park, two blocks down, one across and headed back home. Findlay was slowing down perceptibly, and they had to wait for her several times. When they came back in through the front gate, she headed straight for her water bowl and drank like a camel after the long haul to Timbuctoo.

Opening the front door, Stephen heard his phone ringing. When he came home in the evenings, he abandoned it next to his keys on the granite top in the corner of the kitchen where he was allowed space for his stuff. He picked up the urgent little device, looking at the caller's name to decide if he'd answer. At work he picked up all calls. At home, he answered only if he should or wanted to. *Ronald Priest*, said the screen. Stephen pressed the green button.

"Hi there," he said.

"Hey Stephen, you well?"

"I am, but I have been wondering why, when I ring you, the person who answers the phone says, 'Covenant.' Is it an instruction to the sinners?"

Ronald laughed. "No," he said, "It's the church's name. The Church of the Covenant of Jesus Christ, Middelburg Chapter."

"When I was a student, I worked at a steakhouse where we were supposed to answer the phone by saying, 'Dmitri's for the best steaks in town, hello.' But no one ever did. Except Dmitri, and he made more money than the rest of us put together."

"You think we should say the whole name?"

"I'll ask Dmitri when I see him. What happy fact makes you phone me after hours?"

"There are no after hours. The devil keeps his porch light on."

Stephen laughed. "Of course. What makes you ring me during normal time?"

"I hope I'm not bugging you for nothing, but there's something interesting I saw today."

Stephen made encouraging noises and the priest continued. "There's never enough money for the Lord's work, so His poor servants become beggars. Earlier this year, Mpho was due for an upgrade on his phone, and he knew mine had its challenges. It was the size of a brick and, well, it didn't work so great. I think it was Satan himself who had the idea to keep me from instant communication with my flock. So that boy gave me his old phone. Stuck it to the devil."

"That was nice of him," said Stephen, who hadn't had a new phone in decades. Every upgrade he was entitled to went to one of his kids and he got the hand-me-down.

"Sure. This afternoon I was looking up a number and saw something that may be interesting to you. Some of the numbers Mpho put on the phone are still there. There's an entry for someone or something called OneDrive, whatever that may be, and the number is weird. It's *Frankie@Singapore*. And for the address it says *YodaCU3P*. I thought maybe it's a code or something, and you may know what that means. It may help you."

Ronald, of course, knew of the laptop and the search for what was on it.

While the priest spoke, Stephen's heart skipped a beat. "Father Ronald," he said, not disguising his excitement, "I think I do know what that may be. I hope it's what I think. I've needed a lucky break because we were running dry. Hold thumbs for me that this is what I've been looking for; and be sure, please, to thank your boss. I'll have a word with Him myself a bit later."

Ronald chuckled and they hung up. Stephen immediately redialled. The phone rang once only and an ultra-laid-back voice drawled: "Whydawg."

"We come in peace Whydawg." Stephen tried his best Doctor Spock voice.

"Mr. Wakefield?" said the voice, completely different now. Not the crisp tones of the Queen, but certainly Johannesburg-Business.

"Don't drop the dude voice on my account."

The man chuckled. "We have a game tonight. I thought it was one of my team. We always talk tactics first."

"What kind of game?"

"We play a game called *Scythotic Dronoids*. Five on a team. My team is South African, all over the country. The other team is mostly in Europe. You have to be in the same time zone because the game lasts hours."

Stephen thought about that. "I play bridge?"

"Same thing," said Cleo. "It's best to be in the same time zone."

Stephen laughed. He and Lisa never sat together at a bridge table. She said it was a game for boring old men and dried-up aunties who smoke too much.

"Sorry to bug you late," he said.

"I'm actually sitting here still trying to get into your site. It's driving me nuts."

"Well, here's a thing; try *Frankie@Singapore* for a username; and *YodaCU3P* for a password." Stephen heard the clicking of a keyboard under fast fingers, and then a whoop of delight.

"You beauty! For an old guy you still have the moves," the programmer said. Stephen's heart leaped.

"You're in?"

"Dig, ma bro," Whydawg drawled. Then added in sobering tones: "Oops. What's this?" Stephen heard more clicking, and when he couldn't wait any longer asked: "Well, what is it?"

"Text," said Cleo. *A nod for van Straten*, Stephen thought. "But it's encrypted," Cleo completed the sentence. Stephen's heart slowed and headed for the pit of his stomach.

"What do you mean?"

"It's in hieroglyphics," the voice on the phone replied. "Literally: Birdy, Eye, Water, Sideways-man. Gap. Birdy, Wriggly-snake, Birdy, Sun, Boat, Wriggly-snake. First word four letters. Second word six letters. I bet that says *Mpho Mamela*," Cleo mused. "Birdy is M; and Wriggly-snake is A. Fuck I'm good."

"Cleo, can we un-encrypt it?" Stephen asked, hoping, but not following the stream of consciousness on the other end of the line.

"We? I doubt it. But me? About as easily as you can change the font in your letters to the Academy. Can you do that, by the way?" Cleo asked the relic-from-before-computers.

Stephen chuckled and Whydawg went on: "He will have used a commercially available encryption engine, and that's a Why-Bother. Especially when I know two of the letters already. I'll download it in English on a stick for you. It's not much, about twenty megs, but it's too easy to intercept if I mail it to you. It's a spy thing, isn't it?"

Stephen admitted that it was. "I'll pick it up from you at about eight-thirty?"

"Dude, not from me. I'll be killing Scythotic Dronoids till the early hours, long after you go beddy-byes. I'll leave it with Chessie. Fetch it any time. She gets in at eight." He thought about that, and corrected himself. "Eightish." Then added: "Nine is safer." Stephen remembered Chessie from his previous visit. Her hair was a bucket of tar, her clothes the colour of a raven, her shoes clunky and black, and her skin as if she'd never seen the sun. She glowered at the world, daring it to try its luck.

Stephen immediately phoned Jonny, who answered after the third ring.

Stephen told him the news, and feeling guilty, said: "I'm getting the files in the morning and it shouldn't take me long to find out what's on them. If it's what we think, we need to talk, and it would be good if you could be here."

"So you want me to get up before dawn and drive three hours in case you find something that may interest you? And I must leave Skapie all alone for another day?"

You must leave Skapie alone for always, Stephen thought. On the phone he said, "Hell, Jonny, now that you put it that way. Wait till I've read the files and then I'll ring you."

"Just pulling your leg, man. I was coming through in any event. I'll see you in the morning. I'll bring my kitbag and sleep over. Save me a few miles a day." With that he rang off, leaving Stephen to wonder if he was being serious about staying over in Johannesburg.

The next call was to Shakes. "We got into the files. I don't know what's in them yet, but I will in the morning. I'll let you know."

Shakes chuckled. "How'd you do that?"

"Oh, I was lucky." He'd tell the whole story later.

Lisa, unused to him spending much time at home on the phone, came looking for him. She overheard the last line. "How are you lucky?" she asked.

"We've been trying to get into Mpho Mamela's laptop. And we've just managed."

"Yes, lucky you," she said, managing to make the whole thing sound trivial in just three words. None of the competent women whose names were on the blackboard would've been impressed either.

"These dogs don't look so lucky. They're starving. Aren't you, my Chip Chaps?" she asked them. They sat in a semicircle watching her. As she spoke, they bashed their tails on the floor and Angus let out an anguished whimper, as if fearful that dinner would be cancelled tonight. When Stephen headed for the kitchen, the hungry dog streaked ahead, skidded to a halt next to the food bin, and drooled on the floor. The two old ladies followed at a more leisurely pace, nevertheless not letting him out of their sight.

The ginger kitten and the judgmental grey cat watched the undignified procession, disapproving, but not saying a word.

Chapter 27

Lisa slept like a baby, a real one. She didn't know when she was cold and didn't wake up when she was—she just shrank into a tight ball as if she were a frightened hedgehog, until Stephen would get up and put another blanket on her. Then she'd warm up and slowly unfold back into human shape. Noise didn't wake her and she'd gaze in wonder at the wet garden after a night of rain. "Did it rain?" she'd ask, delighted, even if there'd been an Armageddon-grade storm.

Worry wasn't something she did at night; but excitement kept her awake. Not for Christmas morning, but for things she really looked forward to, such as trips to Austria. Then she spun in her sheets like a dreidel at Hanukkah, partly in anticipation and partly in anxiety: How magnificent to see the snowy peaks where the von Trapps once roamed; and does the visa have all the right stamps?

She woke when Stephen came to bed after midnight, a sure sign she was restless. A few hours later she lay in bed waiting for the coming of the gold-throned dawn. The first rays of the new day were her get-out-of bed pass. She was in the shower before Stephen had stirred.

"You're a lunatic," he said as she came back into the room, pink and clean and smelling of lemon verbena. "What time is it?"

"Did I wake you?" she asked. Stephen chuckled, but with his eyes still firmly shut. It was their long-standing joke that she never answered a question. She came to sit on the edge of his bed.

"It's a quarter to six," she said. "I've got things to do."

"Sure." he patted her arm. "Can I help?"

"No. You lie in your bed like a lump, and I'll get busy."

"See you in a few hours for breakfast?" he teased.

"Watch it," she warned, prodding the end of his nose with an extended index finger. Then he fell asleep again and she did the things that kept her busy. Much later they sat at table over fruit and coffee.

"Your flight is at seven-thirty," he said. "I'd get there at six, but you want to be there earlier?"

"Yes, definitely. You have to get to the airport three hours before an international flight. It says so on the ticket."

"Have you ever done that?" he asked. She'd seen the world from Acapulco to Zurich, and knew her way around the globe better than Shakespeare. And still she felt compelled to follow to the letter all the instructions on the travel agent's standard printout.

"Not when I'm travelling with you," she conceded. "But we have arranged to meet at the check-in desk at half-past-five."

"It will be rush hour. We must leave at twenty to five. That should do."

"I can go on the train," she said for the sake of form. She knew he wanted to come with her, drop her off at the terminal.

"No, it's no hassle," he said, knowing that not to be true. "I'll be home at three. That okay?" He put down his empty cup, pecked her on the cheek, picked up his keys, and went to get a memory stick from Chessie.

This morning the lady-goth had a streak of purple in her hair, from the crown on the back of her head to the fringe that dangled over her left eye. She sized him up, waiting for him to try a wrong move, and said in a perfectly clear, bright voice: "Good morning, Mr. Wakefield. Cleo left this for you." She handed over a memory stick that looked like a USB connection only, as if the memory part of it had become detached and fallen off. As Stephen palmed the little thing, she added, "Let me know if there's anything else we can help with." And then she smiled.

Well, there's just no way of knowing folks, Stephen thought. Aloud he said: "Thanks so much. I appreciate your help and please thank Cleo for me when he comes in." He smiled too, but people expected that of him.

On his way to the office, his phone rang. Jonny's voice on the speaker said: "Hey, boss. I got away a bit late. I'm probably an hour from you. Manage without me till then?"

"Don't rush. I've only just got the stick. I haven't looked at it yet."

In his office he opened his laptop and slid the little device into a port. He keyed the wavy flag and the E key, and up came the index page. *Removable Storage (E)* looked right. He clicked on it and a file opened. *Mpho Mamela* was its name. Cleo had guessed that in three seconds flat. There were three subfiles: Bank Deposits, Correspondence, and Accounts. Stephen opened the first one.

There was only one document in the subfile, and it was named Jan 2015. It was a list of payments, the first dated January 2015, for an amount of R122,344.76. Next to the payment was the name Tolémon Trust. Stephen knew who that was. He'd drawn the deed establishing that trust, and had chosen the slightly silly name himself, because at the time his son had been a big fan of Pokémon. There were nine other payments, each a month apart, for an amount of R25,000. Against those payments the name was even more obvious: T Mpongose.

Stephen opened the Correspondence subfile, which turned out to contain thirty-odd documents. He scrolled through them one by one, finding that they were letters sent and received by an email address appearing only as Rover777GT@gmail.com. How Mpho would've gotten hold of them was a mystery. The first few letters were addressed anonymously but very soon one began, "Dear Thuli." And not long after that the reply was sent to "Dear Padi," which was the Minister's first name. The letters told a sad tale of a straightforward bribe. The Minister, who wrote from Intombilami69@gmail com, said: "Okay, agreed. Deposit R30mil in account, Branch Code 361278, Account number 69627008041 and send me confirmation. When I get it I'll sign the consent and you can send someone to pick it up." The letter was dated the day before ministerial approval for the transaction had been granted.

Stephen felt only tired disappointment at how the world went about its business. This letter on its own was enough for what Shakes and his mates wanted. Both their adversaries would be buried deep. With a sigh he opened the next document, wondering what else could be important enough for Mpho to have kept. He was clearly a sharp young man and would be unlikely to have wasted effort on stuff that didn't matter. And he hadn't.

The next few letters showed where Thuli had got the money from to pay his pal the Minister. They came from J. Zarubin@Vulconia.co.za. When he was in his office, the author of the letter was Josef Zarubin; and the office was the chrome-and-glass corner suite on the top floor of Vulconia House in Bryanston, from where that company traded at least thirty percent of all the coal produced in the country. Just short of eighty million tonnes a year. Even at current rock-bottom prices that was half a billion dollars every twelve months. From its branches around the world, it traded many times more than that.

The letters were full of details about interest rates, repayment periods and sales commissions. Taken together they told of a complex scheme of deception. Stephen was astonished at the bold dishonesty of it all. One of the letters confirmed the transfer of thirty-five million Rand to a bank account, again with banking details. Stephen thought two things: *These guys weren't very careful* and *thirty-five!* So much for honour among thieves.

As he carried on reading, he soon realised that there was a second series of letters, from the time when the company was about to list on the stock exchange. The correspondence was still with Vulconia, and it took Stephen some time to figure out. When he did, he whistled through his teeth, and sat back in his chair in the thrall of a depleting astonishment.

After a while he turned back to the screen and opened the final subfolder. The accounts were detailed but didn't tell him anything he hadn't already read. While his nose was buried in the detail, his door burst open and in strode Thuli, his ego on a leash this morning. Stephen felt a surge of guilt such as he hadn't experienced since he was twelve and his mother had walked into his bedroom while he was minutely examining a *Playboy* magazine his friend Hans Hauptman had lent him. He'd learned greater facial control since then but still felt as if the man across the desk could read the screen from the reflection in his eyes.

"Any progress?" Thuli asked without any preliminaries. His abruptness gave Stephen the perfect cover for his embarrassment.

"No," he said simply, staring back. The silence lengthened while Thuli waited for a more extensive reply, but that ploy hadn't worked with Stephen these last three decades. Eventually Thuli said, "Okay," then he turned on his heel and marched out, without another word.

As the door was swinging to, Stephen muttered under his breath, "Arsehole," perhaps loud enough for Thuli to hear. The door immediately swung back open, and in walked Jonny.

"Who's an arsehole?"

"My visitor who just left," Stephen said, recovering from the shock of seeing the door open again.

"He always speaks highly of you," Jonny said, wide-eyed and innocent. Stephen laughed, relieved.

"Sit down, my Captain. We can't talk here but I've got lots to tell you; and we need to see the General as soon as we can." Jonny sat in the visitor's chair while Stephen dialled. "Shakes," he said, "are you back?"

"I've just landed. You need to talk?"

"I do. As soon as you can, and if Ernst and Zola are around, they should come as well."

"It's serious?"

"It is."

"My office in an hour?"

"See you there. Jonny is with me."

Stephen looked at his laptop, pulled the whole file from the memory stick into a folder marked *Holiday Snaps*, and hit *save*. He pulled the device from the port and gave it to Jonny. "Backup," he said.

Stephen stood, slipped his phone into his pocket, picked up his keys, and asked his big friend: "Can I buy a travelling man breakfast?"

"Never a bad idea," Jonny agreed. They strode in silence to the front door on the ground floor, and as they were leaving, Jonny said, "Don't look up but see who's watching?" Just before they rounded the corner, Stephen glanced over his shoulder and saw the CEO at the top of the stairs staring after them.

"Fuck it, Big Jon, I feel like I'm in a spy movie." He wasn't exaggerating.

They kept schtum all the way to Stephen's car. With the engine running and the big vehicle slowly nosing out of the basement, Stephen looked sideways at his passenger. "Son," he said, "have I got a little story for you."

Chapter 28

By the time Stephen pulled into the parking bay in Shakes's building, Jonny was well-fed on sausages and bacon that, together with a plate of hash-browns, fried black mushrooms, and grilled tomatoes, had kept the big man quiet while he listened to the whole story the old man had to tell him. Stephen signed the security guard's book, confirming that, once again, he didn't have a gun, and that he'd left his laptop in his office. The lift delivered them to the granite mausoleum on the ground floor where the koi still drifted lazily in the timeless karma of their never-ending daydream. The pretty receptionist recognised him and smiled.

"Morning, Mr. Wakefield. Mr. Hlongwane is waiting for you. I'll let Zondi know you're here."

Jonny and Stephen walked over to the postmodern chairs, but hadn't decided whether to sit before Zondi came clicking into the room on her dainty high heels. This morning she wore black slacks that looked as if she'd airbrushed them on, and a pale blue blouse with an elaborate swirl of frills and lace that didn't quite hide the curve of her bosom.

"Mr. Wakefield," she smiled with perfect teeth, Stephen noticing that her heels again made her was almost as tall as he was, but still several inches shorter than Jonny. "Would you come through please?" she asked, turning to walk in short steps ahead of them while Jonny's eyes followed her appreciatively.

This time she led them a different way, to heavy double wooden doors that swung open to a large room, the main boardroom, dominated by a ten-seater table. Its top was a four-inch thick rhomboid of pale wood, inlaid with strips of metal, the whole assembly floating on six brushed stainless steel legs tilting inward from the edges. Both sharp ends had been rounded to create the best seats at the head and foot of the table. The central diamond-shaped portion was covered in black leather and bristled with electronic equipment and connections. Flash Gordon had made his plans to defeat the Zogons at a table like this. The chairs were works of modern art, deep and soft, adjustable in the eight directions of an unpredictable corporate wind.

At one end of the room was a window, the light from it cleverly muted by a series of folding blinds of varying degrees of transparency. Against the wall closest to the door stood a plinth with an enormous bouquet of indigenous wild flowers in a heavy black-and-white marble vase; and the longest wall in the room was covered in the bold, disconcerting black-and-purple slashes of a William Kentridge original.

At the head of the table sat Shakes, at the foot was Zola, and on the far side closest to the sideboard on which coffee and dainty biscuits had been set out, there was someone Stephen hadn't met. Shakes stood up as they came in.

"Stephen," he said, shaking our man's hand. "Thanks for coming. And Jonny," he said, shaking hands with the other, "good to see you again so soon."

Stephen noticed that Shakes didn't wince, which could only mean that Jonny had left his miners' handshake in Crosby.

"You know Zola," Shakes motioned across the table while the visitors shook hands there as well, "and let me introduce you to General Patrick Maduna."

Stephen had imagined General Maduna to be a man filling his uniform to the brim and sweating under the lights of a television studio when reporters asked him awkward questions. But before him was a short man in his forties, stocky and as athletic as a prizefighter. His hair was cropped short and on his right cheek there was an old scar, maybe, thought Stephen, from duelling at the Police Academy. He looked tough enough for that. The paleness of his complexion and the texture of his hair betrayed the recent presence of an Umlungu in his lineage. When he kept notes, he wrote with his left hand; and he looked as if he only ever broke into a sweat under extreme conditions, like Roger Federer. His smile came as an oasis in the desert of his habitual seriousness; it showed a perfect set of well-maintained teeth, and a dry sense of humour bordering on the prudish.

"Ernst is in Cape Town," Shakes said. "He's standing by, but I don't want to conference him in. Patrick here says it's too easy for others to listen in."

Stephen nodded and sat down. Jonny poured himself a coffee, popping first an oval of Greek shortbread into his mouth, and, while adding sugar to his brew, a biscuit roll with one end dipped in chocolate. He balanced another three delicacies in his saucer, and just before taking his seat beside Stephen, snuck one more piece of shortbread into his mouth.

"Shall we kick off?" Shakes asked, when everyone was settled.

"We got lucky," Stephen began. "We managed to get into Mpho Mamela's files." He gave them the shorter version of how that had happened.

"There are three things of importance in the files. The first is a straightforward bribe: Thuli paid the Minister a thirty million Rand bribe. The details are easy to understand and come from an exchange of email correspondence. But I don't know how we'll authenticate the letters."

"Do you know the email addresses?" Patrick Maduna interrupted.

"I do. It's Rover777GT@gmail.com. That's Thuli Mpongose. And there's Intombilami69@gmail com. That's Minister Padi when he's at home." At the mention of the second address, the policeman snorted in disapproval. *MyGirl69*, was not a moniker he approved of.

The senior police officer told Stephen: "There have been great strides in making email less anonymous than it once was. I have no doubt that we, my Department, will be able to trace those correspondences back to their origin, and positively identify the holder of the accounts."

"Good news," said Shakes.

"Well, we have more information," Stephen continued. "The Minister asked for a thirty million Rand bribe to consent to the transaction, and Thuli paid it. We have the bank account details, and the date and amount of the payment. That should be relatively easy to trace?"

"Absolutely." Patrick nodded. "Will you let me have those?"

"We have the whole file here with us. I think we should give you a copy and I'll highlight where the initial interesting bits are," Stephen suggested.

"That works." The policeman nodded.

"It gets more interesting. And more complicated." Stephen looked around the table at his attentive audience. "Perhaps I'll just tell you my conclusions, and then I can sit with Patrick's people later and take them through it step-by-step?"

"I think that's a good idea," Zola replied. "I'll also read the file and we can compare notes about our conclusions."

"Very well," said Stephen. "Thuli got the money to pay the bribe to Padi, from Vulconia. Patrick, we know them well, but in case you don't, they're multinational commodity traders. They're big here, massive in the States, and monolithic in the East. The letter from them to Thuli is quite open and straightforward. It's structured as a special loan: They lend thirty-five million Rand and get a very healthy return that is repaid as an additional charge on their marketing fee."

Zola nodded; what Stephen said was obvious and made sense to him. But the other two were struggling with the details. Stephen explained: "Sethemba mines about sixteen million tonnes of coal a year. Half of that is sold directly to Eskom under a long-term supply agreement. The other half is sold on the open market offshore, through a sales agent, Vulconia. They charge a marketing fee which is usually no more than one and a half percent. But they agreed with Thuli that the company would pay a higher fee while the loan was being repaid."

"Shit," said Shakes. "It's a swindle."

"A swindle with many parts," agreed Stephen. "First and foremost, Thuli got thirty-five million and paid over thirty. The rest probably went into his pocket. Patrick's people will be able to tell us in no time flat. The second part is that the rate on the so-called loan is over the top. Way over the top. Vulconia really ripped the ring out of it. Because it was so lucrative they never wanted it to end."

"I'm going to go after them for this," Shakes said, interrupting Stephen's flow.

But Zola shrugged.

"For what? They'll say they made a deal with the CEO about a marketing rate and they made an up-front capital payment for it and that's why the fee is so high. It's not even a particularly unusual arrangement."

"Exactly right," Stephen confirmed. "And it brings us more bad news. When I read this I couldn't believe the fee was this high, so Jonny and I checked the contract." He saw Patrick looking at him quizzically, and explained: "I write most of the company's contracts and I have them all on my laptop. I keep the Word document I prepared, and the PDF version of the signed contract is sent to me by the secretarial department. I keep that too, in case I ever need to refer to it again. I wrote the clause for a simple one and a half percent, reducing over time to one point two percent. But the signed document has been changed to reflect a different arrangement—the one set out in the correspondence. It's for two point one five percent, reducing slowly to a minimum of one and a half. The bad news is it's signed by Thuli for the company, and there's a resolution of the Marketing Subcommittee of the Board approving the contract in those terms."

Stephen let that sink in; then emphasised his conclusion: "The committee is either grossly incompetent or is in on the scam."

"Ah, fuck," said the old soldier. "Which is it, do you think?"

"Shakes, it's difficult to think that this isn't a deliberate fraud," Stephen said. "Thuli is just the ringleader, he's not alone."

"And of every buck they steal, our consortium pays forty-five cents!" Shakes seldom lost his good humour, but at that moment it wasn't anywhere in sight. Into the deafening silence that followed his remark, Stephen said tentatively: "I'm not finished yet."

"Ah no," said Zola, looking despondent. "Does it get worse?"

"Afraid so," Stephen went on. "Vulconia loved being paid too much on already generous fees. The percentages may seem small but the trades are huge and the numbers vast. Anyway, what happened next was that the company listed. With Vulconia as one of its major shareholders. In the listing it took up an eleven percent stake. That makes them the third-largest shareholder. But here's the thing, the correspondence tells how they went about it."

Stephen looked to see if everyone was following. "Vulconia agreed with Thuli that they would subscribe at what they called a discounted subscription price. They would publicly pay the full price, but the discount would be paid to them by a continuation of the higher commission. They agreed that the coms would stay at two point one five percent, more than a quarter higher than they should be."

"Shit!" Shakes shouted, throwing down his pen, which skittered to the leather island in the middle of the table. "These fuckers used our money to buy our shares!" Zola and Patrick just looked at him; of course he was right. Jonny knew the story already and seemed to be eyeing the cookie tray again.

"Shakes, I have to make you even crosser," Stephen ventured. Shakes dipped his head and looked enquiringly from under a deeply furrowed brow.

"Of course, the arrangement is illegal for many different reasons and can lead to huge problems with the Stock Exchange, but the real issue is that Thuli wouldn't agree to such a thing without a return. What he got from it was two percent of the company's stock. Part of the deal with Vulconia was that they transferred two percent of the shares they bought to Thuli. Him and his pals, I'm not sure exactly who. But the thing is, two percent of the company was transferred to Centaur Nominees for the Tolémon Trust. Jonny and I checked this morning with Centaur—this is publicly available information."

"What trust is that?" Zola asked.

"It's a trust I helped Thuli establish. I was fooling around with the name. Tolémon was supposed to sound like Thuli-man. It's a blind trust, but it's set up for Thuli and his family."

Stephen paused and looked around the table. "Gents," he summed up, "Thuli got two percent of our company by ripping us off. At our present market cap, that's about one hundred and ninety million Rand."

"Don't forget the five in cash," Zola added laconically.

"Quite right." Stephen nodded. "Also, Centaur told me this morning that the Trust has sold about forty million Rand of the shares since the listing. That's where the Ferrari and the black BMW and the SL Merc and the penthouse in Cape Town come from."

A brooding silence settled in the room. Jonny cleared his throat and started speaking.

"This brings us to the next thing: Mpho Mamela. He was a young man in the Accounts Department, and Thuli knew if you dance a two-step with the Prince of Darkness, you'd better keep accounts. So he paid Mamela to keep accounts for him. A second set of books that had nothing to do with the company's accounts, but were dependent on the company's export sales. The books were there just to keep track of what Vulconia was *owed*." As he said the last word, Jonny made quotation marks in the air with both hands. "And he had to keep track of what had been *paid back*." He traced more quotes.

"Mamela was in love with a boy who tried to steal a few Rand from the company, but was so bad at it he got caught immediately. The CEO insisted that he be charged, and now he's in prison. Here's what me and the boss"—Jonny's eyes darted in Stephen's direction—"think happened: We think Mamela tried to threaten or blackmail Mr. Mpongose into helping him get his friend released. But the CEO refused and they had a fight. There's someone who overheard the end of their disagreement. And we think Mr. Mpongose hired someone to kill Mamela to keep him quiet."

"Ikubu Gobevu." General Maduna hadn't spoken for a while.

"Precisely," confirmed Stephen, "But here we are speculating. For the financial stuff I may be wrong here and there about minor details, but for the bulk of it I'll take poison I'm right. However, our theory about a murder and why it happened remains conjecture. How it happened we don't have a clue."

The policeman replied: "You do have an argument between Mpongose and the deceased, and someone who overheard some of it. And you have two witnesses who identified Gobevu in a restricted area where he shouldn't have been, an hour or two before the incident. And I have photographs and witnesses putting Mpongose and Gobevu together in a car a few days later. And you have compelling financial reasons why Mpongose would want Mamela to be silent."

"Yes," Stephen added, "and we have bizarrely peculiar behaviour from Thuli; and a conclusion from things said by Mamela to Frankie Mabena that Mamela was about to confront the CEO."

"I'd say there's plenty to start a case on." Patrick said. "But we must move cautiously. I want to put my IT people onto those emails; my banking detectives will follow the trail of the payments; and I want my commercial branch to sit with you, Stephen, to understand what exactly was done. We must also track down exactly who was in on the fraud."

"Sure," said Stephen. "We'll flush out the guilty ones easily.

There are only two or three possibilities, in any event."

Patrick went on: "I want to move on all these people at the same time so that nothing slips through the net. We'll coordinate an arrest of Mpongose, his Minister friend, this Josef Zarubin of the coal trading firm, and all the people in the Marketing Committee. I'll try to move on Gobevu at the same time but he's the trickiest. We know where he stays, but he often doesn't go home at night. So we'll probably wait for him to be at home and then do a clean sweep in the early hours of the morning."

When the meeting broke up, Shakes came over to Stephen and said, hand on his shoulder, "Thank you for doing this. I'm deeply in your debt. I owe you."

Stephen felt a little sheepish and said, "That's okay. It's good to see the good guys win for a change."

General Maduna walked past Stephen on his way to the door. "By the way," he said as they drew level. "We moved Frankie Mabena into a single cell at the Mondeor police station yesterday. He's alone in there, and he has a bed and food and blankets. The Parole Board will hear his case on Monday, and he will be released. He shouldn't ever have been in prison."

Stephen couldn't put a finger on why his heart surged so at the news. It must be that thing again about being human.

Chapter 29

It wasn't quite three o'clock when Stephen pulled up outside the house, leaving the car in the shade of the big pin oak that spread its green canopy protectively over the drive. Inside Lisa was packed and ready to go, but anxious as one is in that dream where you know you have forgotten something, but don't know what. A meeting with your most important client? The tickets for the show? Your final exam?

"Have I got everything?" she asked him at the front door, staring at her bags.

"Do you have your passport and your credit card?" Stephen asked by way of answer. "If you have those two, you'll be okay, and you can buy whatever you have forgotten."

"I don't want to forget anything," she chipped in in her best school-ma'am voice. This wasn't the right time to argue any kind of point, so Stephen limited himself to asking: "Are you taking a camera?"

"No, I'm just taking my cell phone."

"Do you have a charger?"

"Check."

"European adapter?"

"Check."

"Taxi money?"

"Check."

"My best interests at heart?"

"Don't be stupid." She spun on her heel, as if remembering something, and marched briskly down the passage toward the bedroom. Stephen went into the kitchen and put on the kettle. When the tea was made, he carried it on a tray to the little table outside on the veranda; and went to look for his wife.

"Come have a cup of tea," he said, when he found her.

"That sounds like a good idea," she smiled, glad for the

distraction, and followed him outside. Stephen was used to her not lingering over tea. She drank it scalding hot, while he let his cool down first. But this afternoon she threw it down the hatch even faster than usual. No sooner had she put down the cup than she jumped up again, rushing to check on something else that had crossed her mind.

Stephen waited for ten minutes, and even though it was only a quarter past four, went to look for her again. "Do you think we should go?"

"Yes. I think maybe we should." Ray Charles would've been able to find the relief in her face with his stick.

She had one suitcase only, a sky-blue Cellini with many zips and a handle, on four wheels. She'd tied a bright red ribbon to the handle, lest she couldn't pick it out on the luggage carousel in Vienna. Stephen picked it up and headed for the car. Lisa had her handbag, the same one in which she usually carried the details of her life. Today it was extra full. Stephen was halfway down the steps when she started saying goodbye to her animals.

"Bye-bye my darlings. Bye-bye Chip Chaps. Stephen will look after you well. Bye-bye my angels." Each one got a hug, a stroke and a kiss. The dogs, that is. The cats disapproved of public displays of affection, although they didn't say. Stephen had watched this performance many times. Lisa was so happy where she was, she never wanted to leave; and she was so looking forward to going, she didn't want to stay. The compromise she'd agreed with herself was to leave in a whirlwind of conflicting emotions, in equal parts happy, sad, excited, and anxious. By the stop street at the bottom of the road, she was on holiday and all-smiles.

Soon she reminisced about previous trips. "When we flew to Istanbul, they give you a little candle in a packet with your dinner. It felt like you were sitting at a street cafe near the water somewhere."

"Did they give you an open flame on an aeroplane?" Stephen

asked, astonished.

"No, it's a little light globe that looks like a flickering candle flame, and that's inside a tiny packet. You can spoil the fun by looking inside—you would—but from the outside it looks as if there's a candle burning on your tray table." Stephen looked at her fondly. What else could he do?

Even though they'd left earlier than planned, the traffic was heavy. But they had a clear run all the way to the airport, and as they drew up outside in the drop-off zone at International Departures, Lisa asked the question she'd asked every single time he'd dropped her in this spot: "Will you be all right?" Stephen looked at her even more fondly. What else could he do? Well, he took her bag out of the boot, pulled her tight into an embrace, gave her a kiss, and said, "You have the best holiday, now. I'll look after all your animals, and I'll see you when you get back. Have a fantastic time." He slipped back in behind the wheel, started the engine, and watched her and her blue bag disappear into the terminal. She was only about twenty-five minutes early for her arrangement, which wasn't bad by her standards. He wondered whether she'd be first of the threesome to have arrived.

The way back was just traffic, and Stephen drove on automatic pilot while he thought over the events of the day. He felt no emotional attachment to the outcome. Of late he'd really disliked Thuli, but in a way he felt sorry for him. It must have been hell to watch somebody like Stephen slowly unpicking the threads of your life. No wonder he'd behaved like a pork chop. Stephen didn't feel so much surprised as disappointed. He also felt completely removed from what had happened or what would happen next. It was as if he were standing on the outside looking in: He no longer had a dog in the fight. He was delighted about Frankie, thinking that some good had come out of this sorry affair.

As he crested the Linksfield Ridge, it struck him again that Thuli had stolen two hundred million Rand, but had insisted that

Frankie be sent to prison for having tried, but not managed, to steal a few hundred bucks. *Steal a few cents and they put you in jail; steal a few million and they put you in charge,* he remembered Mpho Mamela's mantra.

The evening went by quietly. He got an SMS from Lisa to say that they were checked in and in the lounge, drinking Chardonnay. *And giggling, no doubt,* Stephen thought. For his dinner Lisa had made butternut soup, which Stephen warmed up and ate, while reading the newspaper at the table. There had to be some benefits to being a bachelor. For the dogs' dinner, they lined up in excitement; and for the cats', they did their best not to show any interest.

After supper Stephen watched television, a program about Green Peace, but from an unusual perspective. The programmer with the science qualifications and a neatly trimmed beard told his audience that, kilojoule for kilojoule, for every one person killed by nuclear power, the oil industry killed nine hundred, and energy from coal killed four thousand. *How could he possibly know that?* Stephen wondered. But the serious-looking man said that burning fossil fuels was the most polluting thing humankind would ever do. The only way to get away from that, he told his audience, was with nuclear power. Which Green Peace had effectively kiboshed. *Gee,* thought Stephen, and went to bed.

Chapter 30

Stephen had always been a light sleeper. When his daughter was a toddler, she found the nights particularly dark. In the tiny hours when large shadows and small noises made her uncertain, she'd creep into his room, a quiet little mouse on tippy-toes, and whisper, "Dad" in her smallest voice. Stephen was instantly awake and ready to help.

For all of his adult life he'd been awake in the dark more than once every night, listening to the wind sighing and the house creaking, and the dogs of the neighbourhood calling for answers. For the last twenty-five years in the patient old house near the zoo, particularly on moonlit nights, he also heard the lions grunt their complaint. That had been the pattern of his sleep always: he'd be aware of how the night was getting on, dipping into sleep without difficulty, but surfacing regularly just to listen to the sounds and to go along with the slow passage of the hours.

He'd been asleep for no more than an hour when suddenly he woke. He was aware that there had been a noise, but couldn't remember the shape of it. He lay still, straining to hear. The house was quiet and nothing outside moved. The grey cat lay on his legs and, sensing that he was awake, purred softly. Just as he decided he'd imagined the noise, he heard it again, now remembering what it had been: a deep thump as of someone landing after jumping over a wall. Stephen sat up quietly and turned on the CCTV monitor next to his bed. Eight cameras fed pictures of the outside of the house to the screen. There was nothing out of the ordinary at the front gate, where three of the electronic eyes were focused. The time flashed on and off in the right hand top corner: 1:17. He looked carefully at all the images in turn, but everything was still. He was just reaching out to turn the screen off when he saw it; the shadow of a man running doubled-over flashed across the corner of the camera covering the pool and veranda area. Stephen's heart whipped into panic, and he reached for his phone. His eyes remained glued to the screen while he speed-dialled the security company, thankful for Lisa's plan to feed that number into his telephone under AAA Cap.

While the phone rang on the other side, two more shadows slipped past the pool camera, and now Stephen saw movement on a second screen, the lounge sliding doors. "Cap Control Room, good evening," said a voice on the other end of the line.

'Evening. This is an emergency. I have intruders in my garden."

"Please identify yourself," asked the voice, official and alert.

"Stephen Wakefield. I'm at 35 Abelwold Street, in Saxonwold."

"I'm in touch with our unit now, please hold on." Stephen held on, watching the screen like a hawk, seeing shadows of movement in several of the frames. "Our unit is on the way. We'll be there in seven minutes. How many intruders?"

"I have seen four on the CCTV screen so far. I don't know how many more there are," he said, noticing that his voice was perfectly steady, as if he were ordering a cup of coffee at Motherland. That notwithstanding, his heart was racing and his stomach had tied itself into a knot.

"Do you have a keypad on your front gate?" The security man guessed correctly that in Saxonwold there would be a big wall around the house and a heavy motor gate.

"Yes. The access code is zero-five-zero-three."

"Thank you. Please stay inside the house. We're on the way." Even while the man was speaking, the dogs woke up and started barking furiously.

He knew those dogs well. Sometimes they gave voice to their excitement about the events of the day, maybe a pigeon flying by, maybe the way in which the wind was moving the branches; sometimes another dog dared walk by their gate and they wanted to know why; sometimes their bark simply said that they were bored and had forgotten how to stop barking. But now their tone told him they were angry beyond measure. Almost at the same time he heard an awful crash, definitely the front door. Someone had smashed something heavy into it.

"Jesus!" he half-shouted, and almost immediately the sound came again, except this time Stephen heard the door fly open in a burst of splinters, and he also heard the secondary thump of it jarring open against the jamb. The internal alarm went off, a piercing electronic whistle, and Stephen heard heavy boots running to the passage, to the locked security gate. Out in the garden he heard two quick shots, followed by a third one.

"Christ," he said to himself, his insides now twisted in a paroxysm of terror. Making a mental calculation, he realised that the security crew would be there in, at best, five minutes, but whoever was down the other end of the passage could be in his room in less than a minute if they weren't put off by the security gate at the top of the passage. They'd smashed through the front door in two hits, and if they tried the same with the security gate, it wouldn't last long. As if on cue, a heavy metallic blow rang out. Someone was going at the gate with a hammer or a crowbar.

Stephen leaped up and rushed to the sunroom door that led off from his bedroom. The original architect's plan had been that the main bedroom would have its own separate sun lounge for the adults of the house to sit in privacy. But Stephen and Lisa didn't much go for privacy when the kids were around, and the room had soon turned into a repository for abandoned toys, the dress-up box, old sports equipment, and out-of-date electronic gadgets. His son, when he still lived at home, had spent hours in there playing TV games on the set that still lurked in one corner.

Stephen rushed to the plastic bin that held old tennis rackets, hockey sticks and cricket bats. There was also a set of golf clubs. Outside another shot went off, the dogs were hysterical, the alarm was shrieking and heavy blows were raining in on the security gate at the far end of the passage. So far it was still holding.

Stephen reached into the bin and his hand closed around the handle of a baseball bat. He'd bought it many years ago on a business trip in New York. It was a Louisville Slugger, but a junior version, made for a young man of about twelve. It was thirty-two inches long, Stephen remembered the long-ago salesman telling him, ten inches short of a senior bat. Its machined aluminium length balanced its weight to perfection: a light pick-up with all the substance and power in the sleek head. Without thinking, Stephen pulled the bat from the bin and ran back through the room to the door at the foot of the passage. As he got there he heard the final crash as the security gate gave way and smashed open against the wall. Almost immediately heavy footsteps started pounding down the corridor toward his room.

"Fuck, man," Stephen panted, out of breath with an uncontrolled adrenalin surge. He stepped to the right of the doorway, staying inside the room and hugging the wall closely. He lifted the bat over his right shoulder, holding it by the handle, left fist at the bottom and right fist on top. *I have only one chance*, he thought. *I have to get this right.* The alarm shrieked, in the distance one dog was still barking frantically, there was much shouting as if from several people, and the heavy tread down the passage was almost at the door.

The grey cat that had been sleeping on Stephen's legs had slunk deep into the corner where Stephen was now waiting. He crouched down low on all fours, hating all this noise, panic-stricken and not knowing the way to safety. His feline instincts chose that exact moment to tell him to get the hell out of there. Without any warning he streaked out of the corner and out the door, straight under the approaching feet. The cat let out a terrified shriek and the heavy boots stumbled, their momentum bringing the shape of an enormous man through the doorway. He was at least six foot four and built like a steam train, but he was looking down, trying to keep his balance. He'd thrown up his left hand in front of him, and had lowered his right, to readjust his weight and keep from going over. Stephen had time to register the bulging arms and shoulders under what appeared to be a leather jacket, but he was already swinging. The groove of a million topspin forearm shots over the years kept Stephen's eyes on the spot he wanted to hit, and drove his hips into the weight of shot. The end of the slugger traced a tight arc and collided with the man's right cheekbone and temple with the sound of a cleaver hitting a haunch of meat. Stephen followed through with his swing, concentrating all his power on that one bit of swinging metal at the end of the bat.

The huge man staggered and something went flying out of his hand, Stephen didn't know what. The force of the blow had redirected the huge figure's momentum to the left and he went down headlong into the carpet. All Stephen could think was that the man would jump up again and attack him, and in the instant of his falling, Stephen stepped over him from behind, raised the aluminium bat high and started swinging for the back of the now unprotected head under him.

"Stephen, no!" shouted Jonny's voice from behind him. The bat was already whistling through the air when Stephen pulled the blow. He stopped the swing a few inches short, and turned to see Jonny running toward him. Someone had switched on the passage and hall lights, and Stephen saw the concern in his friend's face. His confusion was such that right then it didn't seem at all unusual that Jonny would be there in his house.

"Fuck it, Stephen! Are you all right?" The big man was out of breath from an exertion Stephen knew nothing about. An enormous hand reached out and steadied Stephen who was swaying slightly, as if he'd had a drink too many.

"Yeah. I think so," Stephen said, feeling all of a sudden like an old man. He handed the bat to Jonny, why he couldn't tell, but almost wasn't able to hold it still enough for the other to take it: he was shaking like a leaf.

"Thanks, boss." Jonny took the bat, bent down over the prone figure on the floor, and in one smooth action handcuffed him. "Put on the lights," he said.

Stephen fumbled with the switch and the lights came on. On the floor, eighteen inches from the unconscious form on the floor lay a handgun, blue grey and deadly. "Point three eight," Jonny mused. "Our man was serious." He picked the gun up by its butt, between his thumb and index finger and said to Stephen:

"Turn off that alarm and come with me. Your dogs are chewing on someone, and all the policemen are too scared to go anywhere near."

Stephen dumbly followed the big fella down the passage and out onto the veranda. They took the shortcut through one of the sliding doors that had been smashed out of its tracks. Stephen could hear the dogs all the way: Findlay barking hysterically, and a low dangerous growling he could hardly associate with either of the other two. Half on the paving and half on the lawn a man lay whimpering fearfully.

Cindy was attached to his left leg and Angus to his right shoulder, and Findlay was barking right in his face. If he kept still, so did the two who had a mouthful of him. But if he tried to move, the growling got louder and both dogs angrily shook their heads from side to side, ripping their fangs in deeper. The man on the ground was Thuli Mpongose.

Stephen went over to Findlay first. He put his hand on her head, patting her, and bent down low to talk into her ear: "There we go. That's a good girl. Come on now, quiet." She settled down some, but still let out the odd sharp bark while he talked to the others.

Cindy was next, simply because she was the smarter of the two and had always been more obedient. He took into his hand her left ear that was standing bolt upright, and softly massaged it. He leaned in close, his face right next to hers, and spoke quietly: "Okay, thanks my Chap. Let go now. Come on, let go."

And she did.

Angus, surprised by what was happening, let go on his own. But they were, all three, still deeply pissed off and said so, Cindy deep in her throat and chest, growling like the wolf she looked so much like, and the other two with sharp little barks.

Only then did Stephen look up and notice that everywhere the lights were on, and that there were several policemen in uniform bustling about. On the lawn lay four handcuffed men, not trying to move, under the watchful eye of three constables with guns in their hands. On the veranda, half under the cement table, lay someone who wouldn't ever move again. And right in front of him lay Thuli Mpongose, bleeding freely from his leg and shoulder.

"Don't let those dogs near me!" he pleaded fearfully, grey in the face and eyes white with terror. Jonny stared at him, bent down, and yanked him to his feet. Stephen saw the man wince in pain. With the same smooth action he'd displayed in the bedroom, Jonny slapped the cuffs on his CEO. Then he shoved him roughly in the direction of the group of prisoners on the lawn, where one of the constables grabbed the bleeding man and, none too gently, thrust him down onto the ground next to the other four.

Stephen felt as if he were standing in one corner, away from it all, and watching the people, himself included. He didn't have any idea what was happening, but it didn't worry him in the slightest. Jonny was there, and for the time being it was enough just to glide in the big man's wake, like a porpoise next to a boat in the green waters off a distant coast somewhere far from land. It will all make sense later, he knew.

Into the scene he was watching strode another man, short but powerfully built. He looked perfectly at ease, as untroubled as if this kind of thing happened to him every day. He was talking on a mobile phone, and as he came toward Stephen his features resolved into the familiar face of Terence, the Rolls-Royce driver.

"Evening, Mr. Wakefield," he said in a calm, respectful voice. Then he remembered that the old man had asked him several times to be on first name terms. "Uh, Stephen," he corrected himself. "The boss wants a word." So saying, he passed the phone to Stephen.

"Hullo?" Stephen asked stupidly, not knowing what to expect.

"Stephen?" Shakes's voice on the line was full of concern. "Are you okay?"

"Yes, thanks. I'm fine."

"Terence has told me what happened. I'm so sorry. But it's all under control now. It will all be fine."

Stephen wasn't sure what the man was talking about, but said: "Thanks, Shakes. Much appreciated," and gave the phone back to Terence. The chunky ex-combatant rang off and turned to Jonny.

"We have to get him out of here immediately." He nodded his head at Thuli who was lying on the ground with his eyes closed and his mouth clamped down tight. He was sweating and was clearly in pain.

"Is he. . . ?" Jonny asked, and Terence nodded again.

"Okay, time to move," Jonny said, turning to the policemen who were standing guard over the prisoners on the lawn. "We have to get that one," he pointed at Thuli, "to a doctor. There's an ambulance outside. One of you go with the Lieutenant and get him to medical care. Go with him in the ambulance. Both of you."

Stephen watched from inside his chrysalis as the talking and the flashing lights and the toing and froing went on and on. Outside the front door that hung in splinters from its hinges, the driveway was like a disaster movie, set in LA in a suburb where the drug lords lived. There were five SAP vehicles, three of them patrol cars and the other two vans for keeping prisoners in a cage at the back. All but one of them had left their blue lights strobing, throwing shadows off this real-life pantomime with its many moving parts. Two ambulances, one with its emergency lights on, stood outside in the road next to the three Cap vehicles—tough black double cab bakkies belonging to the neighbourhood watch. The ambulance into which Thuli had been put pulled away slowly, letting out one mocking electronic squawk.

When the crowd finally thinned out, and only Jonny and Terence were left behind, Jonny looked at Stephen and said thoughtfully: "Tough old bastard, aren't you? Maak vir ons 'n koppie koffie?" *Make us a cup of coffee?* "Then I'll tell you what happened here tonight."

Stephen flicked the switch on the Nespresso machine and while he waited for it to warm up, set out three cups with milk and sugar. He took his black and bitter, but was willing to wager that the other two wouldn't.

"Important stuff first," said Jonny, taking a cup into his huge mitt. "The man who came for you in the bedroom was our dear friend, Tuesday Ikubulala Gobevu." He paused, took a sip, and gazed at Stephen from under a tight frown.

"He's no longer with us," Jonny completed his sentence without any cadence or emotion. Stephen looked at him, not understanding; and, seeing the puzzlement in his friend's eye, Jonny said, "He's dead."

Understanding dawned on him slowly, and when it did, Stephen asked: "Did I. . . ?"

The big man across the table just nodded. Astoundingly, Stephen felt nothing. No reaction, not even when Terence drawled: "Goodbye, Ruby Tuesday."

"That's why we had to get Thuli out of here so fast," Jonny continued. "We didn't want him to know his soldier was dead; not before we had spoken to him properly and in detail."

"Is that where he is now?" Stephen asked.

"Yes," replied Terence. "General Maduna is questioning him. He's the best in the business."

Stephen nodded, then asked the thing that had been seeping upward in his mind for the last few hours: "What were you two doing here?"

"We were staking out your house," Jonny answered. "Shakes is a man of tactics; and he says to be a good tactician you must think like your opponent. The last time Mpongose found out somebody might oppose his schemes, he had him killed the next night." He paused to sip his coffee.

"He found out yesterday morning you were trying to access the cloud storage; and he no doubt thought that with you out of the way, nobody else would carry on with the investigation. Shakes thought that if Mpongose stayed true to form, he'd make a move tonight. We didn't know if he'd be stupid enough to try, but we weren't going to take the chance." Jonny saw the question in Stephen's eye and answered it: "We didn't want to scare you, so we didn't tell you."

Terence took up the story. "We parked a block-and-a-half away, where we could see the front of your house. A police car was parked at Rosebank. They could get here in less than a minute. We thought we had it covered, because we expected one person, maybe two."

"But," said Jonny, "seven of them came. Terence and I took down five, and your dogs one. And you, thank God, looked after the last one."

He hung his head, looking tired all of a sudden. "Fuck, Steve. That was close. I was five seconds behind him, but I don't think I could have stopped him." He kept quiet and then shook his head. "Jesus!" he mumbled.

Stephen leaned across the table and squeezed the man's shoulder. It didn't dent.

"Buddy, without the two of you, they would've got me tonight, for sure. Thanks. Thanks so much." Suddenly Stephen felt tearful, for no reason he could understand other than that he'd looked at the clock on the wall and thought that Lisa would be landing in Vienna soon.

"You've got no doors left to speak of," Jonny said, pointing in the direction of the ruin of the front door. "I think we should stay here with you till you can have them replaced in the morning."

"That's kind. Thanks, I'd appreciate that," Stephen said, realising that he didn't want these two solid peacekeepers to disappear. For the first time in half a century he was scared to be alone. "There are two spare rooms, the kids' rooms, and they have beds already made up."

After another round of coffee and more talk about how things had gone down and what they each had seen and heard, they went to bed.

For once in his life Stephen didn't just drift off into an easy sleep. Every time he closed his eyes he heard the sounds of the front door and the security gate being bashed down; the heavy tread of the killer running down the passage. And, worst of all, the wet crunch of the slugger exploding against the side of the man's face.

At birdsong, a barbet trilled her sweet melody to welcome dawn, waking Stephen and proving to him that he'd eventually drifted off. *She'll be there by now,* he thought and rolled over to close his eyes again.

Chapter 31

Well before the tiny new-age cuckoo in the kitchen would've left her wooden hutch to call eight times, Stephen was sitting outside in the freshness of the early morning. He felt bleary-eyed and washed-out. His cup of coffee stood next to him on the wooden armrest of his stoep chair. The grey cat had slunk up on him, appearing at his feet with an inquiring "Meow?" Without looking too keen, he'd hopped onto Stephen's lap, curled up, and gone to sleep. Stephen stroked the soft fur and tickled behind the cat's ears, and was rewarded with a contented purr.

"You probably saved my life last night, buddy. You hear?" he murmured. The cat said nothing.

Stephen picked up his phone and stared again at the SMS he'd received a minute ago: "Nice flight. Got several hours of sleep. We are in the pension and it's lovely. Vienna is beautiful and icy! Having a quick shower and then we're hitting town. Chat later. Love."

He thought about his response and came to a decision. "Wonderful," he typed. "You have a great time and keep warm. Love you too." He looked at the message; and pressed *send*.

Jonny strolled outside to join him, cup in hand. "Helped myself, hope you don't mind?" he said and settled his huge frame in the chair opposite Stephen. "Terry's in the shower."

"Did you catch a bit of sleep?' Stephen asked.

"Sure did, thanks. Boss, if you don't mind, we are going to get out of here sort of right away. There's a lot to be done."

And there was. Stephen rang three different sets of workmen to replace the front door, the glass-and-wood panel for the sliding door from the lounge to the veranda, and the safety gate. Then he phoned Shakes.

"Hey, Steve," Shakes answered, speaking as if to a sickly elderly aunt. "Are you okay this morning?"

"I'm just fine, thanks. A bit shaken up, to be fair. But okay."

"That's good."

"Thank you for sending Terence and Jonny to look after me last night. I really needed them."

"Hey, buddy. I'm a general and I look after my men. And it nearly went pear-shaped, so I hear." There was a perceptible pause before he added, "They tell me you did well. Thank you." His tone was suddenly that of a military commander, commending his soldier on his bravery.

Stephen, who hadn't hit anyone in his life until the night before, felt a peculiar lack of emotion. He was pleased Shakes thought he did okay, but his soul was still in a bubble on a string tied loosely to his little finger—he thought of the previous night, only a few hours ago really, as if it were an old newsreel in his head. It had nothing to do with him. The General went on: "I'm over-the-top-busy today, but I'm sending you something to see. You deserve to know the end of the story. Terence will drop it off soon."

"Thanks, Mon Genéral. We need to chat about some company stuff too."

"That's right. The news isn't in the papers yet, but it will be there today."

I hope Lisa reads only European papers for the next few days, Stephen thought.

"I have called an emergency board for eleven this morning," continued Shakes. "Hope you can make it? And we need our PR people in immediately after that. Can you call them please?"

"Sure," Stephen replied, thinking how the communications people would handle that instruction: *Without spooking the investors, announce that the CEO has been arrested for murder, attempted murder, and fraud.*

"Stephen, one last thing, and then I must run. Will you be the caretaker CEO until we can appoint a new man?"

They'd discussed Stephen's role in the company before and

he'd made it clear that retirement beckoned to him like a friendly tavern to a party of Hobbits at the end of a long day's journey. Also, Stephen had insisted, he really was a lawyer, not a miner. But this was entirely different.

"Of course," Stephen replied, thinking that he'd sing his last song from as high as swans ever fly. He rang off and walked to the front door where Harold, the trusty handyman who had saved him from hundreds of hours of DIY over the last twenty years, stood scratching his head.

"What happened here?" he asked, chewing on the little stick in the corner of his mouth he used as a substitute for a cigarette.

"An uninvited guest. I wouldn't open, so he opened it himself."

Harold stood listening wide-eyed as Stephen gave him a potted version of what had happened. He left out the part where he killed a man with a baseball bat.

While he was talking, Terence arrived outside the gate in their office run-around, a black Mercedes 500 S. Stephen walked down to meet him, and received a memory stick, much like the one Chessie had given him weeks ago now, it felt like. *Yesterday morning*, he reminded himself.

"Thanks, Terry. See you soon I hope." The tough driver smiled and backed out of the drive.

Back in the house Stephen took his laptop into his study, closed the door, and inserted the stick. A big triangle, pointing to the right, appeared. Stephen clicked on it and an image from a still camera filled the screen: a barren room, much like the one he and Ronald had seen Frankie in. A bare table in the middle and a chair on either side. The camera was positioned so that one chair was on the left, the other on the right. In the far right corner, distorted by the camera angle, was a closed door. In the chair on the left sat Thuli Mpongose. His right arm and shoulder were heavily bandaged, and even through the distant remove of the camera lens he looked exhausted. The time signature in the left top corner of the screen said 05:37. Thuli sat staring at the table.

The door opened and in came General Patrick Maduna with a file under his arm and an aloof expression on his face. The room was wired for sound and Stephen heard the door opening and closing, and the sound of a chair scraping as it was pulled back. Patrick sat down, facing Thuli.

"I want to call my lawyer," Thuli said, husky-voiced, before Patrick had even opened his file.

"Oh. I thought you tried to kill him last night?" replied the policeman. He wore a simple white shirt with a silver SAP badge pinned above the pocket on the left. Thuli said nothing. Patrick sized him up and said: "Look, we can get you a lawyer and we can fool around with procedure and nonsense, but if you take my advice, you'll talk to us right now. There's a lot I want to know; and you know who's next door. He hasn't asked for a lawyer and we may draw some conclusions while you try to be clever."

"He's lying!" screamed Thuli, his face suddenly contorted in fear. "He's just lying!"

"How can you tell? You don't know what he said."

"I know what he's saying. He says I killed Mamela. And that's a lie!" Thuli leaned forward, holding supplicating hands in front of him. "You've got to believe me, it's a lie!"

"Oh? Who killed him then?"

"He did. He killed him."

"Who are you talking about? Just so we are clear?" Patrick asked calmly.

"Ikubu. Tuesday Gobevu."

"How did he even know Mamela?"

"I brought him in, but not to kill anybody, I swear."

Patrick inclined his head in a movement that spoke of disbelieving scepticism "Okay then. Start at the beginning, and I'll see if I believe you," said Patrick, opening his writing pad.

"You have to believe me!" Thuli begged. The policeman simply raised his eyebrows.

After a moment's silence, the haggard man with the bandages started speaking.

"Mamela came to me and tried to blackmail me. He had this boyfriend, this homo boyfriend, who had stolen from the company and who was in Diepkloof, and he wanted me to get this little piece of shit out of there. He said if I didn't, he'd make trouble for me."

Let him talk, don't interrupt, Stephen murmured at the screen. And Patrick didn't. Mpongose went on: "I got hold of Ikubu through some friends I know, and I asked him to come have a talk with Mamela, just to give him a fright. I knew Mamela worked late, so on one Thursday evening I took Ikubu to see him in his office at the mine."

"How did he get into the mine?"

"I put him in the boot of my car. The security staff don't check my car, because I'm the CEO." It sounded to Stephen as if the man was actually still bragging about his own importance. But he couldn't be sure.

"When we were inside we walked to the Admin block, to Accounts, and Mamela was there at his desk. I had checked first that he was alone. When we came in, he saw me but didn't know who was with me. Ikubu walked up to him, and without saying a word, punched him in the chest. A huge blow. Mamela fell over backward off his chair, onto the floor. He was winded and couldn't speak, but he tried to crawl away from us. Ikubu grabbed him by the arm and pulled him to his feet. At this stage I said nothing. I wanted the boy to be scared, not to threaten me again." Across the table the policeman sat without expression, listening.

"Then Ikubu said to Mamela, *we are going for a little drive, you and me.* Mamela couldn't answer, he was still trying to catch his breath. Ikubu picked up the keys, phone, and laptop that were lying on the desk, and marched Mamela out of the building, holding him by his arm. There was no one around, everybody had already gone home. I followed them, and when we got to the front door, Ikubu said to me over his shoulder, *just follow us in your car.* I didn't know what he was going to do, and even at that stage I was a bit worried. He was already taking things a bit far for my liking." Thuli stared at the table top, keeping quiet.

"So what happened?" Patrick asked.

"They got into Mamela's bakkie and drove out toward the mining area. I didn't know where they were going, but I followed in my car. They drove a long way, quite slowly. Mamela was driving. Then they stopped, next to the conveyor belt, half off the road. Ikubu opened his door, and pulled Mamela out the left-hand door by his arm. He fell on the ground as he came out of the vehicle. Ikubu left him there, closed the passenger door, and walked around to the driver's seat." Mpongose fell silent until the general raised an inquiring eyebrow.

"He opened the door, and took out Mamela's laptop and telephone and gave them to me. Then he went back to Mamela who was still lying on the ground, curled up like a baby. Ikubu bent down and grabbed him by one arm and pulled him up onto his feet. He was very strong, and the boy was like a rag doll in his hands. All the while he was talking to Mamela in sort of a low voice. I couldn't really hear what he was saying, but it was about keeping quiet, or else he'd be quiet permanently. He was threatening to kill Mamela."

Again he hesitated, looking more and more like a condemned man.

"Good story so far. What happened next?" asked the policeman.

"Ikubu was enjoying himself, that I could see. The boy was grey with fear. Then Ikubu grabbed Mamela by the wrist, and said to him: *I'm going to stick your arm into the conveyor belt. See if you like that.* Something like that. I don't remember the exact words." The man took a deep breath, steeling himself for the next bit.

"Mamela screamed in terror, and tried to resist, but Ikubu was much stronger than him and just dragged him all the way to the conveyor. He pushed his head under the railing, and all the time I could hear Mamela screaming. I still thought he just wanted to scare him, and I was standing about ten metres away. Ikubu pretended to push Mamela's hand into the rollers of the conveyor, and Mamela screamed again, pleading with Ikubu. He said he'd do anything if we would just let him go. I wanted to interfere, but Ikubu, who was laughing, pushed Mamela's hand toward the rollers again. Whether he did it intentionally or not, I don't know. But this time he pushed too far. It was terrible."

"What was?"

"The one moment Mamela was there, and the next he wasn't. It happened so quickly. His hand had got caught by the rollers, and they pulled him through, in the blink of an eye. The one moment he was crouched in front of the rollers, screaming and begging, and the next moment he was just gone. I ran forward to see what had happened, and in the corner, under the rollers against the support structure, there was just red pulp. That was all that was left of him." Thuli let out several dry sobs. Patrick let him be until he got control of himself again.

"And then?"

"I shouted at Ikubu, something like: *What have you done?* And the man was laughing. He was actually laughing." Thuli shook his head. "And he answered me by saying: *I've shut him up for you. He won't be blackmailing anybody soon.* And then he laughed again."

"Why did you leave Mamela's bakkie in the road?"

"I wasn't thinking straight. All I wanted to do was get away as soon as possible. Ikubu got into the car with me, and we drove back to the main gate. He was chuckling to himself all the time. He'd enjoyed what had happened. Just before the gate, he got out and into the boot again. And when he was back in the passenger seat, we drove back to Crosby."

Jesus, Stephen muttered to himself. On screen Patrick made no comment. He just asked his next question: "And what happened tonight?"

"Well, I was desperate. I thought that Stephen Wakefield was going to try to blackmail me as well. So I arranged with Ikubu to come to his house with me." Thuli said nothing else.

"Why?"

Thuli hesitated for a long time. Then, looking down at the tabletop, he mumbled: "We were going to take him out." In his study, Stephen's gut had tied itself into a knot again. He listened, appalled.

"To keep him quiet?" Patrick asked.

"Yes." Thuli said nothing else.

"Why were there seven of you?"

"It was Ikubu's idea. I had told him that Wakefield had many pictures on his wall, and we thought to make it look like an art robbery. One that went wrong. We knew we wouldn't have much time before the security service was there, so five of the guys would go in and steal the pictures, and Ikubu would go into Wakefield's bedroom and shoot him."

"They're prints! They're worthless, fuck-sake!" Stephen shouted at the screen, involuntarily getting to his feet. "They are prints," he groaned, sitting back sat down again and feeling tired.

"So you went there with the specific intention of killing him?"

Mpongose didn't answer. Patrick left him for a while and then asked again: "Were you going to kill him?"

"Yes," whispered the man, his head dropping until his forehead rested on the table.

Patrick was silent for a long time. Then he said: "What was he going to blackmail you with?"

On being confronted with the thought of his own dishonesty, Mpongose decided that that was the right time to stop cooperating.

"I won't carry on this conversation without a lawyer present," he said, and he wouldn't budge from that position. As if the money he stole were more important than the people he set out to kill.

Stephen ejected the memory stick. *Why don't I feel anything?* he asked himself. And he didn't. In the shower he heard Thuli's words again in his head: *Ikubu would go into Wakefield's bedroom and shoot him.* And still there was a vacuum in his soul: he felt not a thing. He got dressed for the board meeting, got in his car, and drove to the office.

Chapter 32

The morning sun shone brightly for Stephen's drive to the airport. He parked in the second basement at International Arrivals, and waited behind the barricade with Nick and Braam for their wives. They'd stood for almost an hour when the sliding doors opened and the smiling trio came through with their trolleys. It was all hugs and smiles and laughing; and everyone spoke at the same time.

"Hi! Welcome back!"

"Good to see you."

"Did you miss us?"

"Did you have a good time?"

"How was the flight?"

After some minutes of that, and of everyone saying a personal good morning to everyone else, came the consolidation phase.

"We must do this again."

"You must come with us."

"Where are we going next?"

And finally, as the party started breaking up and it was time to let go of the holiday, they moved on to the goodbye-saying phase.

"I'll phone you."

"We'll chat tomorrow."

"See you in Plett!"

Eventually the procession moved off to the basement, staying together up to the machine where you pay for parking, and from there they found their separate cars.

"So you *did* have a good time?" Stephen asked as soon as his seatbelt was on.

"Oh, absolutely! It was the most marvellous thing. We saw such pretty things and we got on so well! It was absolutely fantastic." Then she set about the details, while Stephen smiled, listened, asked the correct questions, and was glad she was back.

The joyful reunion between Lisa and her menagerie was as it usually is after she'd been away for a while. Angus barked in a high-pitched yowling that infected Findlay, who took up the same note. Both of them turned around and around, as if chasing their tails. Cindy, much older and more dignified, walked straight up to Lisa, groaning her usual sounds-like-a-complaint, her tail swishing madly from side to side. Lisa played bongos on their backs, hitting them with her open palms, and saying "My Chip Chaps! How have you been?" All three of them loved being the drum—they spun in front of her like washing in a drier, pushing each other out of the way, hoping to get the next few pats.

Attracted by the caterwauling, the feline members of the household strolled outside and sat on the top step, thinking the dogs were such losers. Showing how savvy and cool they really were, they kept their views to themselves. When Lisa got to them, she swung the ginger kitten high onto her shoulder, much to its irritation. The grey cat saw how things were, and slunk off into the bushes.

Lisa looked up, her face so happy and smiling, and noticed the new front door. "What's this?" she asked Stephen who was lumbering behind her, laden with her case and duty-free shopping bags. He looked at her steadily and said: "Let me make you tea, and then I'll tell you," he smiled, wanting to make her happiness last as long as possible.

While the kettle was boiling, she prattled on some more, handing out the presents she'd bought him: a hand-knitted jersey from Tyrol and fancy chocolates from Belgium.

"Thank you so much," he said, pulling her into an embrace and kissing her forehead.

"Okay now," she said. "What's with the new door?"

Over their mugs of tea, he told her. The joy drained from her face like the colour from an autumn sky of lonely rain. The happiness of a few minutes ago gave way to such anxiety, it almost broke his heart. He'd decided to give her a short and expurgated version first, and tell her the really difficult bits later. But as he spoke, he found his tongue running away with him. When he got to the part where he hit the intruder with the Louisville slugger, a crack opened somewhere inside him, and his soul came pouring out. He wasn't crying exactly; it was just that water was running from his eyes. And, because life sometimes insists on indignity, snot dripped from the end of his nose.

Embarrassed, he got up and fetched a tissue from the box on the counter, blew his nose, and sat down again. He told her of her dogs and how they'd protected him, and ended the sorry tale by giving her the outlines of Thuli's confession. At the end of his story, Lisa, holding his hand across the table, said: "You tell me this now? Why didn't you let me know earlier?"

"I thought about it. But what purpose could that have served? It would've spoilt your holiday. You probably would've insisted on coming back, and even if you didn't, it would have ruined the rest of your trip. And, there really wasn't anything you could have done."

She got up, came around the table, and put her arms around him. She was crying.

"I should've been here," she said. "My God, what if I'd lost you?"

Chapter 33

Two days after Lisa came back, the bell on the front gate rang just after ten in the morning. Looking up at the TV monitor next to the new front door, Stephen saw, as he expected, Ronald's skorokoro. He buzzed the gate open and walked down the steps to meet the priest.

"Morning, Ron. Bang on time. You had a good drive?"

"Yup, thanks," said the priest.

"Come, let me introduce you to Lisa." Stephen led the man into the house, where she was ready and waiting.

"Stephen has told me so much about you. All of it good." She smiled, taking his hand and giving it a firm shake. "Have we got time for tea, or must we go?"

"We have to get going," said Stephen.

"Let me just get the biscuits," Lisa replied, turning back into the kitchen. She came out with two old-fashioned biscuit tins. She gave one to Ronald. He dipped his head, *thank you*, as he took it, turning slightly bemused eyes to Stephen.

"Lisa believes," he explained, "that the universal remedy for all things that go wrong is a tin of ginger biscuits."

"The best ginger biscuits in the world," Lisa chipped. "And you need them, because Stephen tells me you don't have a good woman to look after you."

Ronald was genuinely both surprised and pleased. "Thank you," he said and put his arms around Lisa, giving her a bear hug. She looked as pleased as an American senator in a donut shop.

They bundled into Stephen's car, Lisa sitting on the backseat. "It's how we do it in South Africa," she told Ronald. And she was so much smaller than him.

Stephen drove through light traffic to Mondeor, while Lisa and her new best friend kept the conversation going about where they were born, and where and how Ronald now lived. Into the first gap, Stephen said: "Jonny is meeting us there. He's gone to sort out the paperwork and to see that everything's been arranged."

"He's a really good sort," said Ronald.

"The best," confirmed Stephen.

"Is it true that you're prepared to take Frankie back into his old position?"

"It is. Shakes, our chairman, said that if you want somebody in the Accounts Department who'll never even think of stealing a cent again, you need Frankie. Trevor Hodges, the HR manager, tried to tell Shakes that the insurance policy for the company would be breached if we employed someone with a criminal record in Accounts. Shakes said, nicely at first, that that didn't matter; but Hodges insisted. He's that kind of guy. *Fuck the insurance*, Shakes eventually told him. And then he said: *If you contradict me ever again, you'll be the one who is looking for a job.* Even Hodges understood that." Stephen laughed, thinking back on the scene.

"Well, it's pretty decent of all of you," said the priest.

At the police station he parked and all three got out, Lisa with the second tin of biscuits under her arm. In the reception area, on a wooden bench against one of the walls, sat an old woman respectfully staring at her feet. She recognised Ronald as they came in the door, but her face was expressionless. Ronald knelt and took both her hands in his. She smiled shyly at him. He spoke quietly and Stephen saw her nod.

"Stephen, Lisa, meet Mrs. Mabena," the priest called them over.

She shook hands with them both, holding her right wrist in her left hand, and curtsying as she did so. When Lisa put an arm around her Mrs. Mabena cried, just a little.

"This is such a happy day," she told Lisa. "And I'm so thankful to you and to Father Ronald for helping my son. I don't know how we can ever repay you."

Stephen got the impression that Mrs. Mabena wasn't much used to getting help from anyone, let alone from white people. But Lisa made friends with everyone she came across, and said: "Oh, it's so good to meet you and it's so good to help your son. We're just sorry we couldn't do it earlier." Then the two women sat down on the bench and started chatting, Lisa explaining her theory of ginger biscuits to Frankie's mother.

Stephen and Ronald went to complete the paperwork. At the front desk they asked for Captain Radebe, and were directed to an office down the passage, in the corner on the left. Jonny was waiting for them, sitting in front of Captain Radebe's desk. The Captain did fill his uniform with ease, and it appeared that if ever he were to be interviewed, he'd sweat under the lights like Rafael Nadal on finals day in Palm Springs. He was both friendly and efficient, and a bit intimidated by the fact that there was a priest looking on as he went through the final few strokes of his thing.

"The prisoner has to be released to the custody of a responsible person. Who will that be?"

"That would be me," replied Ronald.

"Will you please sign the forms here? And here? And here?" Ronald signed his tiny, neat signature where the man pointed.

"Well, let's get the boy then," the Captain smiled, capping his pen and reaching for the bunch of keys on his table.

Jonny, Stephen, and Ronald followed him down a passage that smelled of admin, floor polish, and long days. Through a door and down a set of cement steps into the basement they went. At an iron gate, the captain looked up at the television monitor and said, "Radebe," rattling his keys against the bars. Someone at the other end of the controls pressed a button to let them in. They walked past four solid iron doors to the fifth one in the row. The Captain stuck a key in the hole, unlocked the door, and pulled it open. Inside Frankie Mabena, sitting on a single cot, looked up at them with fearful eyes.

"Come, let's go," said the Captain.

"Hello Frankie," said Stephen.

"Morning, my boy," said Ronald.

"Boet," said Jonny. *Bro.*

"Good morning," Frankie all but whispered.

They followed the Captain out through the control gate to the glass door leading to the foyer. There the Captain said: "Okay then, I leave you here. Mabena, don't be back here, understand?"

"Yes, sir," answered Frankie.

Stephen opened the door, and waited for Frankie to walk through. The boy saw his mother at the same time as she saw him.

"Mom," he said, going to her. She stood up, took her boy in her arms, and the two of them wailed like the bride's best friends at a wedding. Lisa, too, stood by with a tear in her eye.

"The company car will take you back home," Stephen said. It had brought Mrs. Mabena there as well. "And, Frankie, when you've been at home for a bit, and you feel like going back to work, phone me. Here's my card. Your old job is waiting for you."

Frankie took the card in his hand, thin and fragile as bone china from the Ming dynasty. "Thank you. Thank you very much," he said again.

When Frankie and his mother, with Lisa's second tin of biscuits, had driven off down the road, and the massive safety officer had come over to their car to say goodbye to the priest and his companions, Stephen stuck out his hand. Jonny took it firmly without squashing his fingers. Stephen looked his young friend in the eye, and nodded sternly.

"To infinity."

There was a brief silence, as if Jonny contemplated the scale of the proposition. Then he dipped his head in agreement.

"And beyond."

Roundfire

FICTION

Put simply, we publish great stories. Whether it's literary or popular, a gentle tale or a pulsating thriller, the connecting theme in all Roundfire fiction titles is that once you pick them up you won't want to put them down.
If you have enjoyed this book, why not tell other readers by posting a review on your preferred book site. Recent bestsellers from Roundfire are:

The Bookseller's Sonnets
Andi Rosenthal

The Bookseller's Sonnets intertwines three love stories with a tale of religious identity and mystery spanning five hundred years and three countries.
Paperback: 978-1-84694-342-3 ebook: 978-184694-626-4

Birds of the Nile
An Egyptian Adventure
N.E. David

Ex-diplomat Michael Blake wanted a quiet birding trip up the Nile—he wasn't expecting a revolution.
Paperback: 978-1-78279-158-4 ebook: 978-1-78279-157-7

Blood Profit$
The Lithium Conspiracy
J. Victor Tomaszek, James N. Patrick, Sr.

The blood of the many for the profits of the few.... *Blood Profit$*
will take you into the cigar-smoke-filled room where American
policy and laws are really made.
Paperback: 978-1-78279-483-7 ebook: 978-1-78279-277-2

The Burden
A Family Saga
N.E. David

Frank will do anything to keep his mother and father apart. But
he's carrying baggage—and it might just weigh him down ...
Paperback: 978-1-78279-936-8 ebook: 978-1-78279-937-5

The Cause
Roderick Vincent

The second American Revolution will be a fire lit from an
internal spark.
Paperback: 978-1-78279-763-0 ebook: 978-1-78279-762-3

Don't Drink and Fly
The Story of Bernice O'Hanlon: Part One
Cathie Devitt

Bernice is a witch living in Glasgow. She loses her way in her
life and wanders off the beaten track looking for the garden of
enlightenment.
Paperback: 978-1-78279-016-7 ebook: 978-1-78279-015-0

Gag
Melissa Unger

One rainy afternoon in a Brooklyn diner, Peter Howland punctures an egg with his fork. Repulsed, Peter pushes the plate away and never eats again.
Paperback: 978-1-78279-564-3 ebook: 978-1-78279-563-6

The Master Yeshua
The Undiscovered Gospel of Joseph
Joyce Luck

Jesus is not who you think he is. The year is 75 CE. Joseph ben Jude is frail and ailing, but he has a prophecy to fulfil ...
Paperback: 978-1-78279-974-0 ebook: 978-1-78279-975-7

On the Far Side, There's a Boy
Paula Coston

Martine Haslett, a thirty-something 1980s woman, plays hard on the fringes of the London drag club scene until one night which prompts her to sign up to a charity. She writes to a young Sri Lankan boy, with consequences far and long.
Paperback: 978-1-78279-574-2 ebook: 978-1-78279-573-5

Tuareg
Alberto Vazquez-Figueroa

With over 5 million copies sold worldwide, *Tuareg* is a classic adventure story from best-selling author Alberto Vazquez-Figueroa, about honour, revenge and a clash of cultures.
Paperback: 978-1-84694-192-4

Readers of ebooks can buy or view any of these bestsellers by clicking on the live link in the title. Most titles are published in paperback and as an ebook. Paperbacks are available in traditional bookshops. Both print and ebook formats are available online.

Find more titles and sign up to our readers' newsletter at http://www.johnhuntpublishing.com/fiction

Follow us on Facebook at
https://www.facebook.com/JHPfiction
and Twitter at https://twitter.com/JHPFiction